Chasing Love

PIPER RAYNE

Cover Design: Whiskey Ginger Goods

1st Line Editor: Joy Editing

2nd Line Editor: My Brother's Editor

Proofreader: My Brother's Editor

2nd Proofreader: Olivia Winston

About Chasing Love

It was over between Bennett Owens and me—until I had no place to go but back to Willowbrook.

Seven years ago, he walked away, and I built a new life for myself, swearing never to look back. But when my husband is arrested, that life collapses, leaving my daughter and me with nothing but a three-month plan to return to the small ranch town before disappearing again.

Bennett's a single dad now. Our girls become inseparable on sight, making it impossible to keep him at arm's length. Especially when I end up working alongside him, where every glance chips away at the walls I've built.

The years apart haven't dulled the pull between us. Bennett remains protective and patient, determined to prove that we deserve a second chance. But he has no idea about the secret I've kept since the day he left.

Because once he learns the truth, he may never forgive me. And like it or not, we'll be bound together forever—by the daughter he never knew was his.

PLAIN DAISY RANCH

CHASING
Love

<u>**The Noughtons Family**</u>
Parents
Bruce and Daisy (deceased) Noughton
Children
Ben Noughton – Gillian Adams
(*The One I Left Behind*)
Jude Noughton – Sadie Wilkins
(*The One I Stood Beside*)
Emmett Noughton – Briar Adams
(*The One I Didn't See Coming*)

<u>**The Owens Family**</u>
Parents
Brad and Darla Owens
Children
Lottie Owens – Brooks Watson
(*Chasing Forever*)
Bennett Owens – Delaney Richards
(*Chasing Love*)
Romy Owens
(*Chasing Home*)

<u>**The Ellis Family**</u>
Parents
Wade and Bette Ellis
Children
Poppy Ellis
Jensen Ellis
Scarlett Ellis

To see more of the Plain Daisy Ranch
family tree visit our website:
https://piperrayne.com/noughton-family-tree

Chapter One

Sean,

I've stared at this blank page for an hour, wondering how to express what I need to say in a way that will make sense to you. With everything I know now, I'm not even sure these letters will mean anything to you. Who knows? Maybe I just need to write them for myself to make sense of everything, to purge the past and start over.

Leia asked me today how a person can love two people at the same time.

In the moment, I had no answer. Memories flooded my mind as I turned the question over and over.

The only answer I could come up with is that love comes in different shapes and sizes and colors. Sometimes it's bright and shiny and hits you in the face with its presence. Other times the colors are muted and seep into each other, living on for a lifetime.

To start, I have to go way back to when I had just moved to Willowbrook. My dad had gotten a new job, and I wasn't happy about moving in the middle of the school year. Thankfully, Poppy Ellis befriended me on day one, claiming me as her best friend.

I was thirteen years old, and summer was in full effect. School had ended, and I was at Poppy's house for a sleepover. Her mom had made us Rice Krispies Treats, and we were laughing, bantering about which candy was better —Hershey's Kisses or the pink Starbursts—when the back screen door creaked open.

And there he was. Bennett Owens, Poppy's cousin.

I didn't have any classes with him, but I knew who he was. Everyone knew the kids who lived on Plain Daisy Ranch. The Noughtons, as everyone referred to them—even though six of them had different last names. It was the family ranch name that stuck.

He was smart, reserved, and popular. Whether it was because he grew up in Willowbrook or the fact that his family was seen by the small town as royalty, I don't know. All the girls would giggle and flirt with him, and he was always surrounded by a group of guys.

"The pink Starbursts are the best," Poppy said.

"Please, nothing melts in your mouth like a kiss," I countered.

Bennett's dark eyes flicked toward me, but the moment was over before it began. He circled back around right away.

"Wrong. Wrong. Wrong." Poppy shook her head.

"Hey, Aunt Bette." He headed over to her, swung his arm around her shoulders, and kissed her cheek. "Mom said you wanted some jars." He set two mason jars on the counter.

"The girls are going to catch fireflies. Want to join?"

He glanced over his shoulder, and his gaze met mine. I pretended not to care, and Poppy grabbed another Rice Krispies square, looking as if she didn't care what his answer would be.

"Nah, I've got plans."

My cheeks flamed. Although we were the same age, I felt years younger than him and a world away from whatever thrilling plans he had. He was probably going to a party to make out with someone. The popular kids had parties while Poppy and I were going to catch bugs.

"Then see ya." Poppy's chair legs scratched against the floor.

Bennett left without another glance, which shouldn't have surprised me. I figured he didn't even know my name.

But later that night, while the sunset painted the sky tangerine as we were trying to catch fireflies, he walked back into Poppy's yard. Poppy was on the other side of the yard, hell-bent on catching one particular firefly that she said was playing games.

"They need air." He came over and handed me a different mason jar. "And I put a wet paper towel at the bottom for moisture, so they don't dry out. Let them go after a day or two. Don't keep them captive just because they're pretty." Then he walked back over the hill, disappearing from view as if I'd imagined him.

Just like that, something shifted. It wasn't a thunder crack or big bright fireworks but rather a quiet click into place. I started noticing Bennett in the hallways when we went back to school. My eyes sought him out at lunch and whenever I was on the ranch. He didn't notice me back though, not for a long time.

And that's why the question stunned me

silent. Sometimes the people who matter most don't crash into your life. They slip in quietly. Like a jar of light you didn't know you needed until you're holding it.

So, I've come to the conclusion that there is room for more than one kind of love in a person's life—each true in its own way, each teaching us something about who we are and what we're capable of giving.

Delaney

Chapter Two

DELANEY

Would Willowbrook be my first choice to run away to? *Back* to, if I'm being honest. Definitely not. It would be dead last. Yet here I am, back in the small town that holds memories of the girl I used to be, the girl who believed her future was as bright and wide open as the sky.

The last time I was here, I was seventeen, naïve, and head over heels in love with a boy who looked at me as if I was his whole world.

Now, more than a decade later, I'm broke, jaded by love, and asking my retired parents to take in both my daughter and me for the foreseeable future.

That seventeen-year-old version of me would be so disappointed in who we've become.

"It's so boring here." My seven-year-old daughter, Leia, flops onto my bed, pulling me from the mental reprimand I've been giving myself since my life took a plunge I wasn't prepared for.

I kneel beside yet another moving box I've been ignoring for the past few weeks and stack her mountain of Hello Kitty plushies on a shelf. "Once summer kicks off, there'll be more to do."

Leia exhales dramatically, staring at the ceiling. "Like what?"

"Horseback riding." I rise and flatten the empty box, trying to sound upbeat. "I'll find a stable so you can ride again."

Moving here with just weeks left in the school year wasn't ideal, but when the DEA bursts into your kitchen one random morning and cuffs your pajama-clad husband, your priorities shift pretty fast. Shelter and food take precedence over friends and familiarity.

"Plain Daisy Ranch would be perfect," Mom says, breezing in and patting Leia's leg to give her room to sit on the mattress.

I narrow my eyes. "Eavesdropping again, Mom?"

"If you two didn't talk so loud, I wouldn't overhear you." She grins, the picture of unapologetic nosiness.

She could be in the eavesdropping hall of fame. God help us all when the time comes for hearing aids, and she can slyly turn those suckers up.

Leia scoots up the mattress, clutching the Hello Kitty unicorn Sean brought home from his last "business" trip. Maybe prison has a gift shop. Hello Kitty in an orange jumpsuit. Stripes would be cuter.

"Mom, I'm not taking her to Plain Daisy. I'm leaning toward Wild Bull. They've expanded from what I see on their website."

Mom waves and grabs the brush from the nightstand, then she taps Leia to get in position in her lap. When Leia just looks at her, she says, "If we don't keep brushing it, you're going to end up with knots."

"It hurts though." Leia eyes me like *tell her to stop.*

"You'll be crying more when knots form. You don't

want to cut off this beautiful hair." Leia winces and her body stiffens as Mom forces the brush through her hair. Then she eyes me over Leia's head. "Wild Bull will cost a fortune. Levi can talk to Nash and get Leia started at Plain Daisy."

If Willowbrook is the last place I wanted to be, Plain Daisy Ranch is the circle of hell in the center. "Levi is not calling in favors for me."

"I miss Uncle Levi," Leia says as Mom guides the brush through her hair. "When's he back?"

"Tomorrow night. He's at a big rodeo." Leia turns her head to look at my mom, but my mom turns her back around, continuing to brush. There's something sweet about watching your mom do for your daughter what she did for you.

"Can I ride a bull like him?" Leia asks.

Mom and I laugh in unison.

"Not yet," I say.

A heavy silence follows. Boxes tower in the corner, keepsakes of a life that was built on lies. The police seized pretty much everything but allowed me to keep Leia's toys, a small kindness I was grateful for. Leia's already lost enough.

"You should go out tonight," Mom says, braiding Leia's hair. "I'll spoil this little one with ice cream sundaes and a movie." She whispers the last part to Leia, whose eyes widen.

"What would I even do?" I flop onto the bed beside them, mirroring Leia's ceiling-stare.

"You've been hiding out since you got here," Mom says gently, careful to approach the subject everyone here pretends to ignore.

"For good reason."

She secures Leia's braid with an elastic, then smooths a hand over her head. "Do me a favor and check on Grandpa, sweetheart." She taps Leia's hip.

"Why? He's probably fishing."

"Exactly. Fishing is fun." Mom winks. "You'll see. Go now."

Leia groans but leaves the room. She knows that my mom isn't really asking. I have the instant urge to yank my little buffer back between me and my mom's inevitable pep talk.

"Be right back. GRANDPA!" she shouts.

"For heaven's sake, don't scream," my mom calls.

Leia's footsteps jog down the stairs, and the screen door bangs shut behind her.

I get up off the bed and unpack another box. "Go on. Let's hear it. Say what you want to say."

Mom joins me, reaching in and picking up items that were packed too haphazardly, since I was only given a small amount of time to move us out of our house. "You have nothing to be ashamed of, Delaney. You did nothing wrong."

"I married him." I set Leia's pink piggy bank on the dresser. Sean used to slip hundreds into it after bedtime on the rare nights he was there to tuck her in and kiss her good night. Which wasn't as often as I would have preferred, but I stupidly believed he was off building our future. "I should have known."

"You loved him," Mom replies, stacking Leia's books on the bookshelf that used to be filled with my own mementos.

There're more than a couple of secrets she doesn't know, but they can wait. One storm at a time if I want to make it through.

"If everyone quit going out in public over embarrassment, the town square would be a ghost town." She strokes my hair. "You have to move forward, for Leia and for yourself."

I stare out the window. This wasn't my childhood bedroom. My parents left Willowbrook right before my senior year of high school and only moved back six months ago to retire. Of course they couldn't pick Florida. They had to return to the one town I swore I'd never return to.

A buttercream yellow Jeep dotted with oversized white daisies turns onto the gravel drive.

I shoot my mom a look. "You called Poppy?"

She shrugs. "She's your friend."

"Her cousin's wedding reception is today."

"It's just a reception. Lottie's already married to Brooks," Mom says with a too-bright smile. "Maybe Bennett will be there."

Goes to show how much she doesn't know. He's a good part of the reason I've been hiding. I'm not sure how our reunion will go, but from the few times my mom has talked about Bennett since returning to Willowbrook, he's really leaning heavy on the whole widower thing—how much he loved Kristie and how her death gutted him.

I'm probably just jealous and don't want to know he was really truly happy with someone else. I wanted him to be thinking of me late at night and going through the what-if scenarios like I do. He probably is, just for Kristie, not me. Which is the way it should be. She was his wife, and I was... well not.

"Stop it," my mom says before kissing my temple. "Lottie will be thrilled to see you."

"I'm not crashing a wedding, Mom."

A knock sounds downstairs. "Hello, Richardses!"

"We're up here," Mom calls, then murmurs, "Sue me for wanting to see you smile again."

Poppy breezes through the doorway, wearing jeans and a T-shirt, her blond hair hanging just below her shoulders in tight waves and not looking all that different from the last time I saw her. Time has been good to her.

She hugs my mom. "I can't believe you're a grandma now! Where's the munchkin?"

"Outside with Grandpa," Mom says. "I need to check that they're not wading in the pond. Lord knows, if Leia asked, he'd probably say yes. You two have fun." She walks out, leaving me with Poppy's raised brows aimed in my direction. "And remember, I've got Leia for the night," she calls from the hall.

Poppy purses her lips with her back to my mom. I really wish she wouldn't have felt obligated to come because of my mom.

"Soo... we're going to ignore the fact you've been back for weeks and haven't bothered to reach out, because I'm in desperate need of a floral designer," Poppy says, plopping onto Leia's bed. "Know anyone?"

"C'mon, Poppy, let's drop the act. My mom bribed you to be here."

"Bribed? No."

"You have Lottie and Brooks's wedding reception."

"I do, but the wrong flowers came in for the reception, and I'm panicking."

I laugh. "I'm sure your cousin Bennett, *the landscape architect*, would be helpful with that."

"Bennett's good with greenery, but you're the flower whisperer." She winks.

Do I want to see Bennett? Hell yeah, from a distance maybe. But to ambush him at his sister's reception? It's not how I thought he'd find out about me being back in town.

"Do you want me to beg?" She brings her hands in front of her in prayer pose.

"I'm not crashing a wedding."

"Just help with the flowers then." She grins, tugging me to my feet.

I sigh. I wouldn't mind having my fingers in the dirt again. The only garden I've mastered lately was my own, and that's probably either being auctioned off to the highest bidder or bulldozed back in California right now.

"Come on."

"I'm not going to the reception." I give her a stern expression.

"Okkkaaayyy." She shrugs. Her smirk says she's going to try to convince me, but on this, I'm going to be stubborn.

I thought returning to Willowbrook would be a quick three-month pit stop to earn some cash and regroup, figure out what the hell I'm going to do with my life now that it's imploded. I'd get Leia and me out of here before anyone discovered my biggest secret that only two people in the whole world know. Visiting Plain Daisy Ranch risks making it many more. I should be slamming my heels into the ground and acting like Leia does when she doesn't get her way, but I allow Poppy to lead me to her Jeep and drive us to The Perfect Petal, the flower shop Bennett started with Poppy.

I'm sure it will be fine. Maybe he won't even remember me.

I'm as delusional as my mother.

Chapter Three

BENNETT

I shouldn't be surprised that Lottie put me to work for her wedding reception. After all, she drunk-married Brooks in Vegas, tried to get an annulment, and somehow ended up being the last one to figure out she was in love with him. That's my big sister for you—chaotic, messy, but always lands on her feet.

"Calm down, it's just plants and flowers," she says, perched on a kitchen stool at my parents' house while Kami, her hairdresser, curls her hair.

"There's a method to planting that you don't seem—"

"I told you, B, I just want to look at the garden every day and know it was planted by people who love us and were wishing us the best of luck on our big day."

"If we want to get technical, on your big day, you were smashed on tequila shots, and your memory is blurred at best."

She glares at me through the mirror. "I'm okay if everything isn't all perfectly uniform like you prefer it. Your garden can be flawless when you finally build your house on the property." Her brows lift in challenge. She's always calling me out on my shit.

I groan because ever since Lottie and Brooks decided to build their house on the family ranch, everyone's been asking when I'm going to build on the lot next to theirs. My dad even suggested we should build mine along with Lottie's and maybe we'd save money. The last thing I want to get into is that topic because that would mean having to address that I'm choosing to raise my daughter in a house with my cousin, Jensen, and his best friend, Nash.

"Anyway," I continue, "the flowers I originally ordered didn't come in, but I've been able to secure some different ones. Poppy is taking care of the pickup and will drop them off just before the guests are set to arrive. I'll start with the plants until then."

Her whole face lights up. "I know I'm being a pain in the ass, but I'm so excited for everyone to plant whatever they choose. It doesn't matter how it turns out."

I shake my head and sigh.

She catches my hand before I can leave. "Thanks, B. I promise I'll pay you back."

"You paid it forward. I owe you, but I'm not sure why you have to be such a pain in my ass about it."

Her eyes get glossy, and her lips pull into a smile. "I'm already an emotional mess. Don't make me cry now that my makeup's done."

I squeeze her hand in return. And I mean it. Lottie and the rest of my family have been there for me more than I could ever repay them. When I came back to the ranch, I didn't expect that months later I'd have a newborn daughter and a dead wife. I didn't have the luxury of pride. I had to lean on the people I love. I've never been good at that, but I was left with no choice.

"You wouldn't be you if you weren't annoyed about something," she teases.

I pause at the front door. "Live my life for a day and get back to me."

I open the door and leave, escaping my sister and her new love glow. The door clicks shut, and I stand for a minute, her words ringing in my mind. Am I always annoyed? I shake my head. Just when it comes to her absurd ideas about guests who have no knowledge about planting and letting them loose in her garden. She'll be lucky if half the plants don't die.

I jog down the steps as Wren's laugh echoes across the field. My mom's chasing her.

"Wren!" she scolds, holding the delicate flower crown Wren's supposed to be wearing today.

Wren circles me, dodging my reaching arms, and darts behind my legs as though I'm her personal fortress.

"What are you doing?" I ask, swiveling to catch her, but she spins away with every move I make.

Mom stops, hands on her hips, exasperated but smiling. "You little wildflower."

Wren giggles, and somehow, I'm able to get my hands on her and scoop her up, spinning her around while she squeals. Her laughter is infectious even to my mom, who is definitely low on patience today.

"Why were you running?" I ask, setting her down.

"I was sitting in that chair forever." She groans, and her eyes roll back, her body wiggling as if she's made of Jell-O.

"The price of being a girl," Mom says, finally placing the crown of flowers with ribbons on Wren's head. "You said you wanted to get all dressed up."

Wren looks up at me with blue eyes that match her mother's. "It's so boring. You just sit there, and you can't move."

"It's called being pampered," Mom says, pinning the hairpiece in place. "I could use a day of pampering. Your aunt has me running all over this ranch to make today the best day ever."

My eyebrows raise. "You complaining?"

She playfully rolls her eyes but smiles. "Never. I love weddings. Especially when it's one of my own." Her gaze flicks to me and lingers a second too long.

"Daddy, what was your wedding to Mommy like?" Wren asks.

My mom's smile tightens because she assumes I don't want to be reminded of my biggest loss.

"Not like Aunt Lottie's, that's for sure." I crouch, meeting Wren's eyes.

She's seen our wedding album, and I've told her all the same stories about the day I married Kristie. What a beautiful bride she made and how perfect that day was. And maybe it was beautiful, in some ways. But I left a lot out because... well, I'll always leave it out. Kristie will always deserve to be on a pedestal for Wren, so I'm not going to tell her the full truth. Not ever.

"Have you seen Poppy anywhere?" I didn't want to worry Lottie, but Poppy should have been here already with the flowers.

"Not yet. Want me to call her?" my mom asks.

I shake my head. "She'll be here soon. Want to help me?" I ask Wren.

"Daddy, I'm the flower girl. I have to show up with Aunt Lottie." Just then, Brooks's truck rolls into the driveway. Wren jumps in the air and propels herself toward him. "Brooks!"

Mom loops her arm through mine as we follow. Brooks steps out wearing a casual suit and lifts Wren with ease, setting her on his hip.

"It's good to see her happy," Mom says quietly. "Are you... happy?"

I glance at her, surprised by her hesitation. My mom

doesn't usually tiptoe around hard questions. "Yeah, Mom, stop worrying about me."

I watch from a distance as Lottie walks out of my parents' house in a dress most people wouldn't think of as wedding attire but fits her style and what she and Brooks are trying to accomplish today—just to celebrate their love.

My mom pauses, and Brooks lowers Wren to the ground, his gaze unable to stray from Lottie. Mom squeezes my arm, and her quick inhale says we shouldn't be watching their intimate moment. Wren shouldn't be either, it should be shared between them, but I can't blame her. Even I can't take my eyes away from them. Their love grew so deep so fast, it spurs a memory from years ago that I swallow back, just like every time it surfaces.

Brooks breaks the distance, opens his arms, and Lottie walks right into them as though she never belonged anywhere else.

"To think how long she fought that." Mom lays her head on my shoulder with a sigh. "That kind of love doesn't come around for everyone."

She doesn't look me in the eye but rather walks away toward the house.

I admire the couple for a second longer than I should. Shame crawls up my spine like a spider because I had a love like that a long time ago.

Then I turn and head toward the planters because there's no sense in thinking about things that can never be.

&a.

A HALF HOUR LATER, I'M ANNOYED AND SNAPPING AT my three cousins who are giving me shit as they're each planting the plant they picked out.

"Six inches," I say to Jude.

"I won't plant it at all if you keep watching over me like I'm a child using a knife for the first time." Jude glances at Ben, and they both roll their eyes.

"I know you think I just play with dirt all day, but there's actually a reason I do things the way I do."

"Here?" Jude asks, stabbing the soil right next to the one my dad planted five minutes ago.

"Yes, but... ugh. Just give it to me." I take the shovel.

That's when I finally spot some of the workers from The Perfect Petal unloading the flowers, while Lottie trails behind them, moving toward the raised garden beds.

"Oh, not there!" I leave my cousins to do what they want with one garden, rushing over to the flowers being put out.

"Hey, it's okay, I'm not picky," Lottie tells me because she doesn't understand how this can all be ruined.

"If we don't plant them right, some won't make it. I told you to let them pick the plants, and I would plant each one. Or someone from The Perfect Petal could handle it."

Lottie laughs and squeezes my arm. "That's no fun. I want it to be their way of planting something for our future. Every time I look at this garden, I'll remember this day."

She keeps talking, but I'm not listening anymore.

Because my eyes catch on a brunette figure near the flower carts.

My heart seizes. My breath stutters. My stomach sinks.

It can't be her. There's no way. I knew her parents had moved back—ran into her mom at the library one day during story time for Wren—but no one told me *she* was back.

"Delaney?" I say, my voice raw.

She looks up and draws back when she sees me. "Hi, Bennett," she says calmly.

Too calmly. As if she's had time to prepare. As if she's had time to brace herself, while all I can think about is how much more beautiful she looks than the last time I saw her seven years ago.

Chapter Four

DELANEY

Poppy has always been persuasive, but she's upped her game in the years I've been away.

By the time her Jeep pulled out of my parents' driveway, she'd convinced me that I should take the open position at The Perfect Petal. She made her case, and I couldn't refuse because the fact is, I need the money. Since I arrived, I'd been focused on getting Leia settled into her new environment, and the few feelers I'd put out for employment had led nowhere. I need a paycheck, plain and simple. If it means I might cross paths with Bennett on the rare occasion he's in his office, then so be it. According to Poppy, he never comes in. My number one priority is Leia and getting us the hell out of this town, and I can't do that without a job.

It all sounded great until I came face-to-face with him. His good looks have deepened with age. Dark hair, eyes a shade of brown that once looked at me like I was his everything. But the warmth they used to hold is absent, and they don't reflect any of the love they once did.

"What are you doing here?" Bennett snaps, as though I'm a thorn in his carefully tended bouquet.

"I work here," I fire back, my back going straight from the tone he's using with me. As if I'm inconveniencing him by returning home. "Poppy just hired me."

Off to the side, I hear Brooks Watson whisper, "Seriously, who is that?"

Lottie shushes him.

Our eyes are locked, and my heart hammers. What was I thinking letting Poppy convince me to do this?

Emmett Noughton shouts from across the yard, "Danson, Ben put it three inches too far left. He's not listening to your rules!"

Who is Danson?

Bennett blinks, shoulders stiffening. "Welcome back to Willowbrook."

With that, he turns away, letting Emmett loop an arm around his neck, and they all mess around just like back in high school. I feel someone's eyes on me, and I turn to see Lottie and Brooks watching me with equal parts polite curiosity and gentle concern.

"Congratulations," I manage to squeeze out of my constricted throat because crashing someone's wedding reception is awkward enough without forgetting my manners.

"Thank you," Lottie replies, but I can barely hear her over all the cousins' roughhousing.

I retreat to the truck for another tray of flowers, dodging arriving guests as tears threaten.

Stupid, Delaney. Stupid. Stupid. Of course he still has that effect on you.

Back at the truck, I'm about to get another flat of flowers, but Poppy comes out of Bennett's parents' house dressed for the wedding, interrupting me. How did she get ready so fast? She certainly doesn't look like she just spent an hour loading flowers into the truck. "I'll carry those. Why don't you run home, change, and come back? Lottie would love it if you were here."

"Can't. I should get back to Leia."

"Are you okay? You look pale." Poppy steps closer, smiling at whoever is behind me, before setting her concerned gaze back on me.

"Just not used to so much manual labor." I laugh it off, but she only looks behind me again.

"Hey, B." Poppy gives him a chagrined smile. Probably for springing me on him.

There goes my heart again, beating so hard I worry it's going to burst out of my chest.

"I hear you hired someone without consulting me?" Bennett says with the same clipped tone as before.

I'm not sure how I thought he'd react to me reappearing in town, on his ranch, but bitterness wasn't on the list. Then again, I could destroy the entire widower crown he proudly wears.

Damn it, there goes my bitterness getting out of control again. And it has nothing to do with Bennett, well, not entirely. It has more to do with my life imploding and landing me here.

"Look! Delaney!" Poppy pivots, hands on my shoulders and turns me to him.

I try to swallow down the desire that still pools deep in my belly for him.

"She's back."

Bennett's eyes barely meet mine for a second before he sets his gaze on his cousin. "Give us a minute, Poppy."

Poppy's arm slackens, and she eyes me for a second. "Am I missing something?"

I scoff and shake my head, playing off the fact that being this near to him again is affecting me. "Nope."

"It's just been a long time. I want to catch up," he says.

"Ohh…" Poppy buys his charm, and she probably still has some hope that we might rekindle the teenage romance we thought would take us down the long road. If she only knew the truth about how twisted our lives have been, but Bennett loves his secrets.

"Sure." She turns to me. "I meant what I said. Bennett can show you back to the girls' house, so you don't even have to go home. Take anything from my closet and come down and enjoy the party."

"Thanks, Poppy." I squeeze her hand. "For everything."

I don't tell her I think I'm going to refuse the position she offered because there's no way I can work alongside Bennett even if he's rarely in the store. I need to stay as far away from him as I can until I can get my daughter and me out of here.

"Of course. See you in a bit." She eyes her cousin. "Get that scowl off your face and behave."

He nods, and she blows out a breath, eyeing me one more time before she disappears under the flowered arch that reads *The Watsons* to where the party is starting to grow in numbers.

"Listen," I say, putting my hand up, knowing I've surprised him.

"What are you doing? Why would you accept the position?" He looks around the space, nods to the side, and walks right past me.

"Is that your way of asking me to follow you to a more secluded spot?"

He turns before the trailhead ventures onto a tree-lined path that would keep us from view of all the arriving guests. "We can't have people see us."

"Oh, sure, let's hide. Wouldn't want anyone to see your dirty little secret, right?" I stomp past him until we're a good way in and no one will see us. We stop where the shade of the trees swallows us from view. "Is this private enough for you, or should we hitch a ride and get out of Willowbrook altogether?"

"You're mad?" His jaw flexes. "*You* show up *here*, unannounced." He points his finger out toward the party. "And you're mad? This is my family's party. What the hell, Delaney?"

I shake my head because I don't have a good answer. "Poppy told me you'd be busy, but I think she still thinks we're a sweet teenage love story ready to be rekindled." My laugh is jagged.

"Fucking hell. When did you get back? Why didn't you reach out? I would've met you for—"

His questions give me no time to answer. "I'm sorry for ambushing you. It wasn't my intent, and I think it's pretty clear why I didn't reach out to you."

His chest rises and falls, and he looks at the opening of the path again, apparently paranoid someone might see us.

I cross my arms. "You do know that if someone finds us hiding out, it will look even more suspicious, right? Unless you've told someone—"

"Fuck no. No one has any idea."

The words and the way he delivers them hit me like a slap to the face. "So, I'm just the childhood sweetheart?"

He drags a hand through his hair and nods. "I've got my daughter to think about."

"I'm not here to blow up your life, and don't worry, I'm going to tell Poppy that I don't want the job. I was just thinking that..." I stop myself from continuing. I'm not putting myself out there for Bennett Owens again. He doesn't deserve to know my vulnerabilities. The fact that Poppy telling me about the floral design position sparked something in me that's been dead for years isn't his business. Bennett doesn't get to know those things about me. Not anymore.

He sighs, and all I want to do is get the hell out of here. "I'm sorry about your husband."

I nod. "I'm sorry about Kristie."

He nods back.

We've never been awkward with each other. Actually that's not true. The last time we said goodbye was pretty damn awkward.

"You should go. It's Lottie's wedding."

He exhales a deep breath and studies me. "Did you want…" Something unspoken flickers in his eyes. "I can show you to the girls' house…"

"I'm not staying. Coming here was a massive mistake." I step past him, desperate to escape.

That look crosses his face. The same one he wore that day he showed up at my door and devastated me. I refuse to go there again.

"I have to go. Enjoy the night. I'll keep my distance until I leave town." I start walking, eager to get away because after seven years, how is that feeling still stirring inside me as if it never died?

His hand closes around my wrist, and I pause, allowing his thumb to run along the inside of my wrist. It feels as if the vines of our tangled past are tightening around me. "Delaney."

His tone is reverent and endearing and like a smooth caress, affirming that I'm not the only one affected by this reunion of ours. I push back the tears that want to spill. My life just fell apart, and the one person I'd love to lean on, I can't because it's a slippery slope, and I'm done being someone's second choice.

Tears threaten again, but I steel myself. I've survived worse than an old boyfriend. I straighten my shoulders and glare back at him. I slip free of his hold and go the opposite way of the party, assured I'll find my way out of the woods and home. "Enjoy your night, Bennett."

Then I turn away, forging through the trees until the music fades.

Coming here was another bad decision to cross off the long list I've made throughout my life.

Chapter Five

Sean,

It's taken me some time to decide if I should continue these letters. Part of me still worries you might be upset hearing about the first boy I ever loved. Ultimately, I've decided that I want you to know him even if it's only on paper. Maybe I'll never even send these. Maybe it will just feel cathartic to get it all on paper, who knows? So, here it goes...

It took an entire year for Bennett to notice me.

My first day of freshman year in chemistry was the moment everything changed. I got lost, turned around in the hallway, and ended up being ten minutes late.

All the good seats were taken, and I

searched the room for an empty chair. Everyone was paired up at the tables, and I feared I'd be the odd one out.

But then Mrs. Pritchett said, "Delaney, you're with Bennett Owens."

My gaze drifted to the back row, and there was Bennett sitting alone, one elbow on the lab table, his gaze on me.

I'd hardly spoken to him since the firefly jar incident. He was taller now, broader through the shoulders. I'd seen him a few times that summer on the ranch, but he was usually horsing around with Emmett and their friends.

Walking farther into the classroom, I felt every stare, and heat flooded my cheeks. I slid onto the stool beside Bennett, and of course, he didn't say hello. He probably didn't want to be my partner either.

Then to my surprise, a couple minutes later, he whispered, "Catch any fireflies lately?"

My cheeks went from warm to blazing. He was making fun of me. I straightened, turned my back, and tried to focus on Mrs. Pritchett, not the scent of Bennett's cedar cologne.

The following day was our first lab project. We were supposed to be measuring chemical reactions that day, but my hands shook so badly that water sloshed over the beaker's rim.

He gave me a reassuring smile and took the glass from me and refilled it to the precise line.

"I wasn't making fun of you," he whispered, eyes on the measurement line.

I noticed that Bennett was painstakingly detail-oriented and a little bit of a perfectionist. He recorded everything, never trusted memory alone, and his notes were meticulous.

I didn't answer, so he continued. "I didn't know what to say. Maybe, I don't know, maybe I'm hanging around Emmett too much." He chuckled and offered me a soft smile.

"It's fine. Don't worry about it."

He set the beaker down and leaned back on his stool. "Come on, if we're going to be partners for the semester, we have to get along. I'm sorry."

"Okay," I said because even though I'd wanted his attention, now that I had it, I had no idea how to handle it.

"Is that your way of forgiving me for my lame joke?"

He lightly cupped my elbow when I didn't look up from my notes, and I finally faced him. There it was again, that quiet internal click, but this time, it felt stronger.

"You're forgiven." I figured that would be the end of it, and we could be cordial lab partners, and my ridiculous crush would eventually fade.

But his smile lit up the room, and I knew that whatever I felt for him had gone from a silly crush to more, but I had no idea what and knew that he'd never pick me because we ran in different circles.

Weeks passed, and thanks to him, I was actually passing. Chemistry wasn't my thing. We traded a few words here and there, but nothing deep. Still, every day, butterflies dive-bombed my stomach when I saw him already seated at our station. He was always there, always reliable.

One afternoon, I felt tension radiating off him through the entire class. When the bell rang, I gathered my things, but his hand curled around my wrist.

"Hey," he said, as if we hadn't just shared forty-five minutes of class together.

I turned, startled to find a nervousness in his eyes that he'd never had before.

"The football game tonight... you going?" he asked.

"Um..."

He hesitated, as though he didn't want to scare me off, before adding, "You should. We could go. Together, I mean... if you want."

A hush settled over me until I realized he was asking me out. Or was he?

"Like a date?" I blurted.

He gave the smallest shrug. "Yeah."

And that's when I knew.

Bennett Owens would be my first love, whether or not I ever became his.

"Okay." I nodded.

His grin spread wide enough to send sparks ricocheting through me. "Great."

I was terrified. The jumping-off-the-edge-of-a-cliff kind of terrified, but I realized fear is often the first sign that something truly matters.

After that football game, Bennett and I were inseparable.

Delaney

Chapter Six

BENNETT

"Daddy, there you are." Wren stands at the opening of the tree-lined path with Poppy at her side. "Why were you in there?" She leans around me, and I sidestep to make sure she won't see Delaney if she's still visible.

"Just had to look for something I thought I dropped." I pat her shoulder to get her to turn around and head back to the party.

"What was it?"

"Just something for the party. You need to go have fun."

Poppy eyes me over Wren's head. I have a million questions for her—but I have a feeling she'll give me the cold shoulder and tell me, as she always does, that if I want answers about Delaney, I need to ask Delaney herself. But Poppy doesn't know our full story. No one does.

"Emmett said he'd dance with me." Wren runs off, and I watch her approach Emmett, who's standing with Briar and their baby, Colter.

"I'll answer one question," Poppy says, both of us looking straight ahead at Wren.

"Why is Delaney back here?"

I'm not sure it's the right question, but I can't wrap my head around why she'd return home.

"You've heard the rumors. Her husband."

"Yeah, but—"

She steps ahead of me and turns around, walking backward with a knowing smile. "That was your one question."

She laughs, and I shake my head at her.

"Poppy…"

"Sorry. You should've thought harder about what to ask." She stops and waits for me to catch up.

"Don't be a brat."

She sticks out her tongue.

"Careful there. Someone might take that as an invitation," Nash says, walking up the drive.

"If only." Poppy laughs and waits for him. "Where's your big belt buckle?"

He chuckles and falls into step with her. "It was Levi's night to win, unfortunately."

"Next time." She punches him in the stomach, and he slings his arm around her shoulders.

They walk toward the string lights and the sound of music, and all I want to do is turn around and go back into those woods to find Delaney.

I begin to follow Poppy and Nash, but Emmett steps out in front of me. I search the dance floor until I spot Wren spinning around with Briar as she holds Colter.

"How you holding up?" he asks.

I push my hand through my hair. "You heard?"

"Everyone heard. All of Willowbrook is practically here. So, she's back, huh?"

I love my cousin like a brother. I'm closer to Emmett than anyone—but I haven't been completely truthful with him. There's one secret I've kept locked away for seven-plus years. A secret only Delaney and I share.

"It's crazy. I mean, she was married to a drug trafficker." Emmett shakes his head.

The top button of his shirt is undone, jacket already abandoned.

"Did you know she was back? I saw her mom not that long ago in town."

He shakes his head. "I think it's only been a week or so. If I'd known, I would've told you."

I nod because I know he would've. Emmett always has my back.

"You seem really affected. Someone said you were rude to her." He arches an eyebrow, appearing confused.

This is where it would be easier if Emmett knew the truth, but I can't do that to Kristie's memory. "Just surprised to see her, I guess."

"It's been what... fourteen years? You had Kristie. And she clearly fell in love with someone else."

My stomach twists when I think of that asshole she married. I couldn't even bring myself to finish reading the story about his arrest. I'd Googled it once—after Brooks told me—but I closed the page pretty quickly. I didn't want to see pictures of the man who replaced me. The man she chose to marry and live happily ever after with shortly after we were through for good. It was selfish and petty, maybe, but it made me sick. So anytime someone brought up Delaney and her husband, I tuned out or walked away.

"You know it's bad if she had to come home. She's living with her parents."

My head snaps in his direction. "She is?"

"God, Danson, did you not read *anything* about her husband?"

"Not really, no."

"Her daughter is Wren's friend, I think. I'm not sure, but

that new girl in school she keeps talking about? Pretty sure that's her."

I rack my brain and remember Wren talking about a new girl she and Kayla adopted into their group, but the last name didn't sound familiar, so I never made the connection. There's no way I would've guessed that girl was Delaney's daughter. Especially one in *Wren's* grade. Obviously, Delaney and her husband wasted no time in starting a family.

The two of us walk toward the festivities.

"If her daughter's already in school, then she's been here a while, and no one knew?"

Emmett shrugs, stopping at the bar where Jude and Ben are arguing about the softball lineup for our team. Ben's questioning why Jude keeps fucking around with the rotation.

"I guess she's been hiding out," he says, signaling the bartender for two beers.

I hate the fact she's hiding as if she has something to be ashamed of. She doesn't. That piece of shit she married does. He's the one who wrecked her life. I can't imagine Delaney ever willingly getting involved in something like that.

And now, I've got a thousand questions.

Was she pressured into that life?

Was she afraid?

Did that asshole hurt her or her daughter?

A jealous rage simmers inside me.

Emmett nudges my shoulder with a beer, and I realize I've missed half the conversation.

"I guess we know who the next victim is," Ben jokes, and all three of the Noughton brothers click the necks of their bottles together, elbows leaning on the bar, watching *me*.

"What are you talking about?" I sip my beer, wishing it was something stronger—wishing I could take a few shots and forget the fact that Delaney is back to sharing the same town with me.

"It just seems fitting, no?" Ben says.

He was a senior when we were sophomores. I'm sure he doesn't really remember how it was between us.

"What does?"

They all raise their eyebrows at me, looking smug and amused.

"That your first love just showed up in town," Ben says.

"Who said she was my first love?" But the pit in my stomach aches because the lie tastes wrong the second it leaves my mouth.

Everyone assumes Kristie was it for me. *The one.* The woman who held my heart so tightly that there's nothing left to give anyone else. But the truth? Delaney had it long before Kristie ever came along.

And even after all this time, I still feel that pull to her. Like every seven years, she comes back into my orbit and wrecks me all over again.

"Delusional," Jude says with a shake of his head.

"Cynic," Ben adds.

"Just a straight-up destiny denier. Sad, really." Emmett tips back his beer.

"You guys don't know what you're talking about." I turn away from them, looking toward the dance floor where Wren twirls around with Nash and Poppy, ribbons spinning from her crown of flowers.

"What about you building your house? Ready to leave the nest yet?" Jude asks.

I roll my eyes. Another topic I don't have the bandwidth for tonight.

"Leave Danson alone. He's got a cushy thing going on over there," Emmett says before sipping his beer, his gaze following mine.

"What's going on with them?" I ask, nodding toward Nash and Poppy. Anything to shift attention off me.

"Heard Levi Richards won at the rodeo today, which just takes us full circle right back to Delaney." Ben laughs.

"I'm out." I walk away from my cousins and down the path toward the dance floor, finishing my beer and dropping the bottle in the recycling.

I ignore the familiar tug that's been pulling my mind back to Delaney for years. Because seven years ago, another girl came into my life, and she owns my heart.

Wren is everything. She comes first. Starting anything with Delaney would be reckless and selfish and probably end up hurting Wren if the truth came out.

I tap Wren on the shoulder. "Dance with your dad?"

Her face lights up, and for a second, I catch a flicker of Kristie in her smile. It hits like it always does—like a punch to the gut. A reminder of the past, of the promises I need to keep.

But I'd never trade what I have now. Being Wren's dad is one thing I'll never regret. It's the most important role I'll ever have.

Chapter Seven

DELANEY

I walk into The Perfect Petal on Monday, prepared to tell Poppy that I made a mistake, and I can't work here.

The shop is cozy and inviting. A spot labeled *The Stem Bar* is nestled between two big picture windows, spilling golden light onto the stained concrete floor. Wooden crates overflow with zinnias, cosmos, dahlias, and of course, daisies. The chalkboard above the main table reads, *Pick 3, Blend 5, and Make it Yours.* Mason jars line the bottom of the table, waiting to be filled.

At the back, a long farm table invites people to sit, talk, and make a bouquet. The shop isn't just about flowers, it's about coming together, which has always been Plain Daisy Ranch's thing.

The sweet scent of the peony display stops me cold. An array of Nebraska-grown flowers in every color sits in tall, galvanized metal tins. Needing a moment, I bend down and inhale.

"You did always love the peonies."

That voice.

Bennett.

For all of Poppy's promises that he's *never* around, it seems like he's *always* around.

I straighten slowly, glancing over. He's wearing jeans, cowboy boots, and a plaid button-down. His hair is styled instead of tucked beneath a hat, but he still carries that rugged ease that California never quite rubbed off him.

"They're like the wedding gown of the flower world."

He chuckles, resting a hip against a table filled with vases and candles, then casually crosses his arms. That's when I see the sign in the back corner.

Plant & Petal Landscape Design hangs above a door.

He follows my gaze and returns it with a smile. "I finally went out on my own."

"You always wanted to. Congratulations." I give him a small smile.

"My expenses lessened when we moved back. Seemed easier to take the risk."

We.

The word slices through me.

"Poppy said she was going to be here. I—"

"She had a bee emergency." He chuckles and straightens, arms falling to his sides.

A red-haired woman steps out from a back area, pausing when she sees us. She watches for a moment before smiling. "Good morning. Sorry, Bennett, I was just looking at an order we need to fill."

"It's okay, Summer. This is Delaney Ric...er..." He waits for me to correct him.

"Moore. I..." I stop myself. No need to unpack all my baggage in front of a stranger.

"Oh, you're Poppy's friend."

I nod.

"Sorry, she said she'd be back soon. The bees just aren't behaving, I guess." She laughs.

Poppy has an apiary on the ranch, and she sells the honey they produce at the ranch's store that Lottie runs.

Bennett glances my way with a crooked smile. Why does he have to be so... distractingly handsome?

"Can you let us know when she gets here? I'm going to show Delaney around," he says.

Summer, unaware of our history, smiles and waves us off, tearing a sheet of kraft paper off the roll and starting on a bouquet. "Sure thing, boss."

"Come on in, I'll show you the offices."

I glance at Summer, then lower my voice as I step closer. "I'm here to tell Poppy I can't take the job."

His shoulders sink. "Give me five minutes to change your mind."

"Bennett," I sigh. The last place I need to be is alone in a room with him.

"Five." He puts up his hand, all long five fingers spread wide.

"Go, you two, I've got this handled!" Summer calls cheerfully.

Bennett waits for me, his gaze steady and unreadable.

"Okay."

I follow him through the doors marked *Plant & Petal Landscaping*. The hallway is short—his office on one side, a small break room on the other.

"There's not a lot to see, but can I offer you a coffee?"

I lean against the doorframe of the break room, shoulder pressed to the wood, watching him pull down two coffee mugs. Each one is pretty and unique with a different glaze. I'm pretty sure they're handcrafted, not mass market.

"You said five minutes."

His dark hair is trimmed shorter than I remember, and the scruffy beard is new, making him appear older. Where did that boy I once loved go? The one with the backward baseball cap and broken-in jeans?

"You don't have to drink it all. Still take it with cream and two sugars?"

God, don't swoon, Delaney. Do not swoon that he remembers the way you take your coffee.

"That was in my younger years. Black is fine now."

He fills both cups and walks toward me. I hold out my hand, but he doesn't give it to me.

"I've got it. Come into my office."

I sigh but step aside. He passes, and I trail behind. Bennett sets the coffees on a table in front of a couch.

His office has charcoal walls and dark furniture. It screams man's domain, but also father with photos of his daughter softening the space. Wren's smile beams from the pictures interspersed with framed drawings dotting the bookshelves.

Then I spot it. On the top right shelf is a wedding photo of him and Kristie.

The knife in my gut twists.

I sit carefully, trying not to think of all the what-ifs. What if I'd made a different choice. What might've been.

He shuts the door.

Great. We're alone with the door shut door in his workplace. Warp me back to seven years ago when my stomach was flat and my tits were perky, and we're in the same exact place.

"You don't need to shut the door."

He doesn't answer, just sits on the other side of the couch, coffee in hand, eyes on mine. Trying to appear as if his mere presence doesn't affect me, I lift my cup, blowing on it.

"I want to apologize for how I acted when I first saw you. You being here... it took me by surprise."

"You're losing your touch. A coffee from a Black Friday, box-store-special coffee maker is your way of apologizing?"

"Would you prefer a bag of Hershey's Kisses?"

"Yes."

His smile deepens, and it spurs a mix of regret and nostalgia inside me. "I'll get right on it."

I glance at the door, then back at him. "I shouldn't have ambushed you. I should've told Poppy no. But she's so convincing, you know?"

He huffs. "How do you think I became half-owner of a flower shop?"

"She's a dreamer," I say, hearing my own yearning for how much I've missed her over the years. We haven't been nearly as close as I would have liked, which is mostly because of me and the secrets I'm keeping.

"She's right to have hired you. I'd like you to reconsider."

"Why?" My head tilts. Why would he want me here every day? To see me and be reminded of everything that went down?

"Honestly?"

I set down the coffee. "No, I like it when you lie to me."

He places his cup gently on a coaster, then looks at mine. "I know."

I blink slowly. "You know?"

"About your husband."

My breath catches.

"I'm sure you need—"

I bolt up from the couch and keep my back to him, trying to hold it together. What little pride I have left feels as if it's hanging by a thread.

Bennett lets me collect my thoughts. I want to ask how much he knows, but at the same time, I don't want to have that conversation.

"I don't need your handouts."

"It's not a handout. Poppy already offered. I don't want you to turn it down because of me."

I turn around. He's leaning forward, elbows on his knees, hands clasped.

"That's not what you said though. You said it was because my husband was a drug trafficker who's in jail, and I had to come live with my parents because I'm a thirty-one-year-old mother who can't clothe and feed her daughter."

Okay, that was a little too much. Way too much.

He stares at me.

"It's good to know the gossip ring of Willowbrook hasn't waned over the years."

"Do you want to talk about it?" he asks.

"No!" I practically screech. "Definitely not with you."

Bennett lifts his hands in surrender. "I just wanted to offer. I mean, we were friends once."

"The keyword there is *were*."

He sighs, then stares at his hands again. "If it makes you feel better, I haven't read anything. I didn't even know you had a daughter until Emmett told me. Apparently, she's friends with Wren."

I close my eyes. I really don't want to start talking about our daughters as if we could somehow have a normal conversation about bedtime routines and how to hide vegetables in their meals.

"Delaney, listen." He stands and steps around the table, closer to me. "Just keep the job. We could use the help and your knowledge. I handled the situation badly, but I don't want you turning it down because of *me*."

Our eyes lock.

"How often are you here?"

He puts a hand over his heart as if I've wounded him. "That hurts." But then he straightens, understanding why I'm asking. "I'm usually out on projects. Rarely here."

I nod. The scent of flowers lingers even in here, and it feels like breathing again. Working with flowers is what I went to school for. What I used to love.

A knock sounds on the door. "B, are you trying to steal my BFF again?"

"Come in," Bennett says, eyes still on mine.

God, how easy it would be to fall into those brown eyes again.

"I'm so sorry. Miss Queen Bee just thinks she owns the hive. Well, okay, she does, but..." Poppy pauses when she sees our proximity. Bennett's arm is inches from mine. "BFF time. See ya, B."

She loops her arm through mine and leads me out of the room.

"Sorry about that. I don't know why he's here. He's supposed to be out working on a bid. That's why I asked you to meet me here." She glances over her shoulder. "Am I missing something?"

It's like déjà vu all over again.

Chapter Eight

Sean,

Leia asked me tonight what love feels like.

Sadly, I don't have a perfect answer for how you know you love someone. Sometimes it's something that builds, sometimes it's fast and explosive. Falling in love with Bennett was slow and sweet. Sure, he did nice things for me. He tutored me through my ACTs, bribing me with Hershey's Kisses every time I got a question right. He rarely showed up at my doorstep for a date without flowers. He complimented me all the time. I'm sure any girl would've fallen for him. But when I think about my time with Bennett, there's one night that stands out from the rest.

It was my seventeenth birthday, and my

grandma had fallen. She broke her hip and was rushed to a hospital in Missouri. My parents had no choice but to go and get her settled. They promised we'd celebrate when they returned, and I said I was fine. Levi was at a rodeo, Poppy had to work, and Bennett had plans to see U2 with Emmett and a group of their friends.

So, I was alone on my birthday.

I made myself a bowl of popcorn and decided to wallow a little, bingeing on rom-coms for the night. I'd just set the popcorn and drink on the table when the doorbell rang.

When I opened it, there he was.

Bennett.

"What are you doing here?" I asked him.

He was in his favorite jeans, cowboy boots, and his backward baseball cap. His hands were tucked in his pockets, and he looked almost nervous. "Come on a ride with me?"

I looked down at my pajama-clad self. "You're supposed to be on your way to St. Louis."

"U2 isn't all that."

"B," I sighed.

"You're more important. And you're not spending your birthday alone."

"What did Emmett say?" I hadn't moved.

Some part of me still wanted to march him right back to Plain Daisy Ranch and shove him into Emmett's truck.

"You don't want to know what he said." He reached for my hand.

I let him come inside so I could shut off the lights and TV. "Where are we going?"

"You'll see."

I quickly changed, closed up the house, and got into his truck, assuming he'd take me to that overlook in Hickory where everyone went to park and... talk.

But when he turned onto the dirt road to the ranch and parked outside the horse stables, I was shocked.

"B?"

"Don't worry, I've got you."

I didn't grow up around horses like he did. Levi found his way to horses, but they always intimidated me.

"Can't we just drive?"

"Not where I'm taking you." He killed the ignition and waited, giving me the choice. That was one of the things I loved most about Bennett. He never pressured me into anything. "If you'd rather..."

"No. Let's go." I opened the car door, nerves fluttering, but my curiosity was stronger.

And I trusted him.

He chuckled, his hand finding mine as we walked toward the stables.

My steps slowed, still unsure when I saw the horses, and he tightened his grip on my hand. We passed stall after stall until he stopped at Junebug. Poppy's horse.

"I thought you rode Cedar." I circled toward Cedar's stall, where his brown head peeked out as though he recognized that Bennett was here.

"I do. But Junebug's smaller. I figured you'd be more comfortable on her."

Bennett adored Cedar. He prided himself on that horse. Part of me knew he wanted me on Cedar for my first ride with him.

"Let's take Cedar." I walked over to the stall.

"You sure? He's taller and stronger. Not that Junebug isn't great..."

I stepped closer until his hands gently caught my hips. "Which one would you prefer?"

"I just want you to enjoy it."

"But?"

A sheepish smile tugged at his lips. "Cedar."

"Get him ready then."

When I said I'd never ridden a horse

before, I meant it. Not even the kind that go in slow circles at county fairs.

Bennett climbed on first, then reached down to help me. "Trust me."

How could I not trust him? He held my entire heart in that moment.

One graceful tug and I was up. Then half on, half falling until he steadied me, his laugh quiet, his warm breath against my neck as I moved into position in front of him.

"Easy," he whispered, his breath tickling the sensitive spot just below my ear.

The horse was taller than I'd expected. His muscles shifted beneath me, solid and powerful all at once. We didn't use a saddle. Just Bennett and me.

I gripped Bennett's arms. "I change my mind," I muttered.

"You want off?"

I shook my head. I didn't want off because I wanted to know what he had planned, what was in the backpack he'd taken from the back of his truck that was now slung across his back.

One arm slipped around my waist. The other braced us both. "I've got you."

We moved slow. Cedar stepped carefully as we headed toward a worn trail in the grass.

Every sway of Cedar's body rocked through me. I couldn't tell if my heart raced from the movement or the nearness of feeling every inch of Bennett pressed behind me. The way he leaned in close. The way his chest rose and fell along my back, the heat of his hand at my waist, the soft circle of his thumb that traced tiny infinity symbols where his hand held me.

The sky faded from gold to bruised violet. It was the most beautiful view I'd ever seen. And somehow, the image still hasn't left me all these years later.

Bennett's voice calmed me the entire ride, telling me what to expect with each shift and turn. What Cedar might do. What it meant when his gait changed.

We reached a clearing on top of a hill near the creek.

He helped me down, and although the ride wasn't as scary as I'd expected, I was glad to have both feet back on solid ground. He walked Cedar to a nearby tree and secured him, leaving enough slack for the horse to graze.

I wandered to the edge of the hill and sat down, tucking my knees to my chest, watching the last of the sunlight streak across the sky. Bennett came up behind me, his long legs bracketing mine as he sat, and I leaned into the warmth of his body and his strong touch.

I heard the click of a lighter, and Bennett placed a cupcake in front of me, candle lit and glowing.

"Happy birthday," he whispered.

"B!" I turned, heart aching in the best way.

"Make a wish." Again, he held the purple frosted cupcake in front of me. "And don't waste it on me, because I'm already yours."

I giggled as I always did at his humor, and he urged the cupcake closer to me.

I closed my eyes tightly and made a wish that I'd always have Bennett. I'd heard what he had said, and I believed he was mine, but I wasn't naive. We were seventeen and in love, with our futures wide open in front of us. He had dreams of going to college, and I was still unsure where my path would lead after high school.

He placed the cupcake back in the box beside another one and pulled me into his arms. He laid back, and I curled onto his chest.

His hand tucked a strand of my hair that had fallen down during the ride behind my ear. "I love you, Laney."

"I know."

And I did. Maybe that was part of it. I

never questioned whether he did. Even before he said the words, I felt it, deep down.

Bennett taught me that real love isn't just about butterflies or fireworks. It's about being someone's cheerleader and letting them choose whether to take the leap—but always being there to hold their hand if they do.

And that's probably why I fell for him. Because that night, and every night after it, he made me feel safe and seen. He was always the calm during a storm for me.

Delaney

Chapter Nine

BENNETT

I'm sitting at the usual family table in the dining room at The Getaway Lodge. Mom is busy talking to the guests, while Wren pushes her eggs around on her plate.

"Come on, eat."

"Why did Uncle Jensen make me eggs? I don't like eggs." She looks at the eggs with disgust.

"Because you need a little protein in you." I finish my plate of over-easy eggs and toast, wiping my mouth and sipping my coffee. I'd love to get out of here before my mom corners me about Delaney being back in town.

"I like pancakes," Wren says.

I huff, knowing she's not going to touch her eggs.

"Wren, you can't always eat what you want." I lean back in my chair.

Delaney's been living in my head since she got back. She starts the job today, and I'm not sure what to expect. I had an appointment that would've taken me out of the office, but the clients wanted to come in for the meeting because the wife is having some women's brunch and wants to pick up some bouquets while she's there.

"Why not?" she asks, interrupting my thoughts.

"Four bites."

"Two," she argues back.

"Six."

She groans and jabs her fork into the eggs.

"Hey, who takes your friend Leia to school?"

She shrugs. "I don't know."

"Her mom?"

"I don't think so."

It's clearly not Leia's dad.

"Grandma? Grandpa?"

Wren puts the eggs in her mouth and gags. Quickly, her hand grabs her orange juice, and she takes a sip, swallowing it down.

"It's not that bad." I can't help but chuckle at her dramatics.

"You're only saying that because you eat that drippy yellow stuff."

"Here you go." Mom slides a plate with two pancakes in front of Wren.

"Thanks, Grandma!" Wren pushes away the eggs, already forgotten, and grabs the syrup, smothering her pancakes.

"Undermining me again." I arch an eyebrow at Mom.

"The guests were looking, and you sound like one of those mean dads." My mom sits at the table with us. "Briar has Colter with her today. If you hurry, you can spend some time with them, Wren."

"We don't have time. I have to get her to school and then get back for work."

Mom studies me for a second. "Oh, going in early?"

There's a note in her tone that suggests she's going to interrogate me the minute Wren leaves this table.

I glance at my daughter, who's now shoveling pancakes

into her mouth, both cheeks puffy and full. My focus shifts back to my mom, and any patience I had this morning is already running thin.

"Just go see Briar and Colter," I tell Wren, wanting to get this over with.

She takes another sip of her orange juice, swallows, wipes her face, and drops the napkin on the table before running off.

"Slow down," I call after her, but she's long gone.

"Whoa, Wren." I hear Emmett behind me, no doubt about to join us. "Babe, here comes Wren," he hollers down the hall, not caring that he just interrupted the guests' breakfast.

"Go ahead." I wave toward my mom and lean back in my chair. "Just get it over with."

"Get what over with?" She keeps her head buried in her phone.

"Why you told Wren about Briar and Colter being here. To get me alone."

"What's up?" Emmett pats me on the back.

"Nothing much. Mom wants to interrogate me about Delaney being back."

My eyes stay locked on my mom, who still hasn't looked up from her phone, but she wears that smug little smirk she always gets when she's caught.

"Funny, me too." Emmett slides into Wren's now-empty seat and eats her leftovers.

"Then go ahead." I sip my coffee and glance at my watch. I've got about ten minutes before I need to get Wren out the door.

"Any old feelings come back?" Emmett asks. "You guys were really into one another back in high school."

"Exactly. High school."

What my cousin doesn't know is that our paths reconnected seven years ago. And now that Delaney's back, I need to make damn sure that fact stays buried.

"Come on, man. Tell him, Aunt Darla. He was head over heels in love. Hell, you skipped U2 just to hang with her."

"It was her birthday. She was alone."

As if I don't think about that night enough. The first time we had sex under the big sky. I can almost feel my hands on her again, reliving that moment as if it was yesterday.

"I'm just saying. I didn't understand it until I got with Briar. Now I get why you were always ditching us for her."

I set down my coffee. Even if I have to sit in the school parking lot for twenty minutes, it's better than letting Emmett drag me through the memories I've tried to bury. "I should go."

"I'd be careful if I were you," Mom says, interrupting me as I stand.

"Excuse me?"

Emmett focuses on her, and she sets her phone on the table.

"Delaney's starting her life over. She doesn't need you putting your selfish needs in front of hers."

I sink back into the chair. "And here I thought you were going to tell me to ask her out."

She shrugs. "I'm not telling you not to, but I'm just saying you better get a grasp on your feelings because you can't just twirl her around a dance floor and convince her to go home with you for the night. But if you want her back—"

"I don't."

She tips her head. "If you do, you need to be one hundred percent sure. She doesn't need someone to add to her problems. She needs someone who will stand beside her while she finds herself again."

I glance at Emmett, whose eyes are crinkled with disbelief. I have no idea why my mom's suddenly Team Delaney. It's not like her to warn us off anyone. She's usually pushing us toward any member of the opposite sex.

"I think I always did that," I say.

"Did you?"

She holds my gaze as if she already knows the truth I've worked hard to hide—especially about what happened seven years ago. My stomach sours at the thought of anyone knowing my carefully crafted story about my marriage to Kristie is a lie.

"Jeez, Aunt Darla. I was here to push him to make a move." Emmett being stunned is rare, and honestly, I'm a little relieved that even he thinks my mom's behavior is weird.

Mom picks up her coffee. "Poppy gave her a job—"

"*We* gave her a job."

"Oh sorry, *they* gave her a job." My mom's eyes widen, and Emmett purses his lips to stop from smiling.

"To be nice. You'd do the same."

"All I'm saying, and Emmett can attest to this, is she's a mother, going through something very public with that husband of hers. Don't just go trying to get into her pants."

Emmett's head swivels toward me. I stare at him for a second, utterly dumbfounded.

This is not my mother. Usually she's full of sarcastic jabs, not handing out heartfelt warnings as though I'm some guy looking for a rebound.

"It was never just about that," I mutter. "First of all, it's her soon-to-be ex-husband. And just... don't worry about it. I'm not sleeping with an employee, nor would I ever do that to her. But it's nice to know what you think of my character, Mom."

I down the rest of my coffee, rise from the table, and set my mug down with more force than necessary. "Have a great day."

Emmett's laughter trails behind me as I walk away.

I really hope this is my mom's way of playing a game and not her actually thinking I'd ever put my own wants before Delaney's needs.

Chapter Ten

DELANEY

I climb back into my dad's truck after dropping Leia at school. She complains every day that she's the first one in class and has to sit and read until someone else shows up. I half wonder if Mrs. Martinez will be calling me at some point, instructing me she needs to come closer to the bell time.

But this is best if I want to avoid Bennett at drop-off time —which I do.

The white piece of paper in my center console draws a groan from me. It's Leia's field trip form that's due today, otherwise, she can't go to the zoo for the end-of-year trip.

You can do this, Delaney. A quick run to the office. In and out. No lingering. Head down.

I spring open my door and walk steadily toward the main doors. Only a few parents are arriving now, and I know Bennett isn't one of those parents who comes right before the bell, even without knowing it. He's punctual and timely and annoyingly anal about being early to places.

I'm buzzed in, and I practically toss the form in the secretary's lap, leaving with a fleeting thank you and a wave before speed-walking away as if I'm in a race back to the truck. A relieved breath flows out of me as soon as I'm safe and secure inside the cab.

But then I look through the windshield, and there he is.

Bennett stands by his truck, one hand braced on the open door, the other gently guiding Wren to the ground. He holds out her backpack, and she's talking to him the entire time her arms slip through the straps.

She looks like him... like... I let the thought die. If I keep denying it, maybe the secret will die inside me. Especially after I came so close to revealing it the other day in his office. My confession was right on the tip of my tongue.

Wren skips off with his hand secured in hers, crossing the drive-in front of the school. When they hit the sidewalk, he crouches and tucks her hair behind her ear, his thumb brushing her cheek with a look so tender, my chest tightens. She swats his hand, and he shakes his head, but his smile and laughter crinkle his eyes.

Her little arms wrap around his neck, and he buries his head into her, whispering something before she draws back and runs for the school doors.

I remain there, engine running, the air conditioning rattling the vents. My palms sweat against the steering wheel as I imagine *what if* for the millionth time.

In my head, I've run a thousand versions of the moment I tell Bennett that Leia is his child. The conversation. My confession. The explanations that aren't enough.

But Leia needs security right now. She needs stability and peace after losing Sean. Her life is in chaos, and I'm finally starting to see my little girl come back to me.

Unfortunately, it's mostly when she talks about Wren. A girl from school she has no idea is her half sister.

Telling him Leia is his means setting fire to the remains of our lives that I haven't even stitched back together yet.

But not telling him... means I'm the person I never thought I would be.

I squeeze my eyes shut as they fill with tears.

It doesn't matter how many times I promise myself I'll do it. I never do. I'm a coward and a liar, but I just want to wrap a protective bubble around Leia and me, stopping anyone else from getting in. She's been hurt enough.

And do I dare allow the man who left me in ruins, who chose another woman, a chance to do that to my daughter?

I open my eyes to see Bennett staring at me from the sidewalk.

Shit.

I freeze, as if I could turn into a puff of air and make myself invisible. But he squints, tilts his head, and smiles. That ache in my heart squeezes again when he walks toward me.

No, no, no.

I wipe my face, brushing away the tears already halfway down my cheeks, but it's too late to pretend I'm not crying. I put one hand on the wheel and the other on the gearshift, debating whether I should drive away before he reaches me.

But he breaks the distance too fast, and suddenly he's right outside my window, knocking gently. "Delaney?"

I don't look at him. I can't.

Because if I do, I know I'll tell him.

And if I confess, it means letting him in.

A mother protects. She doesn't invite trouble. And that's what I was trying to do all those years ago.

I drag my sleeve across my face and roll down the window just enough to feel the warm morning breeze. I get the faintest whiff of his cologne. Clean and grounded, as he's always been.

"Hey," I say, voice rough. "What are you doing here?"

He chuckles. "Same as you. School drop-off." Bennett gives a small shrug, gaze scanning my face too closely. He doesn't mention my red-rimmed eyes, but his brow flickers. Of course he notices. "You okay?"

I nod too fast. "Yeah. Fine. Just tired."

His lips thin, and his gaze drifts to the school. I'm a horrible person.

Tell him. Just tell him and get rid of the guilt.

"You sure?" he asks. "You look…"

Broken? Guilty? Yep, both.

"… like you've had a rough morning," he finishes, his tone softer.

I scoff. "That's one way to put it."

A beat of silence lands between us.

I hate that he can still read me. That part of him still wants to fix my problems.

"You want to grab a coffee?" he asks, nodding toward the little café I know is a block down. "I've got time."

My heart stumbles over its beats.

I need to say no. But my fingers twitch on the steering wheel, and some desperate, tired part of me wants to sit across from him for a few minutes and pretend we're still the people who were each other's everything once upon a time.

I miss his friendship.

If things were different, if Leia wasn't his, maybe I could have coffee with him and tell him all my problems. But that's not our reality.

"I can't," I murmur.

"Won't," he says gently.

All the words I've wanted to tell him since I saw him at Lottie's wedding rise up my throat, pressing against my tongue to come out.

I miss you. I'll always love you. Our daughter has your eyes, and I don't know how to tell you without putting her in harm's way.

Instead, I say, "I need to get the truck back to my dad."

He nods and steps back from the door.

My finger goes to press the window button, but he breaks the distance again, putting his hands on the roof of the truck, leaning in. "If you need or want to talk... I know... I mean, our past and all that, but just... I'm here."

I nod and swallow all the chaos of my emotions. "Thanks, Bennett."

I give him a tight smile, and his eyes lock with mine for a beat before he pushes himself off the truck again. I quickly put it in gear to get the hell away from him before I break.

I give myself one glance in the rearview mirror before I turn the corner, pushing it all away.

Chapter Eleven

Sean,

Leia asked me today if it's better to be the one left or the one doing the leaving.

You've read how Bennett and I started dating, but that question made me think about how we ended. How someone can be the center of your universe, and then one day, poof, they're gone.

It's scary, looking back and realizing that. You wonder if you had held on tighter, had put more effort in, instead of letting it all slowly drift away, could things have been different?

My dad was transferred to Iowa the summer between my junior and senior year. Iowa is far from Nebraska, but to two teenagers, it might as well have been the other side of the world. There's no way two teenagers in love could realistically see each other or make a long-distance relationship work.

But we naïvely thought we could.

The day I left, I stood in my driveway, all my friends huddled on the sidewalk as the movers packed up our house, and all I could do was cry and cling to Bennett.

When my parents told me we had to go, Bennett pulled me into his arms, flush against his body.

"I love you," he whispered in my ear.

My fingers tightened around his shirt. I wanted to kick and scream and tell my parents I was staying. Yell that they were ripping me away from everything I loved. Forcing me to start over in a new town with kids I didn't know.

"I love you." My voice cracked, and his cheek brushed along my temple.

"You're going to love it there. You'll see."

We hadn't talked about how we'd stay together, just that we would. It was just assumed. We made promises to write. He said maybe he could get his parents to let him and Emmett drive up before school started again. At the time, I believed all of our fictions.

It was only supposed to be one year apart.

I'd try to go to college near him, and we'd reconnect as though the year apart had never happened.

"I'll write you as soon as we get there. A letter for every day we're apart."

He didn't say anything, but his arms tightened around me.

"Laney," my mom said from behind us.

He loosened his grip, but I clung tighter, desperate to make the moment last.

"It's okay. We got this." He held my head, kissed my forehead, then stepped away from me.

I believed him because I was seventeen, in love, and certain I'd found my soulmate. Time wouldn't change what we had.

I have to admit—it was ridiculous and foolish of me to think that.

He kissed me one last time before we had no choice but to say goodbye.

Poppy hugged me tightly before I climbed into my parents' car.

Everyone I loved, besides my family, stood on that driveway and watched us drive away from Willowbrook.

I hated my dad for taking the job. For making us move.

At first, the letters came daily. Not long or

exactly romantic, but sweet. He'd tell me about his day and how much he missed me. One of them was about a dream he had of us taking Cedar out and dipping into the creek, him making love to me on the bank.

We texted too, but phones were different then. After I went over our data plan the first month, my dad restricted my texting.

I found a group of friends soon after school started. Bennett got a job at a pizza place in town, and our letters grew further and further apart. Days turned into weeks.

Starting over in a new town was hard. And having the person I loved most back in the place I still thought of as home made everything more complicated. I constantly felt split in two.

My new friends grew tired of hearing about Bennett and all the memories I couldn't let go of. Every month, we drifted further apart.

One night, I called him. He was out with Emmett and some friends and was completely distracted and wasn't really paying any attention to our conversation.

After I hung up, I wrote him a letter, breaking up with him.

I addressed it, stamped it, and mailed it

before I could think twice. It was for the best.

And that was that.

I didn't see him for many years. Not until I walked into that breakroom one day.

Which started a whole new chapter for us— but that's a story for another letter.

I can answer half of that question now.

Leaving is easier, but you still feel like the one left behind, just in a different way.

That doesn't mean the love stops. It leaves you with a thousand what-ifs.

I realized young that life is a book with chapters, and as you move through them, you change and evolve.

Delaney

BENNETT

Two days go by, and I don't see Delaney at drop-off. I've barely been at the shop either, and every time I'm there, she's either with a customer or on her lunch break.

The ache to catch a glimpse of her keeps growing, but it needs to stop because she has way too much on her plate to deal with my bullshit. Her crying the other morning made that clear as fuck.

It also made it clear that a part of me still aches to comfort her, to reach for her, to soothe her pain. But I'm not the guy who plays that role in her life anymore. I lost that right.

And I have to keep reminding myself of that fact.

"Daddy, did you know Levi is Leia's uncle?" Wren asks from the back seat, and I glance at her in the rearview mirror.

"I did. Her mom and Levi are twins."

"She said her uncle is going to bring her to the ranch to ride. Can I meet her there?"

"We'll see."

Her legs swing back and forth while she watches the world blur past the window. "She said her uncle is taking her to a rodeo. Can we go?"

Levi's been in the circuit since he was young. He and Nash are saddle bronc riders with a mutual addiction to adrenaline.

"You've been before. We went and saw Nash, remember?"

"That was, like, two years ago. I was just little then."

She pouts, and I can tell she's gearing up to ask again. She's been on a mission to hang out with Leia since she and Kayla named her their fellow best friend.

But now that I know Leia is Delaney's daughter... I can't pretend it doesn't make it complicated—at least for me. What if Delaney doesn't want to be anywhere near me? What if Leia being friends with Wren is already a sore spot for her?

"Maybe I'll ask her mom when they plan on going." I say it to appease Wren, but some stupid part of me wonders if I could just... accidentally run into them there.

God, what am I thinking? I torched any hope for a future with Delaney back in California.

"Yay!" Wren's feet kick in excitement as I pull into the school lot. "There's Leia! Do you see her, Daddy? Kayla too!" She reaches for her seat belt.

I'm too distracted by her trying to unbuckle herself to see the two girls she's referring to as her best friends. I look at her in the rearview mirror again. "Wren, stay seated until I park."

"But I don't want to miss them!"

I find a spot, park, and before I can blink, she's unbuckled and throws her door open—right into the truck next to us.

"Wren!" I snap, my tone harsher than I intend.

I've been shorter tempered than normal lately because of these feelings that won't leave me alone now that I know Delaney is mere miles away from me. That I could spend my entire day in the shop with her but be unable to touch her, to talk to her. That her smile and laughter might never be pointed at me again.

"Sorry." She leans back in her seat as Principal North steps out of the truck.

I get out, round the side, and immediately see the dent in the principal's truck.

"In a rush there, Wren?" he says with a laugh. "Me too. Dentist appointment this morning." He takes her hand and helps her down.

"I'm so sorry, Principal North."

He waves me off. "Please. This truck's old and beat up. I think the new ding adds character, don't you?"

He winks at Wren, and I'm reminded why he's the beloved principal of an elementary school, and I am not. He has the patience of a saint and the heart of a damn hero.

I grab Wren's backpack and hand it to her. She puts it on, but her eyes keep darting toward her friends. I remember being eager to see my friends at her age.

"I'll call my insurance."

Principal North shakes his head. "No, you won't." Then he turns to Wren. "There's Leia and Kayla. Let's go before we're late." He waves to the crosswalk guard. "Cindy, let Wren catch up to her friends!"

Cindy puts up the stop sign, and Wren wraps her arms around my legs. I barely have time to bend and kiss her goodbye before she's gone with a "love you" trailing behind her.

"I'm really sorry," I say again, rubbing the back of my neck.

"I know. But while I've got you..."

Hearing that from a teacher or a principal is every parent's nightmare. "Yes?"

He laughs, pats my shoulder. "Relax. I was going to say how great Wren is. She's outgoing and smart and always making friends, but I've noticed she's taken Leia Moore under her wing."

He eyes me for a beat. "She's a quiet one. Reminds me of a student I had once who clung to his cousin like a life raft."

I cringe. "Was I that bad?"

He chuckles. "You needed Emmett, just like Leia needs Wren. I'm a sucker for friendships like that. Especially when one shows the other it's okay to be yourself, let loose a little."

"Well, I'm glad she's doing that for her." I shove my hands into my pockets.

I'm not sure who I would've turned out to be without Emmett always pushing me to do things outside of my comfort zone. Even years later, I'm still the quiet guy who generally listens more than I talk.

"So, I'll take the ding."

I nod. "Thanks."

We glance toward the school. The three girls are walking up the pathway hand in hand.

My eyes lock on Leia. Her braid is done the same way Delaney wore hers the other day—wrapped around her head and down one side of her neck. And her clothes... she looks as though she just walked off a kid's fashion magazine shoot.

"It's nice to have a familiar face back in Willowbrook, don't you think?" Principal North cuts into my thoughts. "Feels like memory lane, doesn't it?"

"Ah... a little, yeah."

"You know what I love more than those friendships?"

"I have a feeling you're going to tell me."

He laughs. "When the one who was helped becomes the one doing the helping. Now excuse me, I have to get inside the school to make it before assembly."

He raises his brows as though he knows exactly what he's doing, then nods and walks toward the school. "Good to see you, Bennett."

I watch the girls disappear into the building while his words land with the exact weight he anticipated.

I might not be able to be a part of Delaney's life the way I always wished, but I can't leave her floundering either. I have no idea if she'll be receptive to my help, but I have to give it a try for the woman who held my future in her hands for so many years.

Chapter Thirteen

DELANEY

My stomach is a ball of knots as I step inside The Perfect Petal. There's a UTV parked outside, and I really hope it's Poppy's and not Bennett's.

The bell on the door rings, announcing my arrival.

Again, the sweet scent of the peonies calls my name. Bennett was right, I've always loved them, even if they bring forth the memories that felt so crushing to a teenage girl in love, ripped away from the boy she thought would be her forever.

Poppy comes out of the back with an armful of flowers. "Good morning." She drops them on the table and comes over, wrapping me in a warm, welcoming hug. "I'm so happy you're here."

"Thanks again." We've had this little exchange the last two days.

She pulls away and waves me off, going back to the table with the flowers. "Don't thank me, we need your help."

"Then stop hugging me like you're surprised to see me show up for work every day."

She glances up from her flowers, her brows raised.

"Oh, stop it. I'm sorry for letting us lose touch," I say.

"For not returning my calls?"

"Yes."

"Or my texts?"

"Yes." My tone lightens along with hers.

"And not letting me be your maid of honor at your wedding?"

I pull some kraft paper from the roll and help her put together some bouquets. "If it makes you feel better, I didn't have a maid of honor."

"Oh?" Her interest is piqued. I haven't really told her anything about my past with Sean.

"We went to the courthouse and then on a honeymoon where we had a ceremony with just the two of us at sunset."

"That's romantic." She smiles at me.

"It was a lie."

Silence settles over the shop, and I assume Bennett hasn't arrived yet. Or maybe he's tucked away in his office, keeping his distance.

"I'm really sorry."

I glance at her and nod. "Me too."

The bell rings, saving us from digging deeper into my past. I'm thankful not to have to get into it with her. My past with a man I loved, but apparently never really knew. I'm not even sure if Sean loved me or just played the part. His betrayal makes me question everything I thought I knew. I can still see him dancing with Leia around the kitchen that morning, laughing and carefree mere hours before he was arrested. Was that real?

"Oh, this is so cute." An older woman, probably in her sixties, heads to the stem bar and breathes in the scent of the flowers.

A man follows her, presumably her husband.

Poppy stops what she's doing, smiling warmly. "Welcome to The Perfect Petal. Is there anything I can help you with?"

The man has thinning gray hair, is well-dressed, and clearly is out of place in Willowbrook. His slacks, loafers, and country club polo scream money. And not the ranch kind, but the kind earned in boardrooms.

"I'm looking for Bennett Owens. He gave me this address, but clearly this isn't..." He looks around again. "... his office."

"I'm going to make a bouquet," the woman says.

"Rosie, we don't have time for that."

"Sure, we do. It'll only take a moment."

He sighs and looks at us. "Everything only takes a moment."

Poppy and I chuckle, but he doesn't crack a smile, waiting for us to direct him to Bennett.

"He's not here yet. He seems to be running late, which is odd for him. I'll give him a quick call." Poppy digs her phone out of her apron.

"I guess you have longer than a moment, Rosie. He's not even on time."

"Oh, Earl, relax." I like Rosie's style. "We have nowhere to be. You said you took the day off, right?"

He gives her a tight smile. "Yes, dear."

Poppy's whispering into the phone, but I catch enough to know Bennett's probably pissed. He's never handled lateness well and always thought it made him look bad no matter how many times I told him people understand accidents and things that are out of his control.

I remember only one time he didn't care about being late —when we couldn't keep our hands off each other, and he took me on the conference room table. He used California traffic as an excuse, without the stress and edginess he usually possessed.

"Why don't I help?" I offer, finishing the bouquet I was working on before heading toward Rosie.

"Please do. Otherwise, I'll spend my day off in this flower shop and not on the golf course," Earl says.

"Don't even think about playing golf today." There's a warning in Rosie's voice. This is clearly a conversation they've had before.

Earl blows out a breath, stuffs his hands in his pockets, and wanders the shop.

I'm halfway to Rosie when Poppy says, "He's only five minutes out. There was an accident at the school his daughter attends."

I stop mid-step, my heart lurching.

"Oh, just Wren hitting Principal North's car with the truck door. Nothing with the actual school."

I let out a relieved breath, nodding like I need the reminder that we're safe. No one knows where we went. No one's looking for us.

"I'm not very good at this," Rosie says, laughing as she tries to pair two flowers together. "How do you guys make it look so pretty?"

I sit on the stool next to her. "Well, I went to school for it."

"You can get a degree in flowers?"

She's dressed like someone used to manicures and high-end shops. Flats with gold emblems, a sundress, and a cardigan. Her hair is curled and dyed without a hint of gray. I'm fairly sure her jewelry costs more than the car I owned before the DEA seized it.

"Floriculture, yes."

"Like horticulture?" she asks.

"Yes, that too. But I concentrated in florals because... they're so pretty. And they smell so good." I lift a peony and breathe it in.

"They are. And it seems to suit you." Her gaze sweeps over me.

I cross my legs, a little self-conscious. I used to dine with women like her. Women who wouldn't blink at dropping five figures on a brunch fundraiser.

"What do you mean?" I tilt my head in her direction.

"Your flowy dress, your natural hair, and lack of makeup. One of those hippie types."

I laugh. I don't think she means it offensively, it's just her frame of reference. "I guess so."

If she'd seen me six months ago, she probably wouldn't recognize me. My hair was always straight with maybe a curl that came from a curling iron, never my natural waves like now. My makeup, fake lashes, and lipstick were always on before I left the house.

That's been one freeing thing since everything went down—I feel more comfortable in my own skin again.

"Let's get started. Pick three flowers that call out to you."

She spins her stool, thank God. The longer she looks at me, the more I fear she'll say, *"Hey, you look familiar, don't I know you from the news?"*

She taps her finger to her lips and looks over the array of flowers Poppy must have put out when she opened this morning. She selects a big sunflower, a daisy, and a rose. That's a challenging mix, but we can work with it.

"It's ugly." She frowns at her trio.

"We haven't cushioned them yet. Pick five more from the lower level."

"Greenery is boring."

"Well, it might be boring, but it makes the flowers shine. It's like your backdrop and will barely even be noticed, but you can pick some fillers too. Sweet peas or larkspur might be nice."

"How about we dumb this down for me? I point, you pick. If you want to name them, fine—but I'll forget."

I laugh. "Sure thing."

She points, I pick, and soon I'm arranging the bouquet in my hand, varying heights, centering the sunflower. I add a few unexpected touches for texture, something soft and playful.

I hold it out, and her eyes widen. "Wow. You're amazing at your job. Earl! Come see what this young lady just made!"

"I'd rather not," Earl mutters. "It's been longer than five minutes."

"Sorry," Poppy says behind us. "I'm sure he'll be here any second. This is very unlike him."

"Let's trim the ends. Do you want to put it in the mason jar now or wait till you're home?"

She leans in. "If I carry a mason jar of water all the way home, I'll look like I peed myself by the time we get there."

"Then I'll tie it together and wrap it in kraft paper. All you have to do is add some water and slip it into the jar when you get home. Sound good?"

"Sounds too easy. Don't be upset if they're dead in a day."

I stand from the stool. "You'll keep them alive for a week, I bet."

"No, she won't," Earl calls from the front, constantly within earshot.

I lean down and whisper, "I believe in you."

Her face lights up. "I really like you."

As I walk to grab the kraft paper, warmth blooms in my chest. I'd forgotten how good it feels to make someone smile. To create something beautiful out of what they thought was nothing. *Thanks, Rosie. I owe you one.*

The bell rings, and Bennett barrels in, cheeks flushed. "I'm so sorry, Earl."

"Fifteen minutes late. Might want to get that watch checked," Earl mutters. "Rosie, he's here."

"Again, I'm sorry. Let's go to my office."

Bennett glances at me, then Poppy, before weaving through the tables.

"Perfect timing. She just finished my bouquet," Rosie says. "I'll grab it on the way out, darling."

"It'll be ready for you."

Bennett stops at his office door, and I hold up the bouquet. His mouth lifts in a small smile. Our eyes meet, and for a breath, we hold each other's gazes. Then he opens the door and motions for Earl and Rosie to go in first.

"Man, I can't breathe." Poppy clutches her throat.

"What's wrong?"

"All the sexual tension in the shop. You'd think I had allergies or something." She flashes me a teasing grin.

I bump my shoulder into hers, and she laughs.

God, for a little while there, I forgot all about my problems. And it felt really, really good.

Chapter Fourteen

BENNETT

I open my office door for Earl and Rosie. She takes a seat on the couch while Earl settles into one of the two office chairs in front of my desk.

"Rosie?" Earl looks over at her.

"The couch is more comfortable." She sinks into the leather cushions and crosses her legs, clearly not planning to move.

Earl exhales a quiet huff and switches to sit beside her.

"Can I get either of you anything to drink?"

I'm already flustered from being late thanks to Wren hitting Principal North's car door. Then I saw Delaney with her cheeks pink, a warm smile, and a bouquet in her hand, and something inside me cracked open. She looked happy, which made me happy.

Not a good sign.

"Let's just get this started." Earl leans back and rests his ankle on his opposite knee.

Of course, I couldn't be late for a couple who'd just built a house and are looking for suggestions on what to plant and where. Not that those customers aren't important. They are.

But Earl and Rosie own Blue Prairie Country Club outside of Lincoln. It's members-only, and they're in the running to host a major golf event this fall. Landing this account would be huge. Though if I can secure it, it might mean some late nights and early mornings. I won't have the time I like to have with Wren during the summer, but it could earn me the money I need to build our house, even if I'm not sure whether I want to move into it or not.

I drop the projection screen on the opposite wall and queue up my computer. "You asked me to mock-up the eighteenth hole to see my vision, since that's where a lot of the attention will go. Here are some of my plans."

I show them the slides and sketches, 3D images of what I'd remove and what I'd replace it with. Rosie yawns a couple times and doesn't ask any questions while Earl hammers question after question—how long the plants will last, what happens if one dies. We discuss the greens and the path up to the clubhouse.

"I want flowers," Rosie says out of nowhere. "Green is boring. We need reds and pinks and orange—"

Earl gives me a look as if he's already exasperated. "Can those be incorporated?"

"We could definitely do pockets of flowers in key areas."

"Good. And I want that girl out there to be in charge of it," Rosie says.

She says it so casually, as though she didn't just lob a grenade in the middle of my office.

"Excuse me?"

"Rosie, you can't dictate how he runs his business." Earl shakes his head at his wife. "Just add a few of those flower bed things." Earl waves his hand as though that should take care of it.

I swallow my pride and the urge to argue that it's not as simple as everyone thinks to make plants blend and look natural yet beautiful. It's not as easy as tossing in some petals and mulch and calling it a day.

"Sure, I can." Rosie straightens and narrows her eyes as though she knows the ache that's still alive in me for Delaney. "We're going to pay you a lot of money. I want someone specific on the flowers."

"I can assure you that I'm just as knowledgeable about flowers as I am with the landscaping. I can handle the whole project."

She hums. "I like the girl."

Earl sighs. "I guess the girl is part of the deal," he says with a shrug.

"Just to clarify, you're talking about the dark-haired one?" I sound desperate, because I am.

"Yes, the brunette. She's lovely and has a real eye for flowers."

She's not wrong. I'm not suggesting I handle it on my own because Delaney isn't perfect for the project. She's the best I've ever worked with, but it would put us in close proximity, and the last project we did together had that line blurring fast. It's dangerous. Last time we tried, I had her up against the wall of my office with my pants around my ankles.

Earl gives me a look as if it's out of his hands. His wife has spoken. A contract of this size could change things for the business—put my firm on the map in Lincoln. Increase business and secure a better future for Wren.

"I can ask her," I offer. I'm not going to speak for Delaney. She might say no.

"Let's ask her now." Rosie smiles at me.

Coming into this meeting, I didn't think Rosie was going to run it, but she clearly makes the decisions and is a little pushy when she wants something.

"I can ask her once we secure the contract."

"We'll secure it today if she signs on." She inches forward in her seat. "Should I get her or you, Mr. Owens?"

Earl just shakes his head and shrugs.

"I'll get her." I give her a smile I hope reaches my eyes.

I rise and step out, shutting the door behind me, then lean against it and close my eyes for a moment.

Can I do this? Who cares about my name in this industry? Working with Delaney is going to stir shit up again. We're both unattached, changing the game.

Who am I kidding? She probably wants nothing to do with me, plus she's coming off a mess of a relationship. I can handle a little temptation in order for Wren to have a comfortable life. But seeing Delaney every day, working late hours, pretending it's only professional when everything in me still wants more? It's not going to be easy. I have to though, for Wren.

After my little pep talk, I push off the door and walk into the shop. Poppy and Delaney are laughing about something. They've always been like that, laughing and talking nonstop. It's nice to see, for Poppy too.

"Delaney," I call, raising my chin at her when she looks over.

"We're busy. Get your clients' coffee yourself," Poppy teases, dancing to the music while arranging a bouquet for a wedding shower at The Knotted Barn. Which makes me think of my sister Romy, and I wonder why I haven't seen her lately. I need to ask Lottie about it.

"Earl and Rosie want to talk to you."

Delaney turns to Poppy, then to me. "Um... why?"

"You made an impression. Rosie wants you on the project."

She hesitates, biting the inside of her cheek. I know that look and exactly what memories are flashing through her mind. The way we promised to keep it professional seven years ago, but late meetings turned into lingering touches, nurturing that seed of arousal until we couldn't stand it any longer.

"I don't think that's a good idea." She shakes her head.

"They own Blue Prairie Country Club up in Lincoln. It's huge. This is a massive account for us." Poppy looks between us. "She'll do it."

"You can't make that decision for me." Delaney's forehead wrinkles.

"I can because I'm your best friend. I can because you deserve to have something for yourself. I know we've been separated for years, but you should be happy I haven't flown to California and kicked he-who-shall-remain-unnamed's ass for what he did to you. So yeah, you're taking it. You love flowers, and you gave up that dream for a man who didn't deserve you."

I fight the smile that wants to break out. Poppy's so right, and I would've messed it up if I'd tried to say the same. Principal North's words ring through my head. I'm ashamed that the first thing I thought of wasn't the same thing as Poppy. I was worried that I couldn't be around Delaney, when I should've wanted her to do this. Should've seen this opportunity as Poppy sees it—a way to start something new in her life, build herself back up. Fuck, I'm ashamed of myself.

"It's been so long." Delaney worries her bottom lip.

"Flowers are still flowers," I say.

Her head snaps toward me, eyes wide as if asking how I could be on Poppy's side with this. "Nebraska's different than California. The soil, the weather, what grows, and what dies."

"You know your stuff, and what you don't, I'm here for you."

Her face flickers, and I remember how many times I said those words to her only to not be there for her in the end.

"I don't know. It would take me away from Leia and—"

"I'll do pick-ups or help with dinner, homework. What-ever you need." Poppy urges her to say yes.

"I appreciate that."

"My mom can get her from school. She's there getting Wren anyway. And she'll be happy to not have to entertain Wren until I get off work."

Another sigh.

"Just hear Rosie out. She wants you, bad." I hold my breath, waiting for her answer.

Delaney glances at Poppy, who nods. "Okay. I'll hear what they have to say."

"Great!" Poppy claps her hands. "I've got to run these over to The Knotted Barn. Be right back. I'll put up a sign that says someone will be back in five minutes."

"Sounds good," Delaney murmurs, following me to my office.

Inside, Earl is on his phone, and Rosie is examining my bookshelf.

"She's beautiful," she says, pointing at the wedding photo.

Why does it feel as though the universe is trying to tell us this is a very, very bad idea?

"Your daughter has her blue eyes," Rosie says.

Delaney stiffens beside me.

"Thank you. My wife passed during childbirth."

Rosie frowns. "I'm sorry. That must've been a hard road for you."

I shift in place. "It was. But it's in the past."

"Life moves on whether you're ready or not. No one is stopping that clock." Rosie gives me a sad sort of smile.

"All right, Rosie, enough with the philosophy. Let them live their lives." Earl stares right at Delaney. "So, you're on board?"

"I was just telling Earl before you came in that I felt it. But then I saw the wedding photo..." She points her index fingers at Delaney and me, then brings them together. "I can't figure it out though."

"She thinks she felt some kind of energy between you two." Earl fills us in.

"Oh, no, I mean..." Delaney glances at me, and my expression screams *do not give this woman ammunition to use against us.* "It was in high school. A long time ago."

"Oh? Childhood sweethearts?" Rosie's interest is piqued, that much is clear.

Earl groans and slouches back on the couch.

"Um... I don't know if you'd call us that." Delaney looks at me. I want to tell her that this is her show.

"How long did you date?" Rosie asks.

"Three years. We didn't see each other after junior year—"

"So, let's talk about the contract," I interrupt, wanting to steer us off of memory lane.

"Three years definitely classifies as high school sweethearts, and you know what they say about those who find their mate in high school..."

"Rosie." Earl's impatience shows in his tone.

"We were high school sweethearts, you know. We had this little break when Earl thought he wanted Suzy Park, but he came to his senses. And we've been married ever since."

"Well, we're not together," I say, trying to remain polite.

"Hmm. You never know. I'm sure I felt it."

"What exactly?" Delaney entertains her theories again.

I sigh, glaring at Delaney to stop going along with this. She ignores me.

"Unfinished business. There's more to play out here." Rosie waves her finger between us.

Rosie is a trickster and cannot be trusted. Noted.

"So are you in? He doesn't get the contract without you," Earl interrupts, thank God.

Delaney bites her lip, then nods. "I'm in."

"Great! Let's make another bouquet while these two handle the business stuff. It's so boring." Rosie pretends to yawn, hooks her arm through Delaney's, and whisks her out of my office.

"What just happened?" I don't realize I said it out loud until Earl answers.

"Rosie happened," Earl says, chuckling. "She bulldozed you."

Fuck yeah, she did.

Chapter Fifteen

Sean,

Seven years ago, I was hired by an architectural landscaping firm, and on my first day when I went to the breakroom, Bennett was there, preparing his coffee. I hadn't seen him since I was seventeen.

I knew he'd gone to Berkeley, but I didn't know he'd majored in landscape architecture, and I definitely didn't know he was working at the same firm I had just been hired at. Sure, I probably should have done more research. He was likely listed on their website. But after a long stretch of sending out my résumé and hearing nothing back, I was just grateful for the interview.

When Bennett turned around and saw me,

his coffee mug slipped from his hand. It shattered on the floor, black coffee splashing across the tile.

"Laney?" he asked, eyes wide.

"Please tell me you're the coffee repairman."

It was stupid, I know. But after we drifted apart our senior year, I thought about him so many times. I looked him up once when I was in college and saw his profile filled with pictures of him and a pretty blue-eyed girl. She was obviously important to him. I assumed the love he'd once had for me had long since died.

I figured Bennett would be the type to finish his degree and return to Willowbrook. I never would've guessed he would stay out here, working so far from his hometown. Family was everything to him.

"I am. I'm irreplaceable because I only fix coffee machines bought on Black Friday doorbuster sales."

I laughed, just like I used to when I was around him, and his eyes warmed.

He grabbed some paper towels, and that was when I saw the light hit his left hand, a silver wedding band snug across his left ring finger. My stomach dropped. Of course he'd married her. He'd looked so in love in those pictures.

I pulled off more paper towels and bent down to help clean up the pieces of the mug and the spill.

"Denise is going to kill me. That was her favorite mug."

I didn't know Denise yet, but the way he said it, I knew he'd be out hunting for a replacement tonight before she could figure it out.

"Denise?" I asked.

"She did me a favor, so I figured I'd return it with a coffee. She hates leaving her desk. You'll find out soon enough."

Our eyes locked and held for a long moment as if we were both taking in the fact that we were once again in the same city. Same firm. Same space. It felt too perfectly aligned to be a coincidence. Like something bigger was pulling us back together.

But that ring reminded me he was someone else's now. No longer mine, but hers.

I was so distracted I didn't notice the shard of ceramic until it pierced my skin.

"Shit." I lifted my hand, watching a stream of blood trickle down my finger.

"Let's run it under water." He gently pulled me to my feet and led me to the sink, where he held my hand under the cold stream of water. I winced and tried to pull away, but he kept it steady. "I don't think it's too bad."

Honestly, I'm not even sure I'm telling this right because I was mesmerized by him, studying the man he'd become. The way he'd filled out. His broad shoulders. Strong hands. Had he always been this tall?

He caught me eyeing his wedding band.

"It's not what you think," he whispered.

"It's okay. I looked you up once. The artist?"

His face dimmed, and for a second, my finger drooped. He caught it again, wrapping it in a paper towel. "Kristie. Yeah, but..."

"What happened here? And who are you?" A woman interrupted us, and I looked over my shoulder at her walking in.

But I couldn't keep my eyes off of him for long, so my gaze soon found his again. There was pain in his eyes, something cracking beneath his polished surface.

"Sorry, Denise. The new girl broke your mug," he said, a half-smile tugging at his lips.

That smile was a mask. I was certain of it, and it was the first time I'd ever seen him use one with me. It hurt more than seeing that he had committed himself to someone else. We had always been honest with each other.

"I know it was you, Owens. And I'll happily accept a new one tomorrow." Then she turned her attention to me. "Welcome, new girl. Come see me for paperwork when you're done."

Bennett's eyes dropped to my lips. I felt myself lean in slightly before my conscience snapped me back.

What was I doing? Did I really believe he'd second guess every decision he'd made in his life just because he saw me again after all these years?

I stepped back. He did too. Both of us remembering that we weren't innocent seventeen-year-olds anymore.

Clutching the paper towel to my finger, I scanned the room for a first-aid kit.

Bennett got there first. He sat me down at the table, his knee brushing between mine as he leaned close to apply ointment and a Band-Aid.

We didn't speak. I had no clue what was running through his head. I could barely process the fact he was really there, touching me.

"We're separated," he whispered, glancing toward the door.

His tone was hushed, private. As though no one else in the office knew. Or maybe just a few.

Bennett was never the secretive type. But I could tell this wasn't something he shared easily. It wasn't anyone's business anyway, I suppose. Then again, he was still wearing his ring. How long had they been separated?

"I'm sorry."

"Don't be. You're not the one who cheated on me."

My heart cracked. I wanted to claw out that blonde's eyes for not realizing what she had. She had the man I'd compared every other one to. The reason I could barely make it to a fourth date with anyone else.

And even though he was technically available in the physical sense, I'd never felt more replaceable than I did right then.

That's only because I didn't have a crystal ball to see into the future.

To know that one day, I'd feel that way again, but deeper and more devastating.

Delaney

Chapter Sixteen

BENNETT

The scent of coffee clings to the cab of the truck. Thankfully, it masks whatever perfume Delaney might be wearing. I can't afford to be thinking about her that way, but she's sitting beside me, and every damn thing about her is impossible to ignore. Her fingers wrap around the travel mug, the same fingers I used to trace with my own. She moans softly after every sip, as if it's the best thing she's ever tasted. As if she doesn't know her sounds are slowly driving me insane.

I was late getting Wren to school this morning, distracted by too many thoughts, too many what-ifs about what today would bring. It frustrated me that just Delany's presence in my life again was messing with my usual punctuality, my usual control over my thoughts.

It'd be just the two of us for most of the day, traveling to the golf course then deciding what we're keeping and what we're tearing out and planting new. I should be focused on the job, but the tension humming in the cab is all I'm consumed by.

Twenty minutes until I can flee this truck and the suffocation I feel inside it.

"You still drive aggressively," she says after a car honks behind us.

"Why don't you get in the back seat?" I shoot back.

She shrugs. "I'm just saying, we're not late." She holds up her hand before I can respond. "I know, if you're not early, you're late."

I lift a shoulder. "It's the truth."

"In your lifetime, how many times have you actually been late?"

I shake my head, not wanting to get into this. She was always on my anal habits, wanting to calm me, relax me so I wasn't strung so tightly. And now my mind terrorizes me with the memory of her giving me a blow job, like a game to see how much self-control I had. Turns out none, since her mouth on my dick made all clocks disappear.

"Truth?" I ask.

"Always."

"You always seem to be the one with me when I'm late."

Her cheeks flush, and she hides behind her coffee cup.

"Payback for making fun of my driving," I mutter.

"At least they were good reasons," she says with a smirk.

I stop at a red light, and for a moment, our eyes lock. Something familiar and way too dangerous crackles between us.

"Definitely."

The light turns green. I focus on the stretch of soybean fields outside the window, but she shifts in her seat, adjusting the mug in her hands.

"You looking forward to today?" I'm desperate to direct us away from the memories of when we were so entwined in each other's worlds.

"I'm a little scared actually. Stayed up late researching Nebraska land, zooming in on pictures of the golf course." She cringes.

"You've got nothing to be nervous about. You're killing it at the shop. Everyone's raving about your arrangements. Romy said two women almost fought over one of your centerpieces."

Romy... I need to nail her down and ask why she's been disappearing every few days recently. I know she's dating someone, but it's not someone from around here, that's for sure, or I would've already caught wind of it.

She presses her hand to her heart. "Really? That makes me so happy. Thank you for telling me."

It makes me happy too. But I don't say it. Just watching her light up like this is thanks enough.

"I—I forgot what it feels like."

"What?"

"Working with flowers, on a design project," she says, quieter this time. Her fingers tighten around the mug. "Sean liked me at home with Leia. Which was great. I'm grateful I was able to be home with her. And I had my own garden, but that's not the same as earning someone else's praise. I know it should be. But it's not."

Something hot curls low in my chest. "Did you want to work?"

She shrugs. "Yes and no. I was happy to stay with Leia until she went to school. I helped friends with their yards, went to floral markets with them, but most of the women I hung around hired other people to do that stuff. When Leia started school, I asked Sean about getting back into work. He said we should redo our own landscaping for starters and then maybe look at finding me a job. I was halfway through the project when it all fell apart."

She doesn't say more, and I don't push. She'll tell me what she wants when she's ready.

"He didn't treat me badly, not in the way people usually

think. I just... I didn't feel like I was being controlled until I was out of it and looking back."

"And now?" My hand tightens on the steering wheel, the other on my thigh.

She exhales and turns away from the fields rolling by us. I feel her gaze on me, and I wish I could look at her. Tell her she can trust me. I'm on her side. I'm always on her side.

"I wonder if I saw what I wanted to see. Missed the signs that there was something more going on. After he was arrested, I saw some of the evidence... there was a transcript of a phone call he had with one of his associates." She swallows hard, seeming to gain the courage to say whatever she's going to next. "Sean was talking about how I had no idea what was going on right under my nose, how Leia and I were the perfect cover for him. It makes me feel angry, of course, but now I'm just—embarrassed." She shakes her head. "Oh, we're here." Her fingers brush under her eyes, and she straightens in her seat. "Look at me, pouring all my problems onto you."

My hands clutch the steering wheel. What a piece of shit. I park and turn toward her, catching her wrist before she can reach for the door handle. Instinctively, my thumb runs the infinity symbol along her soft skin. "Pour them on me. I want to know."

She sighs, glancing down at her wrist before looking at the crew unloading behind us. "Even without knowing that Sean was running a high-level drug dealing ring, I just woke up one morning and didn't know the woman staring back at me."

I glance at her, taking in the profile I once knew better than my own. She's carrying something heavy on her shoulders. I thought I understood it, but I realize now that it's different than what I thought.

"He didn't see you," I say before I can stop myself.

She gives me a sad smile. "Maybe not. I didn't see him for

who he was either, though. I probably morphed myself into what I thought he needed me to be. He wanted me perceived a certain way, and I walked right into his trap happily, as if he was my savior."

She climbs out of the truck before I can say anything more. I watch her walk to the tailgate, pulling on gloves, then she changes into her work boots.

There's a distance between us, and I realize that I don't know what to say to make her feel better. I think it's something she has to find within herself. But maybe I can be here to support her while she does, even if I shouldn't be.

"You ever think," she says softly, "how different things could've been?"

"All the time." I meet her eyes. "Every night."

Silence extends over us.

"He was good to us. Never hit me. Never raised his voice at Leia or me."

"Why are you telling me this?"

"I just want you to know. I might've gotten lost in the smoke and mirrors, but he gave us security and a life I never imagined I'd have. Too bad it was all fake, but I thought we were happy. I thought I'd made the right decision. You have to know that." Her eyes are imploring me, willing me to understand, but I don't know why.

She hops off the tailgate and heads toward the workers, our conversation over.

I'm pissed I didn't say anything back, but what would I say? *I'm pissed off that you were happy with someone else. That I should be the only one who makes you happy?* So I let my anger simmer inside me. I was the reason she fell in love with someone who wasn't me. The decision was in my hands.

Delaney walks ahead, boots squelching in the wet grass, her back straight, shoulders tight.

I head after her, carrying the tools, frustration gnawing at me. I should've said something.

I catch up, falling into step beside her. "You know," I say carefully, "there's still time to become who you want to be."

She stops and turns. "I don't think she exists anymore."

"Then don't try to find her. Discover who you are now without any restrictions on you."

Her gaze searches mine. "It feels good to do this. I didn't realize how much I missed using my hands for something other than folding laundry and braiding Leia's hair."

"It's not like I had a choice. Rosie was adamant." I smile to soften my words.

"I want to make her proud."

I step closer, drawn to her as always. "You will. Your talent is going to shine through, and I can't wait to witness it."

She smiles, and I tighten my hands around the tools I'm holding to keep from reaching for her.

The sprinkler system hisses and comes alive. A jet of cold water slams square into her side.

"Shit!" she shrieks and spins, hands on my hips, shoving me in front of the blast.

"Come on!" I move the tools to one hand and grab her wrist, running toward the golf cart shelter, both of us soaked and laughing.

By the time we duck under the overhang, we're drenched.

"I thought you told them to turn it off," she says between breaths.

"I did! Obviously, they didn't do it."

She shakes water off her arms. "Well, great day one."

I look at her, soaking and shining with wet hair and flushed cheeks. "We always make good memories, don't we?"

She tucks a strand of hair behind her ear, her gaze lingering. "Thanks, Bennett. Not just for the protection. For what you said."

"You don't have to thank me for telling the truth."

We stand there a beat longer, water dripping off us, and for the first time since she came back, I'm not thinking about what we lost but wondering if we could find our way back to one another.

Chapter Seventeen

DELANEY

Leia's strapped into her booster seat in the back of my brother's truck, and my stomach is a knot of nerves as we wait for Levi. My mom went behind my back and talked him into getting Leia horse riding lessons at Plain Daisy Ranch. Then Levi went ahead and told her it was happening. So now, here we sit, waiting for him to finish raiding my mom's kitchen before we leave.

He jogs out of my parents' house, still chewing a biscuit from dinner. Levi rents the house behind my parents. Well, he doesn't pay rent. He's never home anyway, and my parents are too all in on his rodeo dream to demand rent from him.

"Sorry," he mumbles, crumbs tumbling onto his shirt as he hops into the cab. He looks back at Leia. "Ready?"

"Yep!" She's all smiles and excitement.

The minute she was old enough, I put Leia on a horse. It's one of those things I wished I was comfortable with, so I wanted to make sure my daughter would be. Then I realized that if I was too afraid to ride, she might be too, so I joined her lessons. I've tried to raise her to be fearless, even if I'm not. But she's still cautious, studies everything before she feels she can trust it.

"You good?" Levi glances at me, half a biscuit still in his mouth, turning the key in the ignition.

"Yes."

"Just making sure. Mom said you wanted to go to Wild Bull, which, for the record, offends me deeply. That guy's a class-A—"

"I get the point." I nod toward the back seat.

"Sorry. Not used to having kids around."

"I know." I give him a small smile.

He manages to get the rest of the biscuit into his mouth without his hands, which is a disturbing talent I didn't know he had.

"You could've eaten before we left."

"Nah, I told Nash we'd be there in fifteen."

Nash. Bennett's roommate, along with his cousin, Jensen.

"Nash will be there?"

Levi side-eyes me at the light. "How do you think I got her in? Why?"

"You're very inquisitive this evening. I'm just curious." I cross my arms and turn toward the window, watching the farmland roll by.

My parents didn't move to the city this time. They wanted more land. So now we're out here among all the farms even though we're not actual farmers. It's quieter out here than in the city of Willowbrook. More peaceful. Less hectic.

"Congrats on the belt. I haven't seen you since you won. Speaking of, where've you been staying?"

He checks the rearview mirror. "Nowhere."

His smirk says otherwise. Probably seeing someone or multiple someones.

"One day a woman's going to knock you on your a— butt."

"I'd like to see that." He laughs as though that's the most absurd idea in the world.

We drive in silence, and I try not to obsess over whether Nash will see some resemblance to Bennett when he meets Leia. The secret I'm carrying feels heavier with every mile. I brought Leia back here to feel safe, to be herself again, and today is about giving my daughter the chance to do something she loved back in California.

Levi drives under the gateway sign with the horseshoe on it that reads *Plain Daisy Ranch*. He turns off onto the road that leads around to the stables. I spent a good portion of my childhood on this ranch, and even though I come to The Perfect Petal every day, it's on the outer edge of the ranch. I've avoided venturing deeper in, afraid that too many memories would crush me.

The second Leia spots the corral, she squeals.

"That's my girl. No scaredy-cat like your mom." Levi beams, proud she shares his love for horses.

"I hope Wren comes," Leia says.

Levi stops the truck. My heart stops too.

"Is she coming?" I ask, forcing my voice to stay level.

Leia shrugs. "She said she was going to convince her dad."

"That would be fun, wouldn't it, Laney?" Levi's got a grin that screams mischief. He knows something.

"Duh." She shakes her head at him.

He laughs and climbs out of the truck, raising a hand to Nash where he stands by the fence. Nash is cute—rugged, tall, blond hair always tucked under a hat, with eyebrows that are darker than his mop of hair. He looks as if he was born to wear tight Wranglers. I'm pretty sure he has a thing for Poppy, but as far as I know, they've never crossed the line.

Levi helps Leia out while my thoughts spin. Her face lights up as though I just gave her an extra hour before bedtime.

"Mom, look!" She gasps and points at two ponies circling the corral.

Levi hoists her onto his shoulders and jogs the rest of the way to Nash. Her joy is contagious, and for a moment, I forget why I was so worried about bringing her here.

"Wren!" she shouts.

A dark-haired girl steps out from the stables wearing riding boots and a helmet.

Levi can't get Leia down quickly enough, and the two girls run toward one another, clinging to each other like long-lost friends. Levi glances over his shoulder at me, but I'm already staring at the barn entrance.

"Wren wouldn't stop begging me," Nash explains. "Bennett's not home tonight, so I figured I'd tire her out. Poppy might swing by though."

My anxiety eases that I only have to worry about Nash or Poppy seeing some kind of resemblance. Even though I've compared their pictures a million times. If someone knew, they might see it, but according to everyone, she's my mini-me.

Leia and Wren run back over to me, and Leia introduces me. The second I look at Wren beside my daughter, I see enough similarities that I'm not sure how anyone hasn't noticed.

"You're the only one who can do braids like my aunt Briar," Wren says. Her hair sticks out of her helmet, unbraided.

"That's why Leia is always coming home and asking me for specific braids, I guess." I squat down. "Want me to braid your hair now so it doesn't bother you?"

"Yes please!" She rushes to the picnic table and sits on the bench, waiting patiently for me.

I dig through my purse for a brush and some elastic bands I always keep in there for Leia.

"I'm going to get this one started," Nash calls to me, then looks at Leia. "You ready?"

"I was born ready," she says, deadly serious.

It makes him chuckle. "That's what I like to hear."

"She can ride Biscuits, Nash!" Wren shouts.

I sit on the table, legs bracketing Wren's sides, and brush out the tangled chaos of her hair.

"She's riding Sparkles," Nash says.

Leia's eyes widen as she spots the black pony, then she turns to look at me. "Mom!"

"I know."

"What?" Wren asks, trying to turn around, but I straighten her.

"Her horse in California looked just like Sparkles."

"Really?" Wren's legs swing under the table.

I want to ask her where her dad is tonight. Is he on a date? He doesn't wear his wedding band anymore. Maybe he goes outside of Willowbrook to date. I hate the jealous feeling that's growing inside me.

"Nash said you went to school with them," Wren says.

"I did."

"You're Aunt Poppy's friend?"

"I am."

"And Daddy's high school girlfriend?"

My fingers freeze.

"I heard Emmett and Daddy talking."

"That was a long time ago."

She shrugs. "I know. Before my mommy."

"Yep." I try to keep the emotion from my tone. This is a little girl who probably misses her mom and doesn't need to hear my jealousy that her dad picked her mother.

"Everyone wants my dad to get married again. They think he's lonely."

I should not be having this conversation with her. I glance at Levi, who's cheering Leia on by the fence.

"Well, that's his decision, right?"

"You're pretty."

"Thanks." My fingers work fast to finish the braid, desperate to end this conversation.

"I told my daddy to ask you out."

My fingers tremble. I wish I could scream at Levi to get over here and save me. "Oh... well..."

Strike me down now for wanting to know what he said.

"Are you almost done?"

I want to ask what her dad said, but I'm sure I won't get the answer I want. Seven-year-olds bounce around topics like a scroll through social media.

I secure her braid and hand her the helmet. "All done."

She smooths her hand down her head and smiles. "Thanks."

Then she puts her helmet on her head, staring at me with those same blue eyes that used to stare back at me through my phone screen when I'd search them out as a reminder that Kristie was what Bennett wanted. She rests her knees on the bench of the picnic table and wraps her arms around my waist, hugging me tightly.

Emotion clogs my throat. I've never felt more like a horrible person. Here I am hugging his daughter, and he has no idea the little girl in the corral is his too.

"You're really nice. Leia's lucky to have you as her mom."

Wren runs off without saying anything more. Nash scoops her up and carries her over to Biscuits.

A few minutes later, Levi saunters over and sits beside me. "How you doing?"

"Why do you keep asking that?"

Silence stretches out between us.

Levi leans back on his hands, both of us staring at the girls. "It's a little unfair, right?"

"What is?"

"You braiding both of his daughters' hair?"

My stomach drops, and I freeze, unable to look over at my brother. "What are you talking about?"

He sits up and lowers his head to shoot me a look. "You know damn well what."

I glance at the girls, then around us. "Levi…"

"Has he seen her yet?"

"How did you know?" I've never told anyone about my affair with Bennett. According to my family and everyone else, I got with Sean, and we were pregnant immediately.

"You forget, I was out in California visiting you right before you dated Sean. I'll give it to you, you put on a really great act, but I woke up once in the middle of the night and saw you crying on the balcony. Then I came back to Willowbrook, and suddenly Bennett and Kristie have moved back. Honestly, I wasn't one hundred percent sure I was right until you just confirmed it."

"Why didn't you say anything?"

"First of all, it's none of my business. Second, I thought you were the one who left him for whatever reason."

I shake my head. "It was him."

"I'm not sure he wanted too though, right?" He arches an eyebrow.

"Please—"

"I'm serious." He holds up his hands. "From my observation, Bennett never looked very happy those months before Wren was born. He always seemed to be somewhere else in his head when we were all together. Her too. I thought maybe it was a marriage thing. What the hell do I know about living with someone for your entire life, day after day? Sounds like complete torture."

"Grow up, Levi." I swat his leg.

"Then you met Sean, and I figured you'd tell me. She looked so much like you when she was younger but now…" He cringes.

"God, Levi."

"Does Sean know?"

I nod. "From the start."

"He loved her like she was his."

"He did." I look at Leia, who is smiling but concentrating to make sure she does everything right, while Wren is relaxed and laughing. They're so opposite.

"But Bennett doesn't see it?" Levi asks, pulling my thoughts away from Sean.

"He hasn't met her."

"Yet."

I wrap my arms around myself as if that's going to shelter me. "It seemed like the right thing at the time." My voice is small, pained.

"I'm not judging," Levi says, a bit softer now. "But you can't keep this secret now that you're back, and you brought her with you."

I close my eyes for a second, fighting the lump in my throat. "You think I don't want to tell him?" My voice cracks. "You think I haven't rehearsed it a million times over? I've come close so many times, but—"

Levi looks at me, his jaw tight. "So why haven't you?"

I stare at my feet and inhale a deep breath. "Because it changes everything. Because once it's out, I can't take it back. And I don't know if I'm ready to take away the small amount of peace I've managed to give her since we came back."

He doesn't say anything for a while. "He deserves to know, Laney."

"And what about Leia?" I say, my voice shaking now. "Does she deserve to have her life flipped upside down again?

To know that the man she thought was her dad, the one in jail, isn't and that her new best friend's dad is? What would that do to her?"

Levi jumps off the table. "Your life already blew up like someone threw a grenade at it. You have to start over anyway. Why not get all the lies and bullshit out of the way and start with a clean slate?"

"You weren't there when Sean was arrested. When I had to pack up her life almost overnight. When she cried because she didn't get to say goodbye to her father or her friends. I told her we were going somewhere safe. That's what this town was supposed to be for her, a fresh start."

"You can't have secrets *and* a fresh start, Laney," he says gently. "The two can't coexist. You know that. You just found out that you were lied to for seven years. Made to believe your life was something it wasn't. Why would you do the same to her? To him? Tell them and be free from it all."

"You make it sound so easy." There are tears in my eyes now.

"She deserves the truth. So does he."

Leia's laughter rings through the warm air, sweet and wild and full of everything I'm trying so hard to protect.

I nod, the tears falling freely now.

"It's going to be messy as hell," he says. "But you'll come out better for it. You all will."

I force a smile and get up from the table.

He pulls me into a hug, as if it's his promise to be there with me.

"I'll tell him," I whisper.

"Sooner the better."

I nod again, but I know the truth.

Saying it and doing it are two very different things.

Chapter Eighteen

Sean,

For two weeks, we kept away from one another. We'd be polite and say hello if we passed in the hall or were in the same meeting.

Then we were assigned to work together on a project that, according to Bennett, would help us make our mark—something that would solidify our futures with the firm or wherever we went next.

It was for an outdoor shopping area, and our boss, Mr. Ewerdt, said he wanted to see what we could do together. As much as I dreamed of us being thrown together, I knew Bennett wasn't in any frame of mind to pursue something with me. He was still wearing his wedding ring, for heaven's sake. Regardless, a small part of me was excited to spend time alone with him.

A week later, we were due to present the following morning, and Mr. Ewerdt didn't like what we'd come up with for the fountain area—the largest attraction at the shopping mall—and we had to scrap it and start over, so we had no choice but to work late.

The office had cleared out hours earlier. We sat at the long table in the design room, sketches in front of us, Bennett on his computer, his mouse clicking as he tried to show me what he was visualizing on the giant screen in front of us.

I pretended to understand what he was saying, but my mind was somewhere else. I had so many questions I didn't have the right to ask. The number one was whether he still loved his wife. Every time I was away from him, I'd reprimand myself for still loving him, knowing he belonged to someone else. But when I was with him, all those talks about letting go and forgetting him disappeared from my mind.

"I'd like lilacs there," I said, getting up from my chair. He moved the mouse to point at the area, but I said, "To the right."

He still wasn't understanding what I meant, so I got up from my seat and leaned over him, asking to take control of the mouse. I felt his gaze on the side of my head—not the screen—as I dragged and clicked the spot I was talking about.

"I moved out the night I found them."

"This is where I want them." I ignored his confession, unsure where he wanted this conversation to go.

Then his hand covered mine on the mouse. The second we touched, it was there again—that pull we never really buried tightening beneath the surface of our skin.

If we had any chance of keeping this professional, we needed to forget the past, forget he was going through a separation, forget the way our bodies were still drawn to one another.

"Bennett," I said, pulling my hand out from under his. Stepping back, I hoped the space would clear my memory too—of those calloused palms that used to run across my body.

"I wasn't a good husband," he murmured.

I leaned against the conference room wall, and he swiveled his chair to look at me.

"I find that hard to believe."

"She wanted to stay in California after college, while I wanted to go back to Willowbrook. The longer we stayed here, the more resentful I grew. Stopped putting in as much of an effort."

I blinked at him. "Why are you telling me this?"

"I just want you to know... she's not the villain in our story. Blame can go both ways."

"It's your business, not mine."

He stared down at his hands. "I'm not sure that's true." His voice was low and unsure. He lifted his gaze to meet mine, and I swallowed to soothe my dry throat.

"Why?"

He tilted his head as if that was his answer. As if he thought I knew. But I wanted to hear him say it. I wanted to hear his confession—that maybe he never forgot me either. I wasn't going to be some rebound after his failed marriage just because I happened to be there.

We stared at each other for a long time, and the air between us crackled. I should've shut it down. I should've left the room—damn the presentation.

But my body betrayed me.

Because instead of walking out of that room, I whispered, "I can't be your rebound."

His breath hitched—the only sound in the

quiet conference room. And had someone asked, I would've said that was all I needed.

My pulse drummed in my ears. I wrapped my arms around myself as if they could protect me from being hurt. His eyes didn't waver from mine.

"We can't do this, Bennett," I said, stepping to the side and over to my stuff farther down the table.

"I hate it when you call me that."

I huffed and shut my laptop. "It's your name."

"Not for you, it's not."

"What do you want me to do here?" Everyone who knew Bennett usually called him B. I'm not sure when it started. I think when he and Emmett used to be made fun of for having such similar names.

"I'm not sure I have the answers."

I stuffed my laptop in my bag and grappled to pick up the papers off the table. "Then I need to go."

I was halfway to the door, hell-bent on leaving him in that room to figure out what he wanted. The tension between us had built over the two weeks we'd been sharing space—there was no denying that—but he'd gotten married. He'd moved on with his life while mine had stalled when it came to love.

"I thought I could forget you," he admitted. His voice was rough and pained, so I circled back around. "That I could move on."

I didn't know what to say, so I remained quiet and still.

"As my marriage dissolved, I started searching."

"Don't." I didn't want to hear that he'd been thinking of me on the nights I'd been thinking of him too.

"But you don't do anything on your socials. You have one black-and-white photo of you, and the rest are only of your work."

I shook my head and closed my eyes.

"Please look at me."

I swiveled back around, glancing at him through my eyelashes, not daring to give him all of my attention.

He looked down as though he regretted what he was about to say. "I couldn't control myself. I was so unhappy, and I craved the connection we had."

More silence stretched thin in the room. I should have left, let him keep his confessions. Because looking back, he was in no place to start something with me.

Bennett did everything by the book his entire

life—and maybe that's why a part of me trusted his decision to rekindle whatever was between us. That his marriage was really over. That he wouldn't have said those things if he wasn't certain.

Now, I wonder if it's just the pull—the invisible string that refuses to break, no matter how thin and taut it gets.

He stood from the chair, and my breath hitched. He was going to break the distance, and I didn't have it in me to fight him.

"When you walked into that break room, I knew."

"Knew what?"

He took another step forward. "That I was stupid to ever think what we had would've faded, no matter how hard I tried to bury it."

Another step, and I remained still. I couldn't breathe. My hands gripped my bag and papers to my chest like a shield.

"I can't keep pretending." He stopped in front of me, just inches away. "I look at you every day and try to convince myself that I don't still want you. That I don't dream about what our future would've looked like."

His words slammed into me.

"You married her," I whispered.

He exhaled as if he'd been holding it in for

years. "You broke up with me... in a letter."

"We were young."

I had chosen safety for my heart. I couldn't live that double life anymore, and he was already pulling away, so I'd made the decision I thought he didn't want to. But that didn't mean I stopped loving him. I was just scared.

"I never stopped loving you," I confessed.

His eyes closed for a beat. When they opened, that brokenness wasn't there anymore. As if he had wondered but would've never asked me.

He brushed a strand of hair from my face, and my body leaned into the touch as if it had been waiting all this time for a physical connection with him. His hand lingered at my cheek, his thumb warm as it rubbed back and forth.

"I've wanted to kiss you every day," he said.

My breath hitched. "Then why haven't you?"

"Because I didn't know if you'd want me to. I know I'm coming to you with some baggage."

"I want you too," I said—and my admission broke something loose inside both of us.

He took the last step, our bodies flush against each other, and pressed his lips to mine.

The kiss was years of desperation unleashed.

His hands went to my waist, pulling me closer as though he didn't trust me to stay in the room. My hands slid into his hair, conveying that I wasn't going anywhere.

All the talking was done.

My back hit the wall of the conference room, and he deepened the kiss, our bodies moving like they remembered everything we thought we'd forgotten.

When we finally pulled apart, he rested his forehead against mine.

"I never got over you," he whispered.

"I never wanted you to."

The room could've burned down around us, and I wouldn't have moved an inch.

For the first time in years, I was right where I was supposed to be.

Delaney

Chapter Nineteen

BENNETT

I walk downstairs, the house quiet since Wren is still half asleep after I woke her up. After pouring myself a cup of coffee, I'm only one sip in when I notice the mess from last night, so I set down my coffee and wash the ice cream bowls from Wren and Nash's sundae making.

I dump out the half-eaten bowl of popcorn, then wipe the spilled coffee from Nash filling his Thermos this morning.

Once the kitchen is clean, I walk back upstairs to make sure Wren is getting ready. She's just sitting up in bed, her hair in a messy braid. Who would've done that? The best Jensen or Nash would've accomplished is a lopsided ponytail.

"Do you want to pick your outfit, or me?" I used to do it, but recently there have been some disagreements on what she should wear to school. And after seeing Leia from the back the other day, I'm starting to see why Wren keeps telling me her clothes are too old and boring.

"You can do it." She rubs her eyes.

"Have a fun time with Nash last night?" This is the usual repercussion of having him watch her. It's like a party, and I'm the mean police officer breaking it up when I come home.

But by the time I returned from Lincoln yesterday, she was already in bed.

"We went and rode Biscuits. He said my balance is getting better."

I pick out shorts and a T-shirt for her and place them on the edge of her bed. "That's good."

"Leia rode Sparkles."

My hands still on the sheets as I prepare to make her bed. "Leia was there?"

I want to drill her with questions and ask if Leia's mom was there. Did Wren talk to her? How was she?

"Yeah, that's why Nash took me. Leia told me she was going to start riding lessons, so I begged him until he was sick of hearing me whine." She giggles.

"Wren, you can't do that. He's doing me a favor when he watches you." I continue making her bed, tugging the sheet for her to get out of bed and get ready.

She gives me a shrug and stands, walking into the bathroom that I had added especially for her. My family made a lot of additions when I decided to move out of my parents' house and into this one. Then Jensen returned and needed a place to stay, and Nash followed soon after. It was never my intention to have Wren live with three adult males, but Jensen and Nash both offer Wren qualities I don't possess.

Nash is the wild party one who diverts responsibility, and Jensen is the one who bakes with her and colors and even does crafts with her.

"Her mom braided my hair," she mumbles around her toothbrush, toothpaste dripping out of her mouth onto her pajama shirt.

Even with pieces slipping out from sleeping with it, the braid is better than I could do. "It's pretty."

I tuck the comforter up and under her pillow, then set the stuffed animals in the perfect order she prefers.

She plops down on the bed, still brushing her teeth. "She's pretty."

Yeah, she is. Delaney's gorgeous, and age has only made her more stunning.

"Did you hear me?" Wren asks.

"Go spit the toothpaste out before it drips on your bed."

She grunts but slides off the bed and goes to the bathroom, coming out a minute later as I'm about to walk out of the room. "I like her. She's nice."

I nod. "I'm glad you had fun." My hand lands on the door handle to give her privacy to change. "Hurry up, okay?"

"Levi made her cry."

I release the door handle. "What?"

"They were talking at the picnic table while we were riding, and I saw her crying. Then Levi hugged her."

"You don't know why?" I'm pretty sure my question is useless, but one thing I've learned as Wren gets older is that her ears are always open.

"No, I was riding."

I figured. It's a mystery I'm going to have to try to control myself from solving because it's none of my business. She's only given me a little glimpse into her life in California, and I don't want to push questions on her, but rather have her trust me when she feels comfortable.

"Let's go. It's going to be a cereal breakfast here if you don't hurry."

Wren rushes over to the clothes I laid out for her. "Uncle Jensen promised me last night that he'd give me extra chocolate chips if I went to bed."

"How nice of him," I mumble. I step out and am about to shut the door.

"I asked Leia if she saw her mom cry."

I pause. Always when I think Wren's moved on to something else, she gives me another morsel of information.

"Oh?" I hear my desperation to find out anything more and wonder if my daughter hears it too.

"Leia said her mom cries a lot. That she tries to hide it and always pretends she's not." She turns around, still not changed. "Why would she be so sad?"

I run my hand down the back of my head, giving myself a few seconds to come up with the best answer I can. "It's been a lot of change for them. Can you imagine moving away from Plain Daisy Ranch? You'd be sad."

"Yeah, but Leia said her daddy was a bad man. The police came into their house and took him away, and she hasn't seen him since."

How did I ever think that little girls didn't talk? Here I've only been thinking about my own feelings that are stirring for Delaney again, while both Delaney and her daughter have a whole heap of problems she's sifting through. How would Wren feel if she saw me being arrested?

"That's sad too."

She shakes her head. "Not if he was bad."

I remember when the world was black and white at that age and not shades of gray.

"Well, now that they're here, maybe her mom will be happier."

That feeling inside me that I could be the one to make her happy rises up, but I'm not sure she'll ever trust me again.

"Go, Daddy, I gotta change." She shoos me with her hand, and I leave, shutting the door.

I hate that Delaney is dealing with so much and wish she'd let me be a shoulder to lean on, but I understand that I haven't earned her trust after I'm the one who severed our tie.

Chapter Twenty

DELANEY

"Why do I have to take them?" I stare at the flowers in Poppy's hands.

"They're from Wren for Aunt Darla's birthday, and Bennett forgot them." She holds them out between us again.

I nudge them back toward her. "And you live right next door to him."

She pushes them closer to me again. "Right, but I'm going out after work."

I push them back her way. "Okay, but you live on the property. You can just drive them over and leave." I give her a once-over. "And you're going out in jean shorts and a T-shirt with The Perfect Petal logo on it?"

"Is that judgment I hear in your tone?" She tries to hand me the flowers again. "And you're getting in your car to leave anyway. What's the big deal?"

"Yes, it's judgment because I know you, and you'd still go home and change even if you were going somewhere you couldn't be late to. Besides, I take the outer drive, which goes nowhere near the residential homes by the lake." I nudge them back at her.

Poppy pushes them closer to me once again. "It's, like, two extra minutes to drop them off. I wouldn't ask if it wasn't really important."

She gives me that pleading look that used to get me to do things I didn't want to when we were younger. "You know what you're asking me to do."

"Come on, you guys have been getting along great. Laughing, joking, driving to the site every morning..." There's a question in her tone.

"He is technically my boss."

She clears her throat. "And me."

"Yes, and you."

Although Poppy doesn't get my heart racing every time she stands two feet from me.

She opens the drawer behind the counter and hands me my purse, then takes out hers. "But I've never shoved my tongue down your throat."

"Is there something you want to ask me, Poppy?" I arch an eyebrow.

She shrugs. "That depends, am I your BFF again?"

"Again? I never replaced you." I position my purse crossways over my chest before helping her turn off the lights in the back.

"Jeez, B, turn your lights off. How quickly did he leave tonight?" Poppy points toward the light streaming in from the back hallway.

I'm closer to the door, so I tell her, "I got it."

His familiar sandalwood scent hits me before I'm through the doorway.

I wish I didn't want him. It would make all this so much easier.

Get in. Get out.

I walk across the room to turn off his desk light, but the picture on the filing cabinet on the back wall snags my attention. It's a picture of him and Kristie in a hospital room. Her belly is swollen, so it was taken before Wren was born. Probably hours before Kristie died. How is he able to look at this every day? Even if it's been seven years.

"It's not what you think," Poppy says from behind me.

I quickly straighten. "I was just... he left his desk light on."

"Delaney."

I put my hand in the air. "I'm fine. It's fine. He clearly loved her. Let's go get those flowers so you can get where you need to be."

Poppy steps in front me, blocking the doorway, and I draw back. She crosses her arms as if she'll wait me out all day. So, I broach the subject first.

"I can't judge. I married someone else too."

"You know, I always found it interesting..." She steps around me, going back into his office. "For a man who says he can't move on because he loved his wife so much, he sure doesn't like to look at her."

"He has pictures of her, of them." I motion around the room.

She nods. "Sure, but none of them face him. Like the wedding photo, tucked into the right-hand corner of the bookcase on a shelf with his nerdy plant pictures."

"What are you suggesting?"

"And this one is behind his desk. Since when does someone turn around to look at a picture in their office?" She picks up the photo I was looking at. "This is for whoever is sitting there." She points at the chair that faces his desk.

"I thought you had to go?" I don't want her giving me reasons to want Bennett, reasons to think he's over his deceased wife and looking to move on.

"BFFs trump my plans."

"I have a feeling your only plan is for me to drop off the flowers." I've heard the Owens, Noughtons, and Ellises all meddle in their family's lives, pushing them to find themselves. This flower thing could be Poppy trying to get me into Bennett's presence with the hopes that we find our way back to one another.

"Noooo," she says, but her smile says otherwise.

"Don't meddle, it's unbecoming of you."

She rounds his desk and hooks her arm with mine, leading me out of the room and turning off the lights. "Meddling? Unbecoming? I gotta knock that California out of you, and I definitely need to get you to The Hidden Cave. You're probably all over the Canary Wall one and two."

"Oh god, I hope not. What would they say?"

"You'll find out... so you get it, right?"

She doesn't let me go until we're out the front doors by our cars. "What?"

"I like to think I know Bennett pretty well, him being my cousin and business partner, and let me tell you—I think he likes to play the lonely widower because it stops people from asking any questions." Her eyebrows lift, and she kisses my cheek. "I owe you for taking the flowers." She stops midway to her car. "Of course, if things go right, you might owe me."

"Oh my god, Poppy, I'm a married woman."

She steps up on her Jeep's doorframe but peeks over the roof at me. "Not really. You told me the papers are signed and just waiting to be processed."

"Go!"

She laughs and climbs into her Jeep, driving off.

I allow myself an extra minute to give myself a little pep talk.

You can do this, Delaney. Just drop them off and go, but whatever you do, do not linger.

Chapter Twenty-One

DELANEY

Memories flood my mind when I pull up to Bennett's house. I remember being here so long ago when it was his family's home. When the Owens family lived here and the Ellis family lived in the girls' house, before they all built new homes. I'm sad that I missed them all deciding to have the girl cousins in one house and the boy cousins in the other. They're all so close.

I should've called first and asked him to meet me outside, but I've only ever used his number that I got off his business card when I was going to be late one morning.

What Poppy said in his office could be true, but seven years is a long time to pretend that you can't move on because you miss your deceased wife so terribly. There's no way he hasn't had sex since before Wren.

I think back to this morning when we were talking about the girls and try to convince myself that he wasn't looking at me in a certain way, but more and more our gazes are snagging on one another, holding. He told me about Wren and her horse, Biscuits, and I confessed that I started Leia on horseback lessons in California to make sure she was never scared of horses like I was when I was a child.

When I reach the front door, I see that the inside door is open, the screen the only thing that separates me from entering his domain. The house he shares with his daughter. The porch light glows softly, and a warm spill of light comes from the living room window.

I knock on the screen door. "Bennett?"

No response.

I press a hand to the door handle, and it's unlocked. I hesitate. "It's Delaney."

I step inside, seeing the plaid couches are gone and replaced by what looks like a new sofa and loveseat. There aren't a ton of feminine touches, but there are pictures along the walls.

"Bennett?" I say a little louder with the hopes that whoever is home will come out from wherever they are. "Nash? Jensen?"

"Hello?" Bennett steps out from what used to be the kitchen.

Words clog my throat. God, he looks good. His hair is a little messy, his flannel sleeves are rolled up, and there's a pencil tucked behind his ear.

"Hey," he says, taking me in.

"Hi. Sorry, I didn't mean to interrupt. The door was open, and no one answered."

He says nothing.

"Flowers," I say, way too flustered, giving away that I was checking him out.

His eyebrows furrow for a moment, and I suddenly want to kill Poppy. Then they straighten, and he rocks his head back. "Oh, shit, yeah. Thanks so much."

"For your mom's birthday," I say as if I have to remind him.

"Of course. I was going to go back and get them after we finished homework."

I point my thumb at the door. "Speaking of, I should probably get home to help Leia."

Just get me out of here because Poppy's suspicions can't stop floating back into my conscious and the vision of coming home to this version of Bennett sounds really nice.

Wren peeks around the corner, and her eyes light up, but she's looking behind me. "Leia's mom?"

"Hey, Wren."

Bennett puts his hand on her back and rubs. "You're supposed to be doing your words."

I lift my hand in a small wave. "I was just dropping flowers off for your grandma's birthday."

Her nose crinkles, and she looks up at Bennett. My stomach sinks.

God, Poppy, you couldn't have used any other excuse?

He chuckles. "Nice, right?"

She turns to me. "Leia isn't with you?"

"I'm sorry, she's not."

Her shoulders slump.

"Hey, is that how you welcome a guest?" Bennett's exactly the kind of dad I thought he'd be. He's the dad I had always hoped Sean would be. More hands-on, offering more guidance.

"Sorry, do you want pizza? Daddy was about to order it." Her voice holds more excitement now.

"There you go." He musses the hair on top of her head, and Wren pulls away.

Bennett looks at me expectantly, his dark eyebrows raised.

"I should get home to Leia." It would be so awkward to stay here and eat dinner with only them and no Leia. It would be a betrayal no one but me would know.

"We could pick Leia up and go out for pizza?" Wren waggles her eyebrows.

Bennett laughs, putting his hands on her shoulders and turning her back toward the kitchen. "You need to finish those words. I marked the ones you got wrong. Study them, and I'll be right in."

My heart splinters into pieces because I've kept this man away from Leia. What was I thinking? But then I remember, he was with Kristie, and they were coming to Willowbrook to be a happy little family. I was tossed aside. Leia and I would've changed this entire dynamic. No one had a crystal ball to see that Kristie's labor would go horribly wrong, and she'd lose her life.

I've thought about if I had told him. Would Kristie have used it against him and made him stay in California, away from his family? Who knows where we would all be right now. But Bennett wouldn't be the man he is right now, and I wouldn't be the woman I am now. Those two things are certain.

"What do you say? Want to get Leia and go for pizza?"

Hell to the no. Unless I want to unleash my secret right here in your family room with your other daughter within earshot.

"I'm sure she's probably eaten. My mom is a stickler for dinner time. But raincheck for sure."

He steps closer, taking all the air with him, and the room shrinks. "Wren's been asking for a sleepover. I understand you might not be comfortable with Leia coming over here with Nash and Jensen, so my parents can host. I'll spend the night over there to keep an eye on them."

He shoves his hands into his pockets and looks wary as if I would never allow it.

"I have no problem with Nash and Jensen, but she hasn't had a sleepover since... well, Sean. Sometimes she still has nightmares."

He nods. "Maybe a day play date or something then? Wren's on me day and night to have time with Leia away from school."

How do I get out of this? Sure, Nash and Poppy have seen her and not said a word about how her features are similar to Bennett and Wren, but I can just picture Bennett serving her pancakes, seeing his eyes reflected back at him.

"I'll take them." The words rush out, and I hope he doesn't grow suspicious.

I know I need to tell him. I just don't know *how* after all this time. How thinking I was doing the right thing back then could feel so terribly wrong now.

"I don't want you to do that." He glances over his shoulder. "We could do something together. I mean… if you'd be up for it. Go to the zoo, the park, or the movies." He raises his hands. "Not a date, just to get them together. Do you know the Millers? We could ask Kayla to come too, and one of her parents if you don't feel comfortable."

I laugh at how unsure and awkward he seems.

"Are you laughing at me?"

I shake my head. "No, not at all. Just weird to see you so unsure of yourself. It's refreshing honestly."

He tilts his head and leans his shoulder against the wall. "Why's that?"

"Because you always have it together."

"You think so, huh?" A smirk teases his lips, and damn, that's sexy. It's been a long time since butterflies fluttered so hard in my stomach.

"Dad, I'm done," Wren calls from the kitchen.

Bennett holds up his finger. "Give me one second." He leaves the room.

This is the perfect time for a getaway. Just text him after and tell him you had to run. Go, Delaney.

They talk in hushed voices, and before I have time to

decide on my exit, Bennett appears in the doorway again. "Can I walk you out?"

"That's not necessary." I step farther into the house, and he looks at me quizzically until I slide between him and the archway. "Bye, Wren. I'll tell Leia you said hi, and good luck on the spelling test tomorrow."

"Bye, Leia's mom."

I hesitate. "You can call me Delaney."

She looks past me at Bennett. He's way too close behind me. Close enough that I can smell sandalwood permeating from him. He must nod or give her some sort of confirmation because she smiles. "Bye, Delaney."

I stand straight, and Bennett is right there, causing me to lose my balance, and his hands fall to my hips. "I got you," he says, his voice soft.

"I have to go to the bathroom." Wren drops her pencil and runs out of the room. Her little footsteps can be heard climbing the stairs.

Our eyes lock, and for a moment, everything from the past disappears. All I want is to have my lips on his.

"She's great," I say.

He holds my stare. "Yeah, she is."

"You're a good dad."

"I try."

I watch him for a beat. The way he looks toward the stairway Wren just disappeared up. The love and adoration he has for her. The unspoken truth pulses in the silence between us.

"It's not your mom's birthday, is it?"

He shakes his head, and mine thumps against the doorframe.

Jeez, Poppy.

"I'm sorry."

His gaze dips to my mouth for a brief second. "Don't be. I

like that you're making excuses to see me." His smirk, that damn slight smile that always drew me to him, transforms his lips.

"Poppy arranged it—"

"Way to bring me down."

My chest rises and falls, and my hands itch to run down the front of his chest. To unbutton his plaid shirt painstakingly slowly, one button at a time, teasing us both.

He clears his throat, and when my eyes meet his, my breathing halts. "Sorry. I've kept you too long." His voice is rough as he studies me.

"No. It's fine."

That's the truth. I don't say how much I wish this were my every day. How my chest aches at the simplicity of his night. Pizza and homework and him a little disheveled and sexy as hell. Leia deserves this. A man who will give her all the stability and love she deserves.

The space between us is charged, crackling with energy.

"Boy, this place brings back memories." I clear my throat and strip my gaze off his in the hopes it cools me down, gives me a moment to remember that I can't act on my feelings toward Bennett.

"Like that night on the porch. You snuck out of Poppy's room after everyone had gone to bed."

I nod slowly. "Our first kiss."

"The best kiss."

"Yeah?"

He gives a crooked half-smile. "For sure. Nothing beats the first."

I can't help but think he's talking about more than just our first kiss. "True."

"I'm trying like hell not to kiss you right now." Again, his attention flickers to the stairway.

His eyes search mine, and something in them looks heavy,

lust-filled. He places his hands on either side of the archway molding, leaning closer to me. My heartrate picks up, and my lips tingle in anticipation. I'm torn between stopping him and pulling him the rest of the way forward.

"Delaney," he murmurs.

"Yeah?" I practically whisper.

He tucks a strand of my hair behind my ear, his thumb lingering a second longer than it should. "You look tired."

I laugh under my breath. "That's what you wanted to whisper to me?"

He smiles. "Forgive me for being gun-shy."

"I'm here, aren't I?"

What am I saying? Walk out of his house right now!

He closes the space between us, and my breath hitches.

"Bennett," I whisper.

His eyes darken. "Tell me later."

He leans in, and every cell in my body screams for him to kiss me... kiss me.

The screen door bangs, and both of our heads whip in that direction.

Nash drops his bag onto the floor. "Man, Poppy's gonna kill me."

Moment officially over.

Chapter Twenty-Two

Sean,

Once we stepped over that invisible barrier, we didn't stop. It was a hot and explosive six weeks of my life. I won't get into the specifics, but it wasn't just the sex. It was the feelings that went along with us being unable to stop touching each other.

We'd have late night talks about the years since we'd seen one another. I didn't even mind hearing his story about meeting Kristie at his first frat party where they bonded over our breakup. Months later, and he was still reeling from it.

He told me about the failed marriage, how he was to blame too. That now that he was with me, he could see she just wasn't his one and only.

God, I think I would've married him if he'd asked and wasn't still legally married to Kristie. I was completely in his orbit and would've never left it if I was given the choice.

One morning, the dream I conjured in my head, the one where we made it, where he divorced Kristie, and we made another go of it as adults, shattered with one ring of the doorbell.

I'd been sent on a business trip to Sacramento for a week to make a bid on a project and couldn't wait for some alone time with him when I returned.

I was repacking my bag, waiting for Bennett to pick me up for a weekend getaway, so I flung the door open, assuming he was early. I was ready to throw myself into his arms, kiss him, and let him sweep me away into a love bubble of just us at a bed-and-breakfast by the ocean. But my feet skidded to a stop before I broke the threshold. Familiar blue eyes stared back at me.

"Hello, Delaney," Kristie said.

Her blonde hair was pulled into a messy ponytail on top of her head. She was wearing jeans and a T-shirt that said "Color Outside the

Lines" with a pair of worn-in Birks.

I looked past her, not seeing Bennett and wondered what was going on.

"Hi."

"Well, I can tell from that response that there's no need for introductions."

"Kristie." I crossed my arms, trying to prepare myself for why she was at my door. Hell, how she knew where I lived in the first place is still a mystery.

"Yes, Bennett's wife."

"Soon-to-be ex-wife, you mean."

She huffed a laugh as if saying, you foolish, foolish girl. "May I come in?"

I stepped aside and opened the door a little farther, allowing her into my space. Looking back at it now, that was a big mistake. "Sure."

"Thanks. You're as sweet and beautiful as Bennett said. That girl next door vibe for sure." She walked over and sat on the edge of my sofa.

"You know about me?"

She laughs, her head falling back. "Yes." She chuckles again. "I've been competing with you for years."

I sit on the chair adjacent to her but stay on the edge because I was pretty sure this conversation wasn't going to be her saying she wishes us both the best.

"I'll just cut to the point because you look like a little fawn caught in the headlights on a dark highway… I'm pregnant."

Any response was swallowed by my shock.

"And it's Bennett's." She rolled her eyes, as if it was absurd that I'd have a facial expression that said I was doubtful. "I'm almost three months along. But yeah, he doubted me too, so he went for a paternity test, and he's the father."

I sat there in shock, panicked and unable to say anything, feeling as if my dream was slipping away.

Her lips turned down. "Sorry to blow up your little lovefest." Her hand fell to her stomach and rubbed a circle as if I wasn't already thinking about the baby growing there. "If it makes you feel better, it hurt me to tell Bennett there's a kink in his plan to reunite with the woman he believes is his soulmate."

Anger flared in my veins. I was over sitting silently and letting her play the game she wanted to play. I'd reached my patience level for her to come to my house with her snarky attitude, acting as if Bennett and I were just a joke, and I was the mistress. She was the one who blew up her marriage by sleeping with his friend. "What do you want? Why are you here?"

Kristie positioned her purse in her lap, unzipped it, and pulled something out, placing it on the table in front of me. "I'm here for her."

The ultrasound picture showed nothing but a little white fleck surrounded by dark with her name printed on the top.

"Cute. You thought I was lying."

I pushed it closer to her, and she picked it up, admiring it for a second, smiling, before placing it face up on the table once more.

Bennett failed to mention how much Kristie enjoyed games.

"Again, why are you here?"

"I've always been irregular, you know. I thought it was a long shot I could be pregnant. I figured there was no way it was Bennett's, but then I remembered that last time when we both decided to try again. I guess destiny had other plans for us."

"Get on with it," I said, annoyed and wanting her to leave so I could talk to Bennett. So we could figure this out. Sure, it would be tricky and uncomfortable, but he could still be a father to his little girl...

She pointed at me. "I see those wheels turning, and I hate to crush your dreams of being my little girl's stepmom, but I don't want her to grow up going from one house to another. I did that my whole life, then my parents decided to reconcile after I graduated from high school. After all the shit they put me through. Fighting over who was paying more, who wasn't doing enough. And the holidays... I sure as hell never enjoyed one since on Christmas morning, the other one would call and cast a shadow of guilt over all my new things because they were home alone. I won't do that to my daughter."

"It's not just your decision."

Her hand went to her stomach again. "True, he could choose you, but I've offered him something he's wanted for a long time."

"Being?"

"Willowbrook. I told him I'll go live in his small little ranch town as long as we give us another go, and his little girl can be raised there like he's always wanted. We both know how important family is to him."

I did. Bennett had gone on and on about us returning to Willowbrook and opening our own landscape architecture firm and flower shop. How we'd live on the ranch with the rest of his family and raise our kids surrounded by love. But I was the wife and mother in the daydream, not Kristie.

"None of this answers why you're here." I wanted Bennett to be the one telling me all these things. How could he come back into my life just to be stripped away again?

"Because he's going to come here and tell you all this, and I'm asking you to let him go."

My heart free-fell into my stomach.

She put her finger on the picture and pushed it closer to me. "It's a fresh start for us. A baby who needs her father and her mother living under the same roof."

My gaze wouldn't leave that ultrasound picture. An innocent life that was going to be born into a tug of war from her first cry. It wasn't her fault. Hell, I wasn't sure it was anyone's fault.

"You're asking me to just step aside?"

"You might not have a choice. I have no idea what Bennett wants. He sure wasn't going to tell me. I'm just asking for you not to fight him if he says he wants me."

"And the baby." I had to remind her that if he chose Willowbrook and his unborn baby, it's not her but his child he was choosing.

She shrugged. "Semantics. There's no baby without me."

I inhaled a big breath. I wasn't going to

give her the satisfaction of telling me what I was going to do. Plus, I had to think about it. Regardless, my choice only mattered if Bennett still wanted me and what we had together. I wasn't going to fall to my knees and beg him to choose me.

"I guess we'll see what his decision is then," I said, hoping it got her to leave my house.

She stood and looked me over as if she really did understand why Bennett was in love with me. For a second, that strong front of hers vanished. "I'm just doing what's best for my baby. I hope you understand."

She picked then to be cordial and nice. I don't know why. I didn't understand her or how Bennett had ever fallen in love with her. The two of us seemed so different.

I didn't say anything but walked over to the door and opened it for her.

She stepped out onto the small entry porch, then turned around. "If it makes you feel better, he really loved you. The first night I met him, when he talked about you and the breakup, I thought, God, no one will ever compare to his precious Delaney."

Except his daughter, I thought but didn't voice.

She turned and walked down the sidewalk to her car, and I shut the door, locking it as if it would keep all the demons from invading my happiness. My back hit the door, and I slid to the floor because deep down, I think I knew what Bennett's decision would be. I wasn't sure I could even fault him for making it.

Delaney

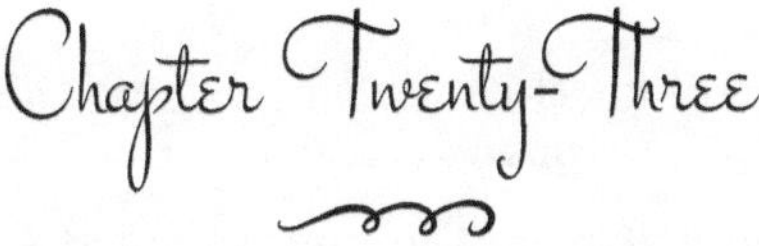

Chapter Twenty-Three

BENNETT

For the past several weeks, Delaney and I have been coming to Blue Prairie Country Club and instructing the crew on the overhaul of the landscaping. Today is the first day we'll be planting.

It's pure and utter torture every time she hops in my truck smelling like whatever perfume or shampoo she uses. I think it's some combination of pear and freesia, and it's intoxicating as fuck.

The best part is that every day it seems like I'm able to chip away a piece of that tense and closed off woman who arrived in Willowbrook. But she's still trying to keep her distance from me, and I can't really blame her. I picked Kristie over her, and the damage and pain that caused won't get washed away with a few flirtatious looks or words.

The rain starts in the middle of our second install—soft at first and enough to make us believe it will pass quickly.

Delaney's kneeling beside a bed of lavender, her hands tucking the roots in the soil gently and precisely. I admire her working longer than I should. She hums under her breath, a song I can't place.

"Are you going to watch everything I plant?" she asks without turning around.

"You have a touch with plants and flowers."

She looks over her shoulder. "That is a compliment, right?"

I chuckle and kneel beside her, digging the next hole for her. "It's a gentleness, like a caress."

She reaches across me, lightly putting the roots in place then sliding the dirt to fill the hole. "It's called nurturing. I like to think the calmer you are, the more it feels at peace with the earth."

I sit back on my ankles, and she puts up her hand.

"I don't want to hear it."

"What?" I hold out my hands, unable to take my eyes off her.

"That it's some new age thinking. I'd like you to know, in my private garden, only two things died, and they were both roses." She sighs. "Should've been a sign."

"I wasn't judging. I love to watch you work."

She side-eyes me, reaching farther to dig the next hole, but I get there first.

"What?" I ask when she doesn't continue the conversation.

"It's just... this needs to stay platonic between us."

"I only said I love to watch you work. I don't see the harm in complimenting you." We start on the second row of lavender.

Honestly, I should be on the seventh hole with the hackberry trees being planted along the fairway, but I can't seem to find it in myself to leave her.

The other night when Wren told me she went riding with Leia and her mom had braided her hair, I was pissed that I'd missed it. Though to see her doing something so motherly with my daughter might've broken that final thread of willpower and had me kissing her.

Delaney stands and stretches, water dripping from the ends of her hair. "Thank you."

I sit back and stretch my arms, watching her tip her head back. "Don't thank me. It was purely selfish reasons that I came over to help you."

I forgot how exciting it is to flirt with her.

"No, for giving me the job. Convincing me to take it." Her voice is soft. "It draws me out of my head and reminds me who I am."

I stare at the water that's coming down a little steadier now, the dark clouds looming overhead. "It's the best. You've been missing out."

She laughs and tilts her head back again, closing her eyes, face lifted to the sky, allowing the rain to wash over her. She throws her arms out at her sides, her chest rising and falling. She's breathtakingly gorgeous, and I want to kiss her more in this moment than I did the other day in my kitchen.

"Why did you allow him to tell you to stop?" I'm taking a chance with the question, but I'm desperate to know since the Delaney I knew would have told him to fuck right off.

She hesitates, and when she does finally speak, her voice is low. "It's not like from day one he said, 'You're not going to work.' It just happened slowly. He was gone a lot, we had the money, and it made sense for me to stay home with Leia at first. But I see now, I let myself shrink to fit a life I never really wanted."

The air shifts around us... thickens, as guilt washes down on me faster than the raindrops.

She looks up at the dark sky again. Rain traces her cheekbone. And for a second, I forget all the shit between us.

"You're here now, and you're definitely making the most of it." I glance at the lavender perfectly planted by her side.

"Well... thank you again." Her lips tip in a sweet smile.

"You're repaying me by looking so gorgeous right now."

Her head dips, and she opens her eyes slowly, blinking at me through the rain that's gotten heavier in the last minute. "Don't do that."

"Do what?"

She twirls her finger, pointing at me. "That. We're coworkers. For real this time. You are my boss, and I am your employee."

I climb up off the ground. "You're so much more than my employee, and you know it."

"Okay, you have hackberries to oversee being planted." She kneels back down on the ground, digging another hole for the next set of lavender.

"I'm really happy you took the job," I confess to her back when I should be staring into her eyes. "It's been a long time since I was this excited to come to work every morning."

"Hackberry trees!" she shouts with a giggle and points away from where we are.

I take my chances because I'm losing control of my usually calculated decisions. I squat behind her, leaning closer. "It's been a long time since I've wanted someone like I want you, Delaney. Like, seven years long."

Her breath hitches, and I lean in closer, inhaling her scent once more to carry me through the next few hours before we're in the cab of my truck again.

"B," she sighs.

"Call me that again."

She shakes her head slowly. "We can't."

I sit down so that I'm facing her, interrupting her work. "I'm here when you're ready. We can go slow. Start as friends if you want, but..." I stop for a second because I haven't really thought this through. For the first time in a long time, I'm going on instinct and feelings. For a split second, I doubt myself, until I look at her. "I want to give us another try." There, it's out there, and I can't take it back. "You know, when you're ready."

I may not have weighed all the pros and cons of my admission, but the moment the words leave my lips, I know them to be true.

For the first time ever, there's something in her eyes I can't piece together. "And if that's never?"

I bring my legs up and wrap my arms around them. "I don't think the word never applies to us."

She holds my gaze. "That's not what you thought seven years ago."

And there it is, the flash of hurt still sparking in her brown eyes. My roadblock to getting her back will be the worst mistake I've ever made and the one I've regretted the most.

"Dela—"

"No, just... go." The pain lining her voice warns me not to push this issue right now.

I open my mouth, but Mark hollers from the edge of the green that he needs me on the seventh hole.

"Hackberries," I murmur.

"Told you."

I get up but then squat beside her. "I want to continue this conversation."

"There isn't much to say."

I stand and wipe my ass although I'm sure my shorts are ruined from the rain and muddy grass. "I disagree."

I walk toward Mark, hoping like hell I'm right about all the signs I'm seeing. That the pulse between us is still alive and just needs a jumpstart.

Chapter Twenty-Four

DELANEY

The Perfect Petal greenhouse sits at the edge of the property, half-tucked behind a row of oak trees. The glass panes fog with humidity from the late afternoon heat.

I've always loved greenhouses. The smell, the humidity, all the growth tucked inside.

Bennett is two rows over, swearing at a broken drip line. His forearms are tanned from our hours spent on the golf course. His muscles flex as he tightens the valve, and I keep peeking at him, smiling to myself. We've been tugging at the invisible string between us lately, and I know I need to tell him the truth about Leia before it goes too far. As much as I love this flirtatious game we're playing, it will end the moment he knows the truth.

"It's nice to see things get to you," I call, leaning my hip along the table.

He glances over his shoulder, the start of a smile tipping his lips. "You should be familiar with that version of me."

I ditch the plants and walk the two rows to him. "Oh?"

Again, another glance, but then he concentrates on the hose. "Let's not pretend, shall we?"

Memories flood of how just one look would have me pressed against a wall or strewn across the kitchen table. I still feel the weight of him pressing me into the mattress. My core clenches when I remember the feel of his intensity. I never questioned how much he wanted me. It always lined his face.

I sit on the stool nearby. "They were good times."

"Yeah," he mumbles, and this time, his eyes don't lift in my direction.

I watch him work for a second, the truth I know I need to reveal to him pressing down on me. I open my mouth to tell him we need to talk, to ask him to meet me away from work, maybe go on a walk. Somewhere I won't be stranded since I'm sure I'll be the last person he wants to be around after I confess.

"I'm sorry," he says before I can speak. "I made the wrong choice."

I hop off the stool. "It's ancient history."

The hose hits the floor, and his hand wraps around my wrist, brushing the infinity symbol over the inside of my wrist with this thumb. But there's no infinity in our world anymore, he just doesn't know it.

"Please... I need to apologize."

Still not facing him, I shake my head. "It's so long ago. It doesn't matter."

"It does. Please... just look at me."

I slowly circle around, and he turns my palm up, continuing to run figure eights around my inner wrist.

"I knew I made a mistake the minute we got to Willowbrook. Our marriage was broken after she slept with Jon, and a baby wasn't going to repair that. I'd fallen in love with you all over again, and Kristie knew it, although she never asked me."

I open my mouth, but he steps closer.

"I'm not sure where I can fit into your life right now, but I've spent the last seven years pretending to mourn a marriage that wasn't real anymore. God, I was so scared when I saw you in Lottie's yard that night. You coming back blew it all up, reminded me of the lie I was living. And—"

"Don't. You don't have to tell me any of this. I moved on. It's over." I move to turn, and he steps forward.

"I'm trying to tell you how much I regret my decision. That it should've been you I picked. I would've made it work with Wren, and you wouldn't be where you are right now."

I draw back, pulling my arm away from his and crossing my arms. "Is that what this apology is about? You feeling like you're to blame for the mess my life is?"

Anger stirs to life inside me, like a rattlesnake ready to lash out. I don't need him to take the blame, as if I didn't choose Sean myself.

"Had I stayed—"

"You didn't though." Tears threaten to break through, but I suck them back. I will not show him how much that affected me.

"Exactly, and I'm telling you I regret it."

"So, what? You want my forgiveness?" I bow. "Granted." I turn around to leave.

"Fuck, Delaney, I'm trying here."

I whip around, the last of my patience long gone. "You're trying to make yourself feel better. Well, you're off the hook. You're not to blame. I made the decision to marry Sean. I'm the one who was too clueless to see who he really was and what he was doing. Not you, Bennett, me." I point at my chest. "I made those mistakes. Me. And I am the one who lives with them every day."

"I'm just saying—"

"You can't fix this!" I shout. "Or me."

The desperation in his eyes guts me. "So what do you want me to do? How do we move forward?"

I close my eyes, and he breaks the distance, slowly, one footstep at a time, gauging my reaction with each one.

"We don't."

"If I could pick any day to do over, it would be that one. I hate what you're going through right now, and yes, I do want to bulldoze my way back into your life and take control. I hate that man for what he did, but at the same time, I want to thank him because had he not, I wouldn't have this third chance with you. And I realize I probably don't deserve it, but that's what I want, to get to a place where we can be *us* again. At least try to be."

I shake my head, panic choking off the air, not wanting him to say these things when he doesn't know the entire story. Doesn't know that I'm not the person he thinks I am. I'm a monster who's kept him from his daughter. A horrible person who allowed another man to raise her for seven years. To love her and tuck her in at night and be her daddy.

"You know we're perfect together. You know we're meant for one another." He brushes his knuckles over my cheek.

"We can't." My fight wanes. The nearer he gets, the more my body leans toward his.

"Delaney?"

"Yes?"

"If I kissed you right now, would you stop me?"

I don't blink. Don't breathe.

And I don't answer.

Because I don't want to stop him. I'm so tired. So sick of fighting to get out of bed every day and put up the front that everything is okay. I just want to forget what a mess my life is for one second and allow myself to get lost in him.

Bennett leans in slowly, his gaze flicking to my lips, the space between us charged. His breath warms my skin when he dips his head and runs his nose along my neck. My hands fist at my sides.

"Bennett... there's something—"

"Later."

I open my mouth, and for a moment, the truth teeters there, on the edge, ready to be set free.

But his lips meet mine, and he seals the secret with a kiss. His hands coast up my sides until one is buried in my hair and the other one is pressed against my back, making it so there's no space between us. His tongue licks along the seam of my lips, and I don't hesitate to open for him.

My nails dig into my palms, my mind screaming to stop this, but then he groans, and my conscience is silent.

He backs up and our eyes lock, but that string tightens, the energy taut and electrifying.

I fist his shirt and pull him closer, needing to feel the solid weight of his chest against mine. His mouth crashes into mine again, tilting my face to deepen the kiss.

God, I remember every kiss before this one. All the memories of us take control of my body. It's as if all the years we lost don't matter. All that matters is right here and right now. His tongue brushes mine, and I moan into his mouth, aching from missing him so much. God, I've yearned for him with a deep hunger I didn't even know I was carrying.

He controls us, pressing me against the frame of the greenhouse and caging me in with his body. His hands are in my hair now, his mouth trailing down to my neck. He nips and bites my collarbone, then soothes it with a swipe of his tongue.

"You feel amazing," I shamelessly confess.

His hardened length presses into my stomach, and all I want to do is wrap my legs around his waist and climb him like a tree, grinding my core along that bulge. His hand slips beneath the hem of my shirt.

"I'm sorry. We should've had this all these years," he murmurs, taking me out of the moment.

The reality of what we're doing and what he doesn't know

is a bucket of cold water over my head. I press a hand to his chest. "Wait."

He stills, resting his forehead against mine and gasping for breath. "What?"

"I can't..." My voice breaks. My whole body is begging me not to let go of him. But Levi's words float back to me. I can't move forward until he knows the truth. "I have to tell you something."

He pulls back, confusion clouding his eyes. "Now?"

I swallow hard, fingers shaking as I lower my hand from his chest, smoothing out his T-shirt. "Something I should've told you a long time ago."

He stiffens and tilts his head, patiently waiting, having no idea I'm about to blow up his life.

"Leia..." Her name trembles out of my mouth. "She's yours."

Chapter Twenty-Five

Sean,

Bennett showed up an hour after Kristie left.

Had she not already outed what he was about to tell me, I would've known something was wrong the minute I opened the door.

His hands were tucked into his pockets, while dark, heavy bags weighed under his eyes, and the look on his face... It's still so vivid in my memory.

That was the moment I knew it was over. His decision was made, and I didn't make the cut.

I stepped aside to allow him in, not giving him my usual kiss and hug whenever we saw one another outside of work. I'm guessing he

didn't even notice because his mind was somewhere else entirely.

My bags were packed by the front door
from an hour before, I'd been prepared for a
weekend of sex and love.

His gaze flickered to them, hurt reflecting
back at me. "How was your trip?" he asked,
stalling.

"Fine. We got the bid."

He nodded, and even with all the pain on
his face, he managed a small smile. "I knew
you'd do it."

I shut the door behind him, and he sat on
the couch, exactly where Kristie had. When I
sat on the chair instead of next to him, he tilted
his head but didn't question me. Instead, he
slid closer to the edge of the couch and took my
hands.

I tried to steel myself. I had taken the
hour before he arrived to prepare myself, but
there was that sliver of hope that he'd still pick
me, even if that would be nothing like the
Bennett I knew.

"While you were away, Kristie reached out to
me." His eyes constantly fought to stay on me.
One minute he looked down at our hands, then
across the room, until they landed on mine
again, only to do the whole rotation over again.

"Oh?" I heard the lack of surprise in my question, but Bennett was so lost in what he was feeling and the decision he'd made, he didn't notice.

He raised his head, eyes on me. "She's pregnant."

I nodded.

"And it's mine. I went for a rush paternity test, and the baby is mine."

I nodded again.

He reached for my wrist and started tracing an infinity symbol. His gaze fell to his hand, probably thinking, like I was, how there would be no forever for the two of us. He clenched his jaw hard, and my heart cracked.

"She's asking for another chance. Wants to raise our baby back in Willowbrook. Try again."

Words clogged my throat, so I waited for him to finish, to put the last nail in the coffin of our future.

"I've thought a lot about it. We could stay here and be coparents, but..."

I waited, and he didn't ask me why I hadn't spoken since he first started this long, drawn-out breakup speech. Part of me wanted him to just spit it out and leave, but if I allowed him to take his time, I could savor the last minutes we'd have together in our lifetime.

"I'm sure you don't want to hear this, but I told you about the mistakes I made too. Doesn't my unborn baby deserve a chance to have her parents be happy together?"

I shrugged, afraid that if I opened my mouth, I'd tell him exactly how I felt. That people coparent every day and make it work. That yes, it's not ideal and doesn't come without a lot of compromise and trials, but everyone would be happier in the end than if he went back to an unhappy marriage. Then again, maybe I had it all wrong... maybe I underestimated the love he'd once had for Kristie. After all, he'd loved her enough to forget about me. The last six weeks, I'd allowed him to convince me it was only me, and Kristie was somehow second prize, but what if I had it all turned around? What if I was always in second place?

"What if we can find our way back to one another?" A squeak leaked out of me, and his eyes narrowed. "Why aren't you saying anything?"

I shrugged. "What do you want me to say?"

He released my hands and stood, going to the front window, pacing back and forth. "Tell me what to do. I've walked more miles this week than the past year, trying to figure out the right decision to make. Whether I should pick us over—"

I never wanted to be a regret to Bennett. I never wanted him to look at us as anything but perfect, but still, I had to know something before he walked out of my life. "Do you have to pick?"

He stopped and turned to face me, the sun reflecting from behind him through the window. The sun that should be on my bikini-clad body at the beach, with him rubbing sunscreen on my skin instead of doing this. "Kristie isn't going to make it easy."

I nodded because I'd gotten that from her short visit, but still, I had a sliver of hope this conversation would be more of a "fuck her, we're going to make this work." I couldn't be more wrong. Now, I just wanted him out of my place and my life because my heart was crumbling in the silence and affirmation that I wasn't enough to fight for.

"Then you should go," I said.

He paced, not refuting my words. "I don't want to end this."

The longer the conversation went on, the madder I became. "According to you, you can't have both."

He stopped again and came over to me,

falling to his knees in front of me. "A baby. My baby," he said it as if he was trying to convince me it was okay that he wasn't willing to try.

"I know." My voice was cold and didn't hold any of the warmth it usually did when it came to him.

He rested his chin on my thigh, his eyes looking up into mine. I weaved my fingers through his hair, knowing it was the last time I'd do so.

"I don't want to say goodbye," he said.

He was just torturing himself and me. His decision was made, so I wasn't sure what he wanted from me. Did he want me to say I'd move to Willowbrook, rent an apartment in Lincoln, and be his little secret so he could have both?

We stared into one another's eyes for a moment, and I ran my thumb across his cheek. "Go raise your child in Willowbrook."

His head leaned into my palm as though he didn't want my caress to end, so I withdrew my hand, and he straightened his head before it fell to the arm of the chair. When he still didn't move, I slid out of the chair.

"I need you to leave." I crossed my arms.

He turned around, surprise flaring in his

eyes. What did he honestly think would happen here? "I thought we were still talking about this?"

I scoffed. "You're just trying to make yourself feel better. You've made your decision, and I'm not going to fight for you to pick a life with me here or with your child in Willowbrook."

"I thought we could talk about it, go over our options together."

If he couldn't come here and be team us, we had no hope in the future when things got dicey, because of course they would. "Okay, Bennett, what exactly do you want to go over?"

He stood and pocketed his hands again, shrugging. "I don't know."

"Exactly. You just want to make this decision guilt-free. You want to walk out that door assured I'm not left crushed and devasted on the other side. Well, I'm sorry, you can't have everything wrapped with a perfect pink bow. Your decision has repercussions." He stepped forward, but I put my hand up in the air. "Just... go."

He hesitated. Even opened his mouth. I thought maybe there was a chance he'd take it all back, but then he turned around toward my door.

His hand was on the doorknob when he glanced over his shoulder. "I love you, Laney. I think I'll always love you."

I didn't say anything. He opened the door and left. I picked up the vase full of peonies he had given me the weekend before and threw it at the door.

The crystal shattered and water spilled all over the front entryway as I sank to my knees and wept.

Delaney

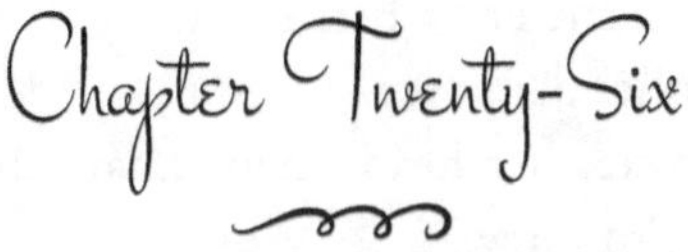

Chapter Twenty-Six

BENNETT

I stumble back from having Delaney pressed against the frame of the greenhouse, her words on repeat in my head.

Leia... she's yours.

Yours.

Mine.

I have another daughter.

"What..."

She moves to the side and walks a row over by the daffodils. "I'm sorry. I should have told you, but you had gone back to Willowbrook by the time I found out, living happily with Kristie, ready to welcome your new baby, and I was still in California."

"You never reached out." My mind is clogged with emotions, trying to sort through them and not be rash in my reaction, but all the years I've had with Wren, I've lost with Leia. Sharp pain presses into the center of my chest. Even if I push aside all the time I've missed, the betrayal I feel... that Delaney kept me from my own daughter and allowed her to be raised by a monster of a man.

My subconscious reminds me that Delaney knew nothing

of the real man she married, but I push the thought aside, uninterested in understanding her viewpoint right now.

Wetness wells in her eyes. Usually, I'd crumble at seeing her upset and want to fix it somehow, but my anger only simmers hotter. How dare she cry when I'm the one who didn't even know I had another daughter.

"I…" She shakes her head, then squares her shoulders. "I have no excuse. I'm sorry."

I feel my eyes practically bulge out of my head. "You're sorry? Sorry? For what? Keeping the knowledge of her existence from me? For never allowing me a relationship with my own daughter? For letting another man raise her? There's a lot to be sorry for." My voice is rising, and as much as I try to calm myself, the blaze burning inside me won't go out.

She wipes her tears with the backs of her hands, and her gaze meets mine with a fire I've never seen. "You left me. You picked her, so what was I supposed to do? Show up at your doorstep, ring your doorbell, and say guess what, you knocked us both up? Hope that you'd pick me and Leia over your original choice? Only to allow my daughter to be inflicted with the pain you left me with when you changed your mind again? I said I was sorry, and I truly am, but I made the best choice I could at that time with the information I had."

I inhale and stare at the ground, hands on my hips, trying like hell to stay calm because screaming and yelling at each other isn't going to change this situation.

"I thought—"

I raise my hands to stop her. "I think I need some time before I can discuss this."

The door to the greenhouse opens. "What are you guys doing?"

I weave around the row of Swiss chard and slide around Poppy at the door. Without waiting, I trudge back up to the shop and see Poppy's UTV she drove down here, then I say fuck it, slide in, and drive off.

I drive around the ranch, unsure where to go, who to tell, or how to process the news that's just been dumped in my lap.

I have another daughter.

With Delaney.

Why does what was always my dream now feel like a nightmare? This is all wrong. The way this is happening is all wrong.

My mind traces back to all the moments I've shared with Wren—the birthdays, the Christmases, the Halloweens. All of those with Leia are gone. She spent them with some other man she believed was her father. Where do we even go from here?

Somehow lost in my thoughts, I end up at the stables where I ditch the UTV for Cedar. Nash glances over, appraising me.

"He good?" I nod toward Cedar's stall.

"Yeah." Nash looks me up and down.

I point at him. "Don't you dare call Poppy," I warn him, not in the mood to talk to anyone. "If anyone asks, you didn't see me."

I saddle Cedar and walk him out of the stall.

Nash pretends not to be watching me, but as I climb up and move Cedar just outside the stables, he hollers, "He needed the exercise anyway."

His laughter rings in the air as I get Cedar into a trot before unleashing both of our pent-up energy.

Cedar was restless the second I trotted him down the path, as though he felt all the wild emotions spiraling inside me. All the fury and hurt twisting me into a knot that I can't pull apart.

Leia is mine.

We gallop past the south fence line, past the logic that tells me to slow down. I let him run. I let him get me as far away from the ranch as I can get.

I lean low into the rhythm, reins tight in my fists. The wind tears at my shirt and eyes, but I don't stop. Not even when my thighs burn.

She kept her from me.

The words thud through my skull, over and over, thumping around with the thundering sound of hooves hitting earth.

Never would I have imagined Delaney betraying me, and certainly not to this extent. If her husband hadn't gotten arrested, then what? Had she had somewhere else to disappear to, would I ever know the truth? Would she have always raised Leia without giving me the opportunity to know her?

Eventually, my mind and Cedar slow, both of us blowing hard, and I turn us back around. A while later, I drop the reins, my chest heaving, as I press my forehead to his damp neck, thanking him for giving me all he had.

"What am I supposed to do?" I whisper, my voice cracking. "How could she?"

Cedar leans into my touch as if he can understand and wants to soothe my pain.

I grip the saddle and stare at the creek, blinking back the sting of memories.

How many times did I come here over the years and wonder about my life choices or recall the moments I shared here with Delaney? Now I feel as if I don't know her at all because the Delaney I knew would never have done this.

"I should hate her," I say, meaning Delaney.

"You never will." Emmett's voice should startle me, but of course fucking Nash called him the minute he saw me take Cedar out.

"Go back."

He trots over on Brutus, meeting me at the clearing by the creek. "You know I won't."

I watch the water moving over the rocks, not even sure how to confess it all. There's more than just Delaney's secret that'll come out now. It's possible that's the reason for some of my anger.

He doesn't say anything else but sits silently, running his hand over Brutus's neck. It's rare for Emmett not to call people out on their shit or feel comfortable in silence, but I'm thankful he's not rushing me.

"Seven years ago, Kristie and I separated." To my surprise, he doesn't gasp and ask for more details. It should be the surprise of his life. So I continue. "I found her in bed with Jon."

"Bastard," he whispers.

He only met Jon a few times when he'd come out to visit me at Berkeley, and they never liked one another. I think it might've been like a competition between them. Emmett felt left out when I went to college, and Jon would throw digs about how much fun we were having. He always was kind of a dick.

"She did it, but honestly, we just kind of grew apart. I think it started before we even got married. That year after I graduated, and she still had her senior year, I stayed back in California because she told me we'd come back here after graduation. Then she got that grant. I was young and pissed off and probably resented her for that. I started working, and she'd disappear when her muse spoke to her, and over time, the planned date nights turned into takeout before we'd go our separate ways. When I found her with Jon, I packed up and moved into a condo on the water, started the divorce proceedings."

Still, Emmett doesn't say anything. Not even to crack a joke.

"Then Delaney started at my company."

His head whips toward me, and I feel his stare on the side of my face.

I nod to answer his unasked question. "We were put on a project together."

A whooshing sound floats out of him.

"Yeah, then one thing led to another."

He chuckles, and I finally face him, silently questioning why he's laughing.

"My lovely wife would have told you it was destiny."

I thought the same for a while. "We started seeing one another, dating in secret. I hadn't told anyone about the separation. I was still wearing my wedding ring and would answer questions about Kristie as if we were still happily married." I shake my head. "I don't even know why now."

"Yeah, you do," he says.

"No, I don't."

"Come on, B, you don't like failure."

I rock my head back. "Okay, first of all, I'm anal and have attention to detail and have to keep a strict schedule because I'm a dad. A *single* dad who needs to be certain everything is organized, otherwise things go to hell."

He clicks his tongue and shakes his head. "You were that way before Wren."

I think back to before I became a father, barely remembering who I was. Whatever version of me existed, I don't have much of a recollection of him. "No."

"Yes," he drawls. "Remember that time I borrowed your notes for biology, and you got all upset because I mixed up the papers?"

"That's what you're using to prove your point?"

He shrugs. "Give me fifteen minutes, and I'll make a list, but seriously, ask anyone. Kristie cheating on you was a failure in your eyes, when let's face it, it was really her decision." I open my mouth, but he holds up his hand. "I get what you're saying about you not being there and working too much, but she actively cheated, B. It was her choice. Pretty hard to come back from that." He waves. "And since she passed seven years ago, you'll need to explain to me why you stole Poppy's UTV, drove to the stables, and decided to exercise Cedar yourself today."

It's just like him to not want more information about that time in my life, only concerned about the present. How many times did I wish I could be Emmett with that carefree attitude, always going after what he wants and never regretting a thing. I feel as if I've been living in the past for my entire adult life.

"Leia, Delaney's daughter..."

"I know who she is. I'm the one who told you about her."

I get back up on Cedar and grab the reins, veering away from the creek, unable to be in a place that only ever reminds me of Delaney. He leads Brutus next to me, and we head to the open field on the west side of our property.

"She's mine," I whisper. It's the first time I've said it out loud, and I'm just as confused on what to feel as I was when I stormed out of the greenhouse.

There's another whooshing sound. With Emmett, his sounds that aren't actual words always convey more than had he spoken a full sentence.

"Yeah."

"Shit, man."

I nod instead of answering.

"Well, I mean, they love one another like sisters. Her and Wren."

"Fuck, Emmett." I nudge Cedar to move away from Brutus, but Emmett only trots Brutus closer.

"Sorry, that's some serious shit."

"You think?"

"What are you going to do?" He stares at the horizon, as if

there are answers to be found there. "Can I give you some advice?" I crinkle my brow, and he puts his hands up in a placating motion. "You're going to sit and stew over this for I have no idea how long. You'll continue to live in the past and rehash every decision that led you here, but what does that accomplish?"

"Me figuring out how to fix it."

He presses his lips together and shakes his head. "No, it doesn't. You're upset that Delaney kept her from you. You're upset another man raised her. Which really just spirals back to you not having time with your daughter. So, stewing over this whole thing is just going to prevent you from getting to know Leia now."

I halt the reins, and Cedar stops. God, is he right? He has a point.

"Say 'thank you, Emmett,'" he says, slowing Brutus.

"For what?"

"Don't deny that I just helped you. I get that you're mad at Delaney, and you have every right to be, but Leia didn't do anything wrong. You and Delaney need to figure out how you're going to get to know your daughter, then decide what the hell to do about the two of you separately."

"I'm not sure there's a chance we could be together now."

He laughs. "Yeah, okay, B." He trots ahead of me. "Now I'll leave you to stew..." He circles Brutus around to head back to the stables. "If you need me to straighten your head out, just call 1-800-Emmett-knows-all."

He leaves me with my thoughts, but he's right. My issues are two separate things. As Wren always is, Leia needs to be the priority. If I only knew where to start.

Chapter Twenty-Seven

DELANEY

"The bastard took my UTV." Poppy opens the door to the greenhouse, and I slip around her, needing to get out of here. "Whoa, what happened?"

All the years pile on top of one another, and the tears trickle a few at a time until I can't control them anymore.

"Delaney." Poppy puts her arm around my shoulders. "Tell me what's going on."

My back shudders, and the longer she holds me, the more the weight feels almost unbearable.

"Levi is a dick," I murmur, backing out of her embrace.

She looks around. "Levi? Is that where Bennett went, to kick his ass?"

Her utter confusion only reminds me how much I've allowed our friendship to wane. "No."

My brother told me to let the truth out, but look where I am now. There's so much I have to deal with now. This isn't freeing. It only buries me under another truckful of rubble. I was feeling so good about myself, as if I was useful again and not only good for being pretty on someone's arm and a good mother. But I have no one to blame but myself.

"I don't understand."

I turn away from her and walk back toward the shop. "You'll hate me just like him, so I need to go. I'll call you later, and if you want to talk to me, you can pick up."

She probably won't. I've deceived an Owens, so I'm pretty sure everyone from Plain Daisy Ranch is going to hate me as much as Bennett does.

"I'd like to talk to you now."

I shake my head. "I need to get Leia."

We reach the shop, and I walk in, going behind the counter.

"Heya, you two," Summer says, but her smile falters when she sees me crying. "Did the peonies die?" she teases since I might be slightly obsessed.

"Not now, Summer," Poppy says and waits for me by the door.

I get my purse from the drawer behind the counter and quickly put it on as I cross the store. Poppy doesn't stand in my way as I walk out the door, but she follows me.

I click my key fob, unlocking the door, and I'm about to slide into the driver's seat, but Poppy shoves me aside, getting in first.

"What are you doing?" I shout, struggling to find my footing. "Poppy!"

"First of all, you're not driving in this condition." She twirls her finger at my face. "Second, I'm Team Delaney first and always."

"It's been years of me dodging your phone calls and texts. And on this one, you're going to take his side, believe me. And you'd be right to."

She secures the seat belt and puts out her hand. "Give me your keys."

"Poppy!" My voice rises, but her hand doesn't lower.

"We can do this the easy way or the hard way."

"What are you going to do?"

"There's a lot of twine in that shop. I can bind you and toss you in the trunk. Summer owes me two favors, and I'm not opposed to using both of them to get you through this."

I look at the store to see Summer's face pressed to the window. No doubt she would help Poppy.

"Fine, but I need to get Leia."

"Leia's at school for another two hours."

"I'm picking her up early."

"Why?"

She keeps her hand out, waiting for me to give her the keys, then I hear a UTV coming down from The Knotted Barn. I drop them in her hand because the last thing I want is for Bennett to return her UTV. I can't face him right now.

I round the front of the car and get into the passenger seat right as Romy and Lottie turn the corner in a UTV of their own. Oh god, the catalyst of my decision all those years ago hits me. They're Leia's aunts, and I've stripped them of a relationship with her too.

"Can we go?" I ask quietly, but Poppy rolls down the window.

Fuck, I'm not in the mood for this. Are they here to kick my ass? Surely Bennett went to his family for support after what he just discovered.

"I gotta go. Flowers are in the cooler." Poppy rolls up the window and puts the car in reverse.

They both step out of the UTV with their eyebrows furrowed as they watch us drive away. I hold it together, pretending I'm not about to have a breakdown.

Once we're off Plain Daisy Ranch, I finally release a breath —until I realize Poppy isn't driving me to the school. She's turning onto the county road toward Hickory.

"Where are we going?" I ask.

"You'll see."

"I'm not in the mood for games."

"I know."

The truth rests on the tip of my tongue, knowing I should just tell her, get it over with. It's my car, so I won't be stranded, but every time I open my mouth, shame silences me.

Fifteen minutes later, she pulls into an ice cream shop I'd forgotten all about, a place I should take Leia to.

Poppy parks and turns off the ignition. "There's nothing a sundae can't fix."

"You couldn't be more wrong." I stare through the windows at everyone smiling inside.

"Listen, I'm not going to push you. I mean, Nash says I'm super pushy, but I want to be here for you. You're my best friend, and I know we've had some distance, but that changes nothing for me. I was so happy when you came back. Let me be your person." Her shoulders dip. "Until B comes to his senses."

I put my hands in hers. "You'll always be my person, and believe me, he's not going to come to his senses. Any hope that you had for us to get to where we were in the past is dead and buried."

"I doubt it, but let's go."

We head into the ice cream shop because I always drown my sorrows in sugar. Maybe I should ask them if they have a loyalty card since I'll probably be here a lot after today.

Once we're settled in a booth and have both ordered our sundaes, me a peanut butter one and Poppy salted caramel, she sets her gaze on me.

"I don't feel as if it's my place to tell you the whole story, so I'm just going to tell you my part, which does mix with his, but..."

She holds up her hand to stop me. "I feel like I need to remind you that what you tell me won't be repeated. I know

Bennett is my cousin, and we're a really tight family, but I'm not going to tell anyone what we talk about."

I nod and muster up the courage to tell her. "Bennett and I ran into one another in California."

Her head tilts. "When?"

"Seven years ago."

She nods and slides back in the booth.

"Leia is his daughter."

She inhales a sharp breath and nods again. "Not Sean's?"

I shake my head.

"Bennett cheated?"

I shake my head, and her forehead scrunches, not understanding how that's possible. It's such a thin line between what's his story and what's mine, but I trust Poppy to keep it between us.

"He and Kristie were separated. She cheated on him. I got a job at the same company as him during their separation. One thing led to something more, and we started dating. Until Kristie came back and told him she was pregnant with his baby."

"So Wren might not be his?" she whispers, thank goodness, but you can never be sure who's listening in these small towns.

"She's his. He had a paternity test to make sure."

"He left you for her, knowing you were pregnant too?"

And there it is, the assumption that I sought him out and told him.

I shake my head. Poppy's smart, so she puts it all together.

"You didn't tell him?" Again, my head shakes, tears springing to my eyes, and she nods. "Gotcha." She seems to process that for a few moments. "And Sean?"

"He came after Bennett and Kristie went to Willowbrook, after he'd broken off what we had. Sean moved into the apartment next to mine. At first it was friendship between us, but I knew he wanted more. He started doing really nice things for me. Expensive dinners, trips, gifts. He adored me, or so it seemed. I think I really needed that after Bennett left, and maybe I just got caught up in it. When I found out I was pregnant, I contemplated telling Bennett for a long time. I looked them up on socials. Bennett wasn't really posting, but Kristie was chronicling her pregnancy, and he looked really happy. I didn't know what to do." Tears free fall down my face. "Would he even accept our child? Would Kristie? I picked up the phone a couple times, started text messages, but I never followed through. I have no excuse other than I was scared and mad, but I didn't do it from spite. I did it because I was trying to protect my child."

"Here you go, ladies." The waitress pretends I'm not falling apart in the booth, which I'm grateful for.

Neither of us touch our sundaes.

"I was truthful with Sean. He said it changed nothing and that he'd raise her as his own. I didn't know then that he had his own agenda for our marriage. He was offering us safety and security, a future that Bennett couldn't, or didn't, want to give."

Poppy dips her spoon into her ice cream, bringing a heaping helping to her mouth. "Man, I had some suspicions about some things, but you just blew them away."

"Suspicions?"

"I'm just gonna say... Leia doesn't look like Sean, but what was I going to do, ask you why your daughter bore no resemblance to your husband's olive skin?"

I dig into my own sundae, but the ice cream doesn't cool my overheated body.

"Well, now I know it all," she says.

"Some of it," I say. "You should probably hear his side."

She scoffs. "No, thank you." She piles another spoonful into her mouth.

"Poppy, I never told him that Leia was his." I stress the truth in one sentence.

No matter all the other stuff that went down between us, I took something away from him without giving him a choice. Took something away from Leia.

"I hear you." She wipes her mouth with a napkin. "And I told you before you got in the car, I'm Team Delaney."

"You can't be on my team. You're his cousin, and I'm in the wrong."

Her brows crinkle. "True, it wasn't the best decision, but I can understand why you did it. I can't imagine how hurt you were. How scared. But that's all in the past. Now you have to move forward. How do you see this thing playing out?"

I've been so hung up on telling him that I didn't really think about what would happen after Bennett knew. Who tells Leia? What about Wren? Do I allow Bennett visitation on his own? I need to tell Sean that he knows. "I'm not sure. I guess I have to wait until Bennett decides what he wants to do."

"She'll be ten before he does something. You need to steer this boat."

I set my spoon down. "Really?"

She's nodding as she swallows the last bite of her sundae. I'm thinking we came here more for her than me. "You want my advice?"

"I'm pretty sure you're going to give it to me regardless."

"And you should feel honored that I'm going to give you my wisdom." She smiles and sips her water as if she has to prepare herself. "The biggest question you need to figure out the answer to is whether you want something with Bennett in the future. You know he's a good dad, you know what kind of man he is, and we both know he'll eventually forgive you for this and will definitely see how his actions played into your decision. But if you want to see where you guys fit, your girls fit, that dictates your next move."

I sigh, since over these last few weeks, there have been times when I wanted a future with him more than anything. But how can I ask for that when I've been lying to him for so long?

She takes my hand. "I'm not saying right this minute, but think about it, okay?"

I nod, and she squeezes my hand.

"You're going to get through this and become stronger and happier, I know it."

I'm desperate to believe her, but I've thought that before in my life and then lost it all, more than once.

Chapter Twenty-Eight

Sean,

After Bennett left and went back to Willow-brook with Kristie, I continued to work at the company. I was in the running to fill his position, but he had been there for so many years that people were constantly talking about him. How much they missed him, how they wished him well with his new baby and his return home. On and on, my coworkers raved about the man, and one day I just lost it. Turned in my notice to Denise at day's end and didn't let them convince me to stay. It was rash, but I felt I needed a clean slate. Hell, I would've left California had I been able to afford it.

I was desperate to forget Bennett, so I agreed to a date with my new neighbor—you. I thought you were nice, attractive, and you always found sly ways to ask me out on dates every time our paths crossed. So, I finally agreed. One date turned into another, and although I forgot about Bennett during our dates, at night, my memories still haunted me. He had moved on, was starting a family, reconnecting with his wife. I had to too. So, I continued dating you and allowed you to spoil me as if I was the most important person in your world. It was nice to feel as admired as you made me feel. Of course, now I'm wondering whether any of it was real.

Then my period was late. I initially blamed it on stress, but deep down, I couldn't forget that one time things got too intense, and Bennett and I didn't have a condom. We naively thought that it couldn't happen as long as he pulled out. I couldn't deny the two pink lines once I saw them though. Since I hadn't slept with anyone else, I knew the baby was Bennett's.

I spiraled and didn't know how to handle the news. I went to the doctor, who confirmed I was indeed pregnant, and I started taking prenatal vitamins and allowed myself to come to grips with growing a little baby inside me. I gave excuse after excuse to you, but you became more adamant about continuing our dates, asking me what was wrong. You were so caring and loving that I finally broke down one night.

That's when you showed up at my door with takeout from my favorite Italian place.

"You need to eat, and I caught you before dinner time, so no excuses." You gave me a smile that I trusted, so I let you in, thinking I'd break the news to you, and you'd give up the fight for me. Who would want to raise another man's baby?

We ate, and you asked me a lot of questions about work and my favorite things. You had this way of navigating the conversation around me. Maybe that's why I felt so important in your eyes. Like you couldn't find out enough about me, and I was the center of your universe.

After I cleaned up the takeout and you took out the trash for me, I told myself now was the time to tell you.

"Thank you for dinner," I said.

You sat on the couch, the same spot Bennett had when he'd told me he was leaving me to be with Kristie. I took the spot next to you and confessed to you the whole situation, and the tears started immediately.

"I was dating this guy who was my high school sweetheart, well, not really, but from freshman to junior... oh never mind, it doesn't really matter, but we broke up right before you moved in. He went back to his wife... oh jeez, I'm not a homewrecker. He was separated, but then she came back to him pregnant. How ironic, he knocked us both up..."

I was a rambling mess, but you never stopped me once. Never asked for further explanation. I liked that. The last thing I wanted was to give you a play by play of my life with Bennett Owens.

"And I'm pregnant," I said it, and it felt really good to tell someone. To no longer harbor my secret alone.

I assumed you'd get up politely, say something nice, and then ghost me, but instead you slid closer. You took my hands and wrapped an arm around me, pulling me into your chest. You allowed me to cry for a half hour, soaking your button-down shirt.

I drew back. "You can go."

"I'd rather stay if it's okay with you?"

"This isn't your problem. It's..." I didn't even know how to say it, but you only put your finger under my chin and brought my eyes to meet yours. I remember that there was no hesitation in your big hazel eyes.

"I want to stay."

It was the words I needed to hear. Now, I wonder if you just saw me as an easy mark.

You didn't ask me what I planned to do. Whether I was keeping the baby or even telling Bennett. You were a pillar of support that I was in desperate need of.

A week later, you showed back up with the same Italian dinner, apologizing that you hadn't been around because you'd been out of town on business. Again, we had takeout and watched a movie.

"Can I ask you something, and if you don't want to talk about it, please tell me I over-stepped?" I remember you asking on our way to get ice cream after the movie.

"Of course."

"Are you telling him?"

It had been the biggest question on my mind. I had even picked up my phone and had Bennett's number dialed three times the other night. Then I made the mistake of searching for him on socials. He didn't have anything new, but Kristie did. A picture of them with Darla, Brad, Romy, and Lottie, all of them wearing to-be shirts, announcing the pregnancy. Bennett's arm was around Kristie, and her arms were around his waist. The rest of the Owens' smiles were big and wide. Where our baby and I could fit, I didn't know.

"I'm not sure yet," I admitted, slightly ashamed I hadn't booked a flight and gone to Willowbrook to tell him already. Or at least texted him a picture of the pregnancy test. Was I really considering having this baby and never telling him?

"Well, I just want you to know, either way, I'm in." Your hand slid over the console of your expensive sports car.

"What?" I thought I had to have heard you wrong.

"I'm not asking to marry you, but you being pregnant doesn't change my feelings for you. I'd like to continue dating and see where this goes."

I turned in my seat. "I'm pregnant."

"I know."

"With another man's baby."

A smile tipped your lips. "I know."

"And I'm fairly sure I'm keeping the baby."

"Okay." You glanced at me before concentrating on the road again.

"We haven't even had sex, and I'm not sure if I want you to see my body all swollen and big the first time."

You laughed and shook your head. "You're going to be a gorgeous pregnant woman, of that I have no doubt."

You parked the car, and we didn't get out right away, mostly because I was trying to wrap my head around the fact that you wanted to date me knowing all these things going on in my life. You didn't care about my baggage, you only wanted me, and that felt really, really good.

"And we can take it slow?" I asked.

"You dictate the pace."

"Okay," I agreed.

You got out of the car, walking around to help me out.

As you know, when I was around five months pregnant, my libido was in overdrive, and I eventually didn't stop you when you tried to progress things along physically. We were like two teenagers working their way through the bases until I didn't care about my stomach or the stretchmarks on my thighs, I just wanted you.

A month before I went into labor, you pulled me aside one morning, since we rarely slept apart unless you were away on business, and told me you'd like to raise the baby as yours. I accepted.

You were my future. Kristie was Bennett's.

I was in love with you, and you gave Leia and me a bigger life than I could have ever imagined. I'll always be thankful for that, even if I might never really know if we were a pawn in you game or whether you ever really loved us back.

Delaney

Chapter Twenty-Nine

BENNETT

As surprised as I am, Emmett gave me some solid advice, so instead of sitting on the news and weighing my options, I head over to Delaney's parents' house to have a conversation with her.

After I park in the driveway, a thought stops me from leaving the truck.

Leia is in there. I've never seen her, at least not her face. Does she have a resemblance to me, to Wren, or is she all Delaney?

I don't want to scare Leia, so I pull out my cell phone to call Delaney to ask her to meet me outside, but before I can press the green button, Levi steps out of the house and walks toward my truck. I drop the phone in the center console and roll down my window.

He's in his usual white T-shirt and beat-up jeans, a sandwich in hand. Levi is a guy you're intimidated by the moment he walks in the room. He holds an air of confidence I've admired over the years, and he makes his decisions whether you like them or not. He doesn't care.

"Hey, Bennett." His free hand runs through his hair.

"Levi."

He nods. So he knows, and I'm sure he's going to be protective of his sister and niece. "Leia is out with my parents at dinner. Delaney will be out in a second. I need to ask you something first though."

"Okay," I say hesitantly. We can't really pretend that Levi couldn't kick my ass. He'd be scrappy, and I'd probably overthink every move I was gonna make.

"You know I have to be the protective brother and uncle right now, but I'm glad she told you."

"You knew?"

He shakes his head, his sandwich long forgotten in his hand. "No. I suspected, but she only confirmed it to me the other night."

She certainly seems willing to put it out there after years of keeping it to herself.

"I have to know, B, what are you looking for here? Because if you try to take Leia—"

I quickly shake my head. "No. I would never."

He nods. "Okay, okay. I didn't think so, but I had to ask, you know?"

"And had I wanted to?"

His eyes lock on mine. "You don't want to know." He chuckles then hits the roof of the truck.

Delaney walking out the front door pulls my attention from Levi. Their screen door shuts, and she takes the few steps down to the driveway.

"Good luck then." He steps away but backtracks. "I have no right to ask this of you, but don't be too hard on her. She's so close to breaking, and I'm trying like hell to see her through this."

It's his expression more than his words that make me nod in understanding. I'd be the same if it was Lottie or Romy or any of my cousins.

Levi holds out his arms, and Delaney gives him a brief hug. He whispers something to her, then glances back at me before he walks into the house. Delaney stands for a moment in the same spot, not moving toward me, so I climb out of the truck and approach her.

"Do you want to go for a ride?" I ask.

She looks up, and my heart constricts. All the anger brewing inside me simmers from seeing her swollen, red-rimmed eyes.

"If you promise not to leave me in a ditch somewhere."

She's just like Levi, deflecting with humor, but I can't find it within myself to match her, so I just hold out my hand toward the truck.

We part ways at the front, me not opening her door for probably the first time ever.

Silence extends through the cab as I start the engine and back out of her parents' driveway. I have no idea where to go, but I'm certain we both want to be alone with no prying ears, so I head to the only spot I know that might be private but isn't on the ranch—a lookout area in Hickory.

Thankfully, no teenagers are making out when we get here. Probably because the sun hasn't completely gone down at this point.

I kill the engine and trace the steering wheel with my fingers, unsure where to start, but I forgot how much Delaney hates silence.

"I have no excuses for what I did, and I understand you're angry with me, but I don't think that there's much else to say to one another. I'm sorry, I am. You know it all now, so how do you want to go about this? Do you want me to introduce you to her? I'd like to be the one to tell her, if that's okay. Should we get lawyers involved, draw up papers around visitation? I'd like to explain myself to Wren, since I'm assuming you want to tell her—"

I place my hand on her shaking, entwined ones. "Breathe."

After a deep inhale, she starts right back in. "I have to know what you want and how you want to go about it. I can't sit here and live in limbo." She turns to face me, a fresh set of tears running down her cheeks. "I know that's unfair of me to ask, that you deserve the time to figure out how you feel, but... she's all I have." A strangled cry leaks out of her, and she covers her face with her hands, her back shaking.

I tear my eyes away from her, the need to soothe at war with my anger. "I would never try to take her from you," I say softly, concentrating on the sky in front of us. "But I want a relationship with her. Regardless, she comes first. She and Wren have to be the priority here."

She says nothing, but I feel the weight of my words heavy on my heart. I thought it might've been our time, we were so close to starting something again, but that has to end. I'm not sure I'll ever be ready now.

"I agree."

"I figure we can do this one of two ways—tell everyone right away or keep it between us for a time. But I have told Emmett, and Levi knows, and when the girls find out, I have a feeling it'll be harder to keep the secret."

I'm not sure they'll even understand the repercussions. Wren won't. I can see her just thinking "yay, I have a sister." Since I don't know Leia, I have no clue how she'll react.

"I'm sure you'd like to tell your parents," she says. "I plan on telling mine tonight."

"They don't know?" I'd thought maybe since Levi did, they would too.

She shakes her head. "Only Sean and I knew all these years."

My head falls back onto the headrest, and I sigh. The man who raised my daughter for the last seven years. Suddenly, all the times she tried to tell me he'd never hurt them physically or verbally make sense.

He was good to us.

"He always knew?"

She peeks over at me but quickly looks down at her hands again. "From day one."

I understand her just wanting to move forward, but I still feel the need to ask. "Did you think I wouldn't have chosen to be part of her life? I mean... is that why you didn't tell me?"

Her shoulders shrug. "Honestly, it was more that you didn't even try with us. You just went back to Kristie, and I was still all wrapped up in that when I found out about Leia. I got very protective and didn't want her to ever have to feel the same way I did when you left me."

I have no excuses for picking Kristie in that moment other than it felt like I was making the right decision for my unborn child. If I had to make the decision again right now, I would have said, "let's coparent, and I'm staying with Delaney," but I didn't.

"How did we get here?"

The past creeps into every crevice of the cab. I open the door, escaping into the fresh air. The click of the truck door sounds, then the crunch of gravel as she meets me at the top of the cliff.

"We have to put our past aside and focus on the girls. Figure out this coparenting thing," she says, wrapping her arms around herself, standing six feet away from me.

The last time I felt this disconnected with her was when I told her about Kristie being pregnant and ended it.

"I have so many questions." I can't stand here and pretend that I've come close to forgiving her. I'm not sure how or if I'll ever get over what she did.

"None of them matter." She turns to me, her arms tighter across her chest and determination on her face. "We were always looking for ways to sever this pull to one another. It's done now, so I'm going to tell my parents tonight and Leia in the morning. I'm taking her out for the day, just me and her. If you'd like, tell your family and Wren tomorrow. I'll see how Leia is handling things, and maybe the four of us can do dinner next week sometime. Does that sound good?"

I nod.

"Okay." She heads back to the truck, but circles around before she gets inside. "And I'll drive myself to the country club from now on. Probably should've from the start."

She turns her back to me again and climbs inside the truck.

There's still so much unfinished business between us, but if she wants to pretend there isn't, then I can do that too.

I head back to the truck and get into the driver's seat. "Can I ask one thing?"

She doesn't answer, but glances at me.

"Can I see a picture of her?"

The anger drops from her face, and she pulls out her phone, scanning through photos before handing it to me.

It takes me a second to look down, but now it makes sense why I've never met Leia. Delaney knew, from one look, I'd have known she was mine.

Chapter Thirty

DELANEY

"So, where are you two ladies going today?" Mom's being extra cheery after I told her and my dad last night that Leia is actually Bennett's.

They took it well, and my mom admitted she'd never wondered until after she ran into Wren and Bennett at the library. She couldn't help but notice how much Wren resembled Leia. I half wonder if this whole town has been whispering behind my back. Of course, my dad said it was a good thing because now she's no longer tied to that no-good son of a bitch, Sean.

"The museum." Leia grins. "But Mom said no to Wren or Kayla going. It's a mommy and daughter day."

Mom ruffles her hair. "Sounds like a fun day. Maybe you can have Wren and Kayla over another time. Summer is almost here. One more week to go."

"Wren said I can go to the ranch, and we can ride bikes, feed the ducks, and horseback ride."

My mom glances at me with raised eyebrows over Leia's head. I ignore the look and grab the brush from the table to get Leia's hair out of her face.

Leia finishes her breakfast while I do her hair, then we say goodbye to my mom and get in the car to make the drive to Lincoln.

She's quiet most of the ride, and I finally push my nerves aside to begin our conversation to gauge where she is with everything.

"What do you think of Willowbrook?" I ask. "Do you like it?"

She turns to look at me in the rearview mirror. "Yeah."

"Do you miss California?"

"Will we ever see Daddy again?"

My heart cracks. "I... don't know." I've always tried to be as honest as I could be with Leia, other than the whole "her daddy isn't who she thinks he is" thing.

"He hasn't even called or wrote me a letter."

I look at her reflection. What am I doing? Thinking I'm going to tell her that her daddy isn't who she thinks between the pretend shopping area and the rope bridge at the museum?

I get off the highway at the next exit.

"Where are we going?" she asks.

"We're turning around, and I'm going to take you somewhere else. If you want to go to the museum later, we can." I stop us at a gas station, get out of the car, and make the necessary call to pull this off.

"Who were you talking to?" she asks when I slide into the driver's seat again.

"Just Poppy."

Returning us to Willowbrook, I follow the roads that lead me to Plain Daisy Ranch, hoping like hell Bennett doesn't see me. But I don't want to tell my daughter the truth surrounded by hundreds of strangers. I have no idea how she'll react.

I park outside the stables and Leia screams, "Mommy, Sparkles!"

"I know."

Poppy walks out of the stables with Nash at her side, holding the reins of Junebug, all saddled and ready for us.

"Thanks, you guys."

"Of course. Nash and I can guide you, then he wants to go workout a horse to give you some space."

"I can't thank you enough for this. I tried the museum but just couldn't do it."

She smiles. "Yeah, this is better. The advantages of living on a ranch." She claps her hands. "Ready, Leia?"

Leia looks back from watching the other worker with Sparkles in the corral. She climbs down from the fence and runs over.

A worker comes out of the stable with helmets in hand. Nash hands the reins of Junebug to Poppy and returns with another horse, and a worker brings out another one. I get up on Junebug first.

"Look at who has become a pro all these years later." Poppy laughs.

I roll my eyes. "Couldn't have my daughter learn if I couldn't ride with her."

"Eh, I think it's that you just couldn't stay away from ranch life." A teasing smile lands on her lips.

Nash helps Leia up onto Junebug so she can ride in front of me. "All good? Poppy will lead, and I'll follow in case anything..."

"Thanks, Nash." I give him a smile.

He nods, and I can't gauge if he knows or not. I'm sure Poppy wouldn't have told him, although they seem awfully close. No, she wouldn't, but eventually everyone in this town will know anyway, so what's the difference?

"Let's go, cowgirls." He smiles at Leia, and she squeals, running her hands down Junebug's neck.

We head up the trail I rode with Bennett so many times,

and with every step, my heart grows heavy. I'm not sure he'll ever forgive me, and I'm not sure I can blame him, so I need to shut off that part of myself. Get rid of the hope that we could somehow be anything but coparents from now on.

I'm so lost in my thoughts, and keeping Leia balanced, that the ride passes quickly. Before I know it, we've reached our destination. Again, Nash helps Leia, and I climb down myself. He takes charge of securing Junebug to a tree.

"We'll be back in a little bit," Poppy says, hugging me.

Nash flawlessly gets up on the horse and offers a hand to Poppy to help her, making it all look so easy. Just like Bennett used to.

The two of them ride off, and I walk us over to the creek and grab a handful of pebbles. "I need to tell you something, Leia, and you're welcome to feel however you want. Your feelings are yours, and there's no right or wrong. I want you to know that, okay?" I pour some of the pebbles into her hand.

She throws one in the water, not saying anything.

"Daddy is most likely going to be in jail for a very long time."

"I know. Marcus said his dad said he'll be lucky to ever get out."

Of course parents have discussed it in front of their kids who have decided to talk to my kid about it. I take a deep breath through my frustration.

"Yeah. I know that makes you sad, but he did some really bad things, broke laws, and—"

"I know."

"I'm sure you must miss him." I sit on a rock and watch her stand at the water's edge, tossing in the small pebbles as if she's trying to get them to go farther with every throw.

"It's kind of like we're on vacation or like Daddy is away on one of his work trips. Sometimes I forget. Then I feel bad that he's in jail."

"That's understandable."

"Do you think they're nice to him?"

I mask my real reaction. "I'm sure he's made friends. He was always talking to everyone, remember?"

She glances at me and smiles. "Yeah."

"I'm sorry that he went to jail." I rest my forearms on my thighs and clasp my hands together.

She shrugs. "Me too. I know you miss him because you're always crying."

So, I haven't done a good job of hiding my tears. She doesn't need to know the real reason I'm crying, and that it's not from missing her dad.

I swallow my nerves and move the conversation forward. "Leia, I made a decision back when I was pregnant with you." I push the words past the lump in my throat. "And there's something I've been keeping from you."

She turns around, a frown marking her sweet face. "Why?"

"Because I was trying to protect you." I hold out my arms.

She allows the few pebbles left in her palm to plop into the creek and walks over. I situate her on my lap, pressing my forehead to hers, and hold her for what might be the last time for a while depending on her reaction.

"What's wrong, Mommy?" She draws back and puts her hand on my cheek.

"Your daddy isn't your biological dad. Do you know what that means?"

She shakes her head.

"It means that your daddy loved you, so, so much. He wanted you very much, and he wanted to be your daddy, but the reason you have your eyes and the way you look is because of another man, someone I was dating before your daddy. Does that make sense?"

Her small forehead crinkles. "Is that why Grandma Kat was always saying it's a shame I didn't get olive skin?"

Sean's mom always used to say how strong their genes were and that she found it odd that Leia didn't share her father's coloring. I have no idea if Sean held that secret or not all this time, though I'm starting to think perhaps she did know.

After Sean was arrested, and I started divorce proceedings, she called me and told me she wanted nothing to do with Leia or me because I wasn't standing by my man.

"Yes, that's why."

Leia's quiet for a beat, trying to puzzle it out.

I run my hand down her hair. "I'm going to tell you some things, and you might not understand at first, but you can ask me as many questions as you'd like. Wren's daddy, Bennett, and I dated in high school."

She nods, a shy smile on her face. "Wren told me."

"And then we met again when we were adults. He was the man I was dating before Daddy and… he's your biological dad."

Her little forehead wrinkles. "Wren's daddy?"

I nod.

Her eyes widen. "We have the same daddy?"

I nod again.

She climbs off my lap and picks up some pebbles. I give her the space she needs to process what she's able to, even if she has no idea how this will impact her life.

She'll probably never see Sean again and now has to deal with someone new coming into the fold.

I've learned over the years never to rush Leia. She'll talk when she's ready.

Ten minutes later, she tosses a pebble. "Does that make Wren my sister?"

"Yes."

"Her mommy died."

"Yes."

"Did you know she never met her?"

"I do."

Another pebble drops in the creek.

"That's sad. I can't imagine not having you."

I have to push back the tears. "I can't imagine not having you."

She throws the last pebble and walks back over to me, sitting on the rock next to me. I try not to read too much into the fact that she didn't sit on my lap.

"Do I have to live with him?" she asks.

"No. Eventually you might want to spend some nights there, but that's way down the line."

"So Mrs. Owens is my grandma?"

I nod again.

"I haven't met Wren's dad."

"He wants to meet you."

Her face turns toward me, alarm flashing in her eyes. "He does?"

"Yeah." I hope one day she doesn't hate me for the decisions I made back then.

"Okay," she whispers, not looking at me.

My heart lifts with relief that this part is over. Sure, we have a long way to go, but she knows the truth now.

God, I hate it when Levi's right.

BENNETT

My parents are big on weekly family dinners, so I figure I'll just tell everyone tonight, then take Wren for a long walk around the lake on the way home and tell her that her new best friend is actually her sister.

"Hello!" I call when Wren opens the door to my mom and dad's place.

Mack, Lottie and Brooks's dog, saunters over, and Wren falls down to her knees, giving him a hug. I didn't even think about using Mack, but he might be my tool to get Wren out of the house.

"Hey, why don't you play with Mack outside?" I say, tossing the tennis ball at her that's always covered in drool from his mouth.

"Okay!"

"I'll go with her," Lottie says before kissing Brooks as if they can't be apart for more than ten minutes.

"Actually, um... I need you here." She stops, then glances at Brooks.

"Let's go, Wren, you'll never guess how far I threw the ball the other day." Brooks kisses his wife's cheek, and I try not to roll my eyes at their PDA since he's doing me a solid and getting Wren out of here.

They leave with Wren rambling to Brooks about the end-of-year school field trip next week and how she wants to see the giraffes eat standing up.

The door shuts, and I turn around to see Lottie standing with her arms crossed. "What's up?"

I bypass her and go to the kitchen where Romy is sitting on a stool with the street corn dip in front of her and a bag of corn chips.

"Way to wait for the rest of us." I steal a chip.

"Bennett has something to tell us," Lottie announces to the room.

"You're marrying Delaney?" Dad holds out his hand toward my mom. "I won."

"I owe you nothing. You said it would happen a month from now." Mom wipes her hand on a dish towel and turns away from the stove. "What is it?"

"Thanks for that." I glare at Lottie.

"You're welcome," she sing-songs. She steals a chip and dips it in the street corn dip. Romy practically growls.

All eyes are on me, and it makes me wonder if I should've given this more thought and gone about it another way. But here we are, so I might as well just put it out there.

"Okay well... Leia... Delaney's daughter?"

"Oh my god, spit it out," Romy says. She's still gobbling the chips.

Lottie covers her mouth and says loudly, "She's cranky."

Off my train of thought, I ask Romy, "Where have you been?"

Her head rears back, and her arms fly in the air. "Will people stop asking me that? I have other friends besides people who live on this ranch."

"Like who?" Lottie asks with a laugh.

Romy shakes her head. "What did you have to say, B?"

I take in my youngest sister. Something is definitely going on with her. I think she might be wearing her pajamas, and her hair is thrown into a messy bun, but it looks like it wasn't even brushed first. No makeup.

"Hello?" Lottie waves her hand in front of my face.

"She's my daughter." I spit it out because I have limited time with Wren outside. "Leia, she's mine." I glance around for a second. "Delaney was in California when I was there. Kristie and I weren't seeing eye to eye..." I push a hand through my hair and cringe. "Actually, she slept with Jon, so I moved out. We separated and had started divorce proceedings. Delaney started at the same company as me, and we kind of..."

"Well, we know what you did, son," my dad says, eyebrows raised.

My mom swats the dish towel at his arm. "Let him continue."

"We started to date, but then Kristie came back and said she was pregnant with Wren. So, I ended it with Delaney, and we moved back here to try to give it another go."

My mom shifts her attention back to the pan of chicken.

Lottie's mouth is wide open.

Romy shoves another chip in her mouth and shrugs. "Nice, big bro, you knocked up two women at the same time. Is he still your favorite, Mom?" she mumbles, pieces of chips falling onto her chest.

"Wait." Lottie puts up her hand. "You just now found this out, or you knew all these years about Leia?"

My lips thin, and I glare at her. "Seriously? You think I'd just tell Delaney to screw herself and our baby?"

At least she looks sheepish. "Well, you left out the part that she hid the kid from you." Lottie leans over the counter and pulls out another chip, not even fighting Romy for the dip, but eating it plain.

"I just found out."

"So, she's not the drug lord's?" Dad asks.

"Apparently not."

Romy snaps her fingers and points to Lottie. "That explains it."

"Yup," Lottie says with a nod.

"What?" I look between them.

"The other day, I had to go over and pick up the center-pieces for that retirement party, and Lottie was with me. Poppy was driving Delaney's car, and Delaney was crying. They didn't want anything to do with us. So…"

"Poppy knew before us." Lottie narrows her eyes. "Who else knows?"

"Emmett," I admit, knowing it will piss them off, but he's my best friend. There's a reason Nash called him to come check on me. "She was crying?"

"Of course she was crying," my mom says.

"Darla…" my dad says, going to her side and wrapping his arm around her back.

"What?" I ask my mom.

She drops the spoon on the rest and turns to face me. "Of course she was crying, Bennett. Her entire world, everything that made her feel safe and secure, has blown up. She doesn't know who to trust, who to lean on. Just imagine, the person you choose to marry, the one you're supposed to be the most vulnerable with has been lying to you the entire time. Isn't at all the person you thought they were."

"And here I thought you'd be on my side. I had a daughter, and she didn't tell me about her for years."

My mom says nothing but gives my dad a look.

I throw my arms up at my sides. "Unbelievable. You're taking her side."

Lottie and Romy glance at one another.

"I'm just saying I'm sure she had her reasons," my mom says.

"Fucking hell. Dad?" This isn't the mom I know.

"I think your mother is saying that we know Delaney well, and this is out of character for her. Did you ask what her reasons were?"

"So, Kristie slept with Jon, your roommate from college?" Romy's eyes narrow as Lottie shakes her head.

"He was always so full of himself." Lottie sticks out her tongue in disgust.

"And you took her back?" Romy frowns.

"Broke up with Delaney for her?" Lottie chimes in.

"I did it for Wren... you know, the little girl throwing a ball to your dog outside." I stuff my hands in my pockets.

"Okay, girls." Dad holds out his hand. "Let's all remember that Bennett just told us that we have a new granddaughter and niece." He tips his head toward my mom then my sisters.

"So what's the plan?" Romy asks around a chip.

"Seriously, how are you going to eat dinner?" Lottie nods at the bag of chips.

Romy rolls her eyes. "Don't worry about me. When do we get to meet her?"

"I already did," Lottie says. "Mom picked her and Wren up from school, and they came by the store. Good thing Delaney's genes are strong."

"She has Bennett's eyes," Mom says, spooning rice into a bowl.

"You knew?" I ask her.

She shrugs. "Suspected. I mean, I saw that Sean guy's pictures, and she sure doesn't look like him. But what reason did I have to think she was yours? You never told us about you and Kristie separating or that Delaney and you were an item in California." She hasn't looked at me once.

"There didn't seem like any point in telling you once I

knew Kristie was pregnant, and we were coming back to Willowbrook together."

"So these past seven years have been what exactly? You unable to move on with your life? Why haven't you if you were able to move on after you separated from Kristie?" She hands my dad the bowl of rice, and he takes it to the table.

"I wasn't trying to raise a daughter by myself back then."

"Oh, okay," Mom says, putting the chicken in a separate bowl and holding it out for Lottie.

"Just say it," I snap.

My dad comes back in from the dining table and gives me his stern fatherly look. "Watch it."

"You're clearly Team Delaney, so I want to hear your excuse as to why it's okay that she kept from me the fact she was pregnant with my daughter. To have that monster of a man raise her instead of me."

My mom walks by me and goes into the dining room. "Mom?"

She turns around and locks her gaze on me. "That's for you to figure out, not me."

I throw my arms in the air and look at my sisters who aren't agreeing that it's absurd that Mom's being like this. "Aren't you upset that you lost out on time with your grand-daughter? Don't you care?"

She slams the spoon on the table. "Of course I'm upset and saddened, but how will that help right now? Is me being mad or questioning Delaney going to change what happened? No, it's not. The only control I have is what happens now."

The door opens, and Mack runs in, tongue hanging out, stopping at Lottie. She bends and pets him. "Oh, Mack, you missed it. Sorry, buddy, but good news, you have another play-mate coming soon." She eyes me with a smirk.

Fucking hell.

"I'm hungry," Wren says, coming in a minute later with Brooks behind her, assessing the room.

"Let's eat." Dad picks her up and swings her around. Her squeal of laughter loosens the tension in the room.

Dinner is quiet since no one says much, but everyone's gaze roams across the table every time Wren brings up her friend Leia.

Chapter Thirty-Two

BENNETT

Lottie and Romy tell me they'll handle the dishes, so I'm quick to say goodbye to my family after dinner.

"You're not staying for the firepit?" my dad asks.

I shake my head. "No. Wren has school tomorrow."

Mom has been ignoring me while she puts away the leftover food. She shoves a container into my chest. "For Nash."

"What about Uncle Jensen?" Wren asks.

"Him too if he can stoop down to my level of cooking."

She hugs my mom around the waist. "You make better pancakes, Grandma, but don't tell him that."

My mom bends and hugs her. "I won't. Have a good day at school and tell Leia I said hello."

Lottie and Romy shake their heads from behind my mom.

"What about Kayla?" Wren asks.

"Oh, Kayla too."

I sigh. "Okay, go give hugs, we're leaving."

"No s'mores?" Wren whines.

"Not tonight."

Wren blows out a breath, and her shoulders fall.

"I'll make you one to go," Dad says and disappears outside.

"Thanks for getting all that energy out of Mack." Brooks holds up his hand for a high five. When Wren goes to hit it, he lifts his hand out of the way, then puts it lower.

"Just let the girl hit your hand," Romy whines, and we all look over at her. "Lottie already told you, I'm cranky."

Wren says her long goodbyes, but I don't rush her. Sometimes I wonder if it's because she lost her mother and is afraid that when she leaves someone, it might be the last time she sees them.

"Ready?" I ask once she's all done squeezing everyone, including Mack, who got the biggest hug.

"Ready. I hope Grandpa put two peanut butter cups in my s'more." She jogs toward the door and steps onto my parents' deck.

"Check out your property on the way home," Lottie says, just to annoy me.

I break the distance and head over to my mom. "I don't want to argue," I say softly, not wanting to leave without talking to her.

"We're not arguing. We just have different points of view."

I wrap her up in a hug, and she puts her arms around me, patting my back.

"I love you," I whisper.

"I love you too. How long do I have to keep this to myself?"

I pull back from our embrace. "I'm telling Wren tonight. Then I'll talk to Delaney. I'm sure once the girls go to school, half the town will know, so be prepared for questions."

"And am I spinning this story?" I swear my sisters lean in. "People might assume you cheated on Kristie."

"Just tell them I haven't told you any specifics."

She nods. "Okay."

I say my goodbyes, and when I collect Wren from the firepit and my dad, her face is covered in chocolate, and she's holding a fresh s'more.

"Sorry, I had to redo it. It wasn't how she likes it." Dad's excuse for giving her two.

"Whatever, let's go."

I say goodbye to my dad, and we leave. Wren skips ahead around the trail beside the lake.

"Hey, Wren, I have something I want to talk to you about."

She stops skipping. "Look at the ducks!" She points at the two ducks that seem to always be on our lake. "I wish we had some food for them."

"Next time. So, listen—"

"Could I give them part of my s'more?" She goes to tear off a piece.

"No. Come on, let's continue." I nudge her to walk again. "So, Wren, what I want to talk to you about..."

"Is this about building the house? Because I don't want to move away from Uncle Jensen and Nash. I like living with them."

"No, it's not about that, but we can't live with them forever." I shake my head. I do not need to start that line of conversation when there's something much more pressing. "It's about your friend Leia."

I regret the words the minute they're out of my mouth. I can't start the conversation like that.

But it does stop her and make her turn around to face me. She's got chocolate and marshmallow all over her mouth. "Can I have her sleep over?"

Yeah, maybe every other weekend and on Wednesdays.

"I'll talk to her mom, but..." We come upon the small dock that's only used for jumping off into the lake. "Let's go and sit."

She runs to the small wooden dock and sits at the edge, her legs hanging over, finishing off her s'more. I sit down next to her.

"This is sticky," she says, holding up her two hands, fingers spread wide open.

"I should've grabbed a wet towel from Grandma."

She sticks one finger at a time into her mouth, licking it away.

"So, you remember how Mommy and I came here from California after we found out we were pregnant with you?"

"Yeah, I can't wait until we can go on vacation there."

I forgot I'd promised her last year that we'd go there and see the ocean.

"Well, Leia's mom lived there too at the same time."

She turns back to me with her mouth open. "Really?"

I nod. "Remember how I dated her mom in high school?"

Keep this going, she seems to be understanding.

"Well, we became friends then because we worked at the same company. And... well..."

She'll never understand this, and maybe I should've rehearsed it with Lottie and Romy, although they don't have kids to know how I can word this so that she understands.

"Mommy and I were taking some time apart."

Her forehead wrinkles. "Time apart?"

"We still cared about each other, but we weren't living together or planning our life as a family at that time. When Delaney returned back into my life, I was dating her during that time, and I just found out that Leia is my daughter."

She doesn't say anything, her eyes on the water and the two ducks paddling around.

"Grown-up issues can be confusing, so—"

"You mean Leia is my sister?" Her eyes are wide when she turns to face me, one leg bent up on the dock and the other one hanging off.

"Yes."

"That's so cool! Mrs. Martinez said we were like twins."

She did? That flicker of betrayal lashes at me that everyone who has seen the two of them together sees the resemblance while my own daughter was hidden from me.

"Not twins but sisters, yeah."

She stands, and I reach to grab her in case she loses her balance.

"Can we get matching pajamas when she sleeps over?"

"Wren..."

I want to stress the importance of how people might say things in town or at school, and how she needs to be prepared. That some people might think I had an affair because telling the truth that Kristie cheated on me would tarnish what people believed about us in town—that we were happily married, and she was the love of my life. But the real reason I don't want anyone else to know that is because I don't want Wren's opinion of her mother to change.

"I can't wait to talk to her at school tomorrow." She runs down the dock and back to the path.

I follow, making up the distance between us. "Are you sure you're okay with this? It changes a lot, and if you want to ask me anything, you can."

She stops and shakes her head. "No, I'm happy. It's going to be so much fun. Can we get bunkbeds?"

For the rest of the walk back to our house, she fires off questions about her room and how we can separate it to fit Leia. Wants to know if they can share clothes. In the ways I imagined this could go, her being ecstatic wasn't one of them.

Chapter Thirty-Three

DELANEY

Bennett and I decide a public restaurant where the girls can play games is our best option.

Now that I'm parked in the lot, waiting for Bennett and Wren to show up, driving far away seems like it would have been a much better plan.

Leia's been quiet, staring out the window.

"How are you doing?" I ask, turning around in the driver's seat.

"Good. They're late." Her voice shakes with worry, a result of Sean ditching our plans a lot because of *work* obligations. That kind of thing started with telling us he'd meet us there, then he'd be an hour late, and ended in him saying he couldn't make it. I should have demanded more answers.

"They'll be here. We're just a little early." I pat her leg.

Her gaze remains out the window, and I pick up my phone to text him. Just as I'm debating what to say, his truck pulls in next to me.

"They're here!" Leia says, surprise in her voice.

Please, please, Bennett, do not hurt her.

He quickly climbs out of the truck and holds his hands up as an apology. It's so rare that he's ever late.

Leia unbuckles herself, and her hand goes to the door handle.

I climb out of my car while Bennett helps Wren out.

Then it's all four of us in the parking lot of a pizza place, staring at each other.

"Hey, sis!" Wren wraps her arm tightly around Leia.

It takes Leia a moment, but then she clings just as tightly to Wren, and they're both smiling as though we're in the Disneyland parking lot, getting ready to spend our entire day there.

Bennett's gaze lands on me over their heads.

"Leia," I say, and she glances at me.

Wren grabs Bennett's hand as if we're going to go into the pizza place now, but there's one introduction that needs to happen before we do.

"This is—"

"Your dad!" Wren shouts with excitement. "And he's the best daddy. You're going to love him."

Leia smiles softly, but she doesn't move. I'm starting to think maybe we should've done this differently.

Wren is obviously over the moon about being sisters, and she's too young to empathize with the emotions coursing through Leia. She was just told that the dad she's known her entire life isn't really her dad and another man is. A man she's never met and doesn't know.

Bennett hunches down, and Wren stays right at his side, her smile big and wide. "Hi, Leia, I'm Bennett."

"Hi," she says, studying him.

I give it a few minutes, my heart in my throat. After years of wondering how this moment would go, I was far from prepared.

"Well, who's hungry?" I say a little too loudly, showing my nerves.

Bennett doesn't take his eyes off Leia, as if he's looking her over to see what parts of him made it into her.

It's not until Leia turns to me that Bennett straightens and stands, turmoil and anger on his face.

Wren grabs Leia's hand. "Let's go."

Bennett brings up the rear as we head inside.

Wren bounces in place beside the hostess stand. "Can we get our usual booth?" Her voice is full of excitement.

Bennett runs a hand down his face. "If it's open, sure."

She peers past the hostess stand to check.

I glance at Leia. She's quiet, her fingers curled around my hand. Her eyes dart to Wren, then to Bennett, then down to the tile floor.

The hostess grabs the menus and says to follow her.

Bennett holds his hand out for us to go first, his hand brushing the small of my back when I walk past. It's light, barely there, but a pulse shoots up my spine.

Read the room, you traitorous body.

Anything between Bennett and me is done and over.

We slide into the booth, Wren bouncing so hard the salt and pepper shake. "Have you had cheeseburger pizza? You're going to love it."

Leia offers a weak smile before slipping in next to me. She presses her side into mine.

Bennett sits next to Wren, his gaze shifting between the girls and me. He looks as if he's trying to keep his expression neutral, but his jaw tenses. What I would do to be in his mind right now.

The server comes by, and we order a pitcher of lemonade, garlic knots, and two pizzas, one cheeseburger and one pepperoni.

Wren drums her hands on the table. "Do they have that game where—oh—the claw machine! Can we play?"

Leia doesn't say anything. She just watches Wren.

While Bennett tells Wren we'll get to the games in a minute, she excitedly tells him a story of when Nash brought her here with Poppy and how Nash won five stuffed animals from the claw machine.

I use the reprieve from the tension with all four of us to check in on Leia. I squeeze her hand and lean over to whisper in her ear, "You doing okay?"

She nods, faster than I would like.

Wren leans over the table, closer to Leia then to me.

"Wren, sit back down," Bennett says.

I love that Wren doesn't seem to have a problem with her new sister. I was worried what her reaction to sharing her daddy would be.

"Can Leia and I play games after we eat? Please?" she asks.

I glance at Leia, who still hasn't answered. Her lips part as though she might say something, then close again.

"If Leia wants to," I say gently.

Leia shrugs and slides a little closer to me.

Bennett clears his throat. "We can all go together."

I give him a quick glance, surprised he said that.

Wren grins wide, kicking her feet under the table. "Have you played the claw machine? Or the driving game? I have to sit on Daddy's lap 'cause I can't reach the pedals, but it's so fun. Daddy, you have to take Leia."

He smiles, but it's tight. "If she wants."

The waitress drops the garlic knots and drinks on the table, and I'm thankful for the distraction. I think Leia is, too, because she perks up and reaches for one. Wren chatters about their art class and a drawing that a boy did of some animal pooping. Leia lets out a tiny laugh, and my chest loosens.

Bennett's eyes flick to mine, a small smile tipping his lips.

"What did you draw, Leia?" Bennett asks.

She only shrugs again. Her voice is a whisper. "A unicorn."

"Oh, Daddy, it was so pretty. Leia's the best drawer in our class. It had rainbow hair." Wren fills in all the blanks.

"I'd love to see it." Bennett leans back, stretching his arm across the back of the booth. He hasn't had a garlic knot or taken a sip of his drink.

Is his stomach as nervous as mine? Probably more.

Wren changes the topic to the spelling test. "Just wait, Leia, Daddy makes you write out the words over and over again. Do you do that, Delaney?"

Of course Wren has assumptions of how this will go with Leia being her sister now. A defensive part of me wants to tell Wren I'll be handling Leia's studying for the spelling tests.

"Mommy has me write the words in the colors of a rainbow. One time she hid parts of the words around the room, and I had to find them and put them together." Leia smiles up at me as if she's remembering the times we've done that.

I tuck a strand of her hair behind her ear.

I look back across the booth. Bennett's eyes are on both of us. For the first time tonight, there's no tension lining his face. It's softer now.

Thankfully, the pizza comes. Maybe we did make the right decision coming here because the distraction of the food is perfect.

"Just one piece." Wren picks up a cheeseburger pizza slice and holds it out to Leia.

Leia looks at me as if I'll know whether or not she'll like it.

"You should try it," I encourage.

"So should you," Bennett says, picking up a piece and holding it out me like Wren is to Leia. "From what I know, your mom has never tried it either. You guys can do it together."

Challenge twinkles in his eyes. It's playful and just what we need.

"I'm not going to like it," I say. We've been through this many times before. "I like my pepperoni."

"I'll do it if you do it," Leia says.

I strip my gaze off Bennett over to her. "Really?"

Leia has always been a picky eater, so I'm shocked she's willing to even try it.

"Okay," I agree and take the pizza from Bennett, our fingers brushing in the exchange. I don't pay attention to the electricity between us.

"On the count of three," Wren says, holding up her hand.

Leia and I glance at one another, making sure the other person will actually take a bite.

Wren counts us down. "One... two... eat!"

We both close our eyes and bite into the pizza, then put the pieces down on the plates while we chew. Then we face one another again and shrug.

"Do you like it?" Wren asks us, up on her knees.

"It's okay," I say.

"Okay? It's sooo good." Wren shifts her attention to Leia.

"I like it, but I still like pepperoni better," she says.

"I'm proud of you guys for trying something new. Next time, Wren will try cauliflower." Bennett pokes her side, and she sticks her finger in her mouth as though she wants to throw up.

"No, I'm not. Just wait until you see some of the things my..." She pauses and looks at Bennett. "Our?"

Bennett's eyes shift to mine for a moment before he says, "My cousin, who is your Uncle Jensen, is a chef. He's always trying to get Wren to try vegetables. It's a game they play."

The reminder of what we're all doing here together is like someone dropped a pig's head on the table.

"It's not fun. He tries to make it like a game." Wren sits on her butt and eats her pizza.

I'm not sure how we would've gotten through this meal without Wren. She's holding it together for all of us.

We eat quietly for the next few minutes, no conversation to be had.

"Done! Can we play now?" Wren wipes her mouth and drops the napkin on the plate.

Leia hesitates, her hands in her lap.

I turn to her. "Only if you want to, sweetie."

She gives the smallest nod, putting her napkin on the plate just like Wren. "I want to."

Bennett stands and offers money to both girls. Wren takes it instantly. Leia... waits. Looks at me to see if it's all right.

I give her an encouraging smile. "It's okay."

They go to the machines where we can see them.

I go to slide out of the booth. "I should go over there."

"You've barely eaten. They're fine. We can see them." Bennett looks to his left.

Wren is putting the money in the machine to get tokens to play the games.

"I don't know what I'm doing. I want to say the right thing. Be the right person for her." Bennett's confession strikes me.

I nod, staring at the bubbles in my lemonade. "It will get easier. She's just quiet."

"Thankfully, Wren isn't." He looks at me through his eyelashes as he bites into his pizza.

"It's nice that Wren is excited."

He puts down his pizza and sits back in the booth. "How did Leia take it?"

"She's been quiet about it, but that's her normally. I think as we keep this going, we'll know more."

He stares at his plate for a second, and I sip my lemonade

to do anything but wonder how much he hates me. We haven't talked about me keeping it from him, and I don't have it in me to get him to understand why I did it, even if I knew it was wrong. I'm not sure I could forgive someone if the roles were reversed. Right now, we just need to concentrate on building Bennett's relationship with Leia and making this transition as easy as possible for the girls.

"I'd like a day with her, just me and her." I open my mouth, but he continues. "I'm not saying soon, but at some point, I need to get to know her away from Wren. And she needs to get to know me away from you."

I swallow the lump in my throat. "Okay." There's no changing that he's her dad, and she deserves to see what that relationship can be.

His eyes hold mine. "Thanks."

I nod.

The girls rush back over, Wren grabbing Bennett's hand. "Come on, Daddy, we want to drive."

Bennett stands and Wren drags him forward. "Are you coming?" he asks me, looking over his shoulder.

I trail behind toward the arcade. Wren darts toward the driving game, shouting something about beating her own high score. Leia stands close to Bennett, watching.

Then he turns to me. "Do you mind taking Wren on the driving game?"

"Is that okay with you?" I ask Wren.

She grabs my hand and tugs me toward the game. "Have you played before?"

I catch Bennett crouching beside Leia, pointing out the claw machine. "Think we can win something?"

Leia's voice is soft. "They're rigged."

He chuckles. "You sound like your mom."

She blinks at him. And when he laughs, she smiles. A real smile lights up her face, and something shifts deep inside me.

I move to stand beside them.

Wren yells from across the room, "Delaney! Come on."

As I walk toward her, I look back.

Leia's hand slides into Bennett's as they walk over to the machines.

Later, once the girls have had enough of the arcade, we walk out into the warm night, both girls clutching the matching unicorns Bennett won for them.

"Still think they're rigged?" Bennett asks me.

"How much did you spend? You could've bought them for the amount of money you wasted winning them."

"You're missing the whole point of the game." We stop where our cars are parked, the girls talking to each other about how much fun they had.

"What's that?"

"Sometimes, what you win means more because you never stopped trying."

Our eyes hold for a moment longer than they should. And for the first time in a long time, I let myself hope that maybe we'll be able to weather this storm too.

BENNETT

Somehow, Delaney said it was okay for me to take Leia out for ice cream after dinner. Since it's the last week of school, they don't have any homework.

Wren wasn't pleased when I explained to her that it would just be Leia and me. Nash was home and said they'd make their own sundaes that would be so much better than Sprinkle Town's.

As I turn my truck down Delaney's driveway, a nervous knot rests in my stomach.

Will she ever see me as her father? Allow me to see the true little girl behind her shyness? God, I hope so. I keep reminding myself that I need to take baby steps even when I want to wrap her in my arms and hold her tight. Tell her how much I love her just because she's mine. Every time I hold myself back, my anger rises. And it's usually pointed toward Delaney.

I'm not even parked when Delaney walks Leia out of the house.

I leave the engine running and climb out, meeting them halfway.

"Hi, Leia," I say like a stranger when she's my own blood.

She should be running into my arms and me squatting to grab her and swing her around. She should at least be smiling.

Delaney nudges her with a kind hand on her back.

"Hi," she says.

No Daddy.

Patience, Bennett. One day this nightmare will be over.

"I didn't think you'd need the booster. You have Wren's, right?"

I nod. "Yeah, but I—" Why am I embarrassed to admit that I already bought another one for Leia?

'Cause it's presumptuous, you idiot.

"I bought her one. In case I ever have them both." I run my hand down the back of my head and pull on my neck.

"Oh," Delaney says. "That's nice." Again, her hand falls to Leia's back.

"Thank you," Leia says.

It's clearly their thing and how Delaney gives her daughter a silent sign to be polite. So much better than saying it out loud. So Delaney to do that.

"You two should go." Delaney scrunches down and holds out her arms.

Leia walks into them with no hesitation. Jealousy slithers up my spine. Delaney whispers something, kisses her cheek, and stands, guiding Leia's hand toward me.

I hold out my hand, and Leia takes it. "We'll be an hour or so."

Delaney nods, one hand across her stomach, her other elbow resting on it with her hand on her cheek. "Have fun." It was a failed attempt to show excitement.

I remember the first time I ever left Wren for a conference, so I understand her hesitation.

"Butterflies," Leia quietly says when she sees her booster.

I might have asked Wren a few questions, and she said Leia loved butterflies.

Had I known this whole time that she was mine, I'd know that myself.

I wave to Delaney, denying the urge to walk over and tell her it's me, I'll keep her safe and have her back to her in an hour. But soothing Delaney's anxiety isn't my job anymore.

The drive is quiet, and I keep looking at her through my rearview mirror, but she's staring out the window.

I help her out of my truck, and the door to Sprinkle Town squeaks on its hinge as I open it, and Leia steps inside, her gaze roaming every inch. During the summer, there's a line out the door, but since school is still in, and it's a weeknight, we have our choice of booths.

It's seat yourself, and Leia looks at me to make the decision.

"You pick." I hold out my hand, and she scans the room again.

She stops at the booth closest to the door. "Is this okay?"

I smile. "Perfect." We both slide in, and I grab a menu that sits in the metal holder at the end of the table and hand it to her. "Do you have a favorite flavor of ice cream?"

"Cookie dough."

"Has your mom brought you here yet?"

She shakes her head.

"You can pick the flavor ice cream you want and make it into a sundae. Then you pick the sauce, whipped cream, nuts or candy, and of course, sprinkles."

She laughs since the entire place is decorated with sprinkle graphics.

"Do you have a favorite?" she asks, and her question spurs my happiness.

"Yup, but it's kind of boring. Vanilla. But wait until you see how many toppings I get."

She studies the menu again.

"Hey, you two. What can I get you?" Marge poises her pad in front of us.

Leia looks up, and Marge turns her attention to me.

"Marge, have you met Leia Moore? She just moved here not too long ago."

Marge smiles. "I haven't had the pleasure. I know your mommy though. Haven't crossed paths just yet."

Leia smiles softly, and I'm sure Marge is wondering why I'm here with Leia. The news will eventually travel around our small town. People will find out that the perfect marriage I made everyone believe I had with Kristie was a lie.

"What's your pick, Leia?" I ask her.

Thankfully, Marge isn't the nosey type. Sure, everyone in Willowbrook is to an extent, but she's not going to go in the backroom and call everyone she knows.

"Cookie dough and hot fudge and whipped cream and double sprinkles please."

"Good choice." Marge jots it down. "I assume you want a cherry or two?"

"Two please." Leia gives her a soft smile.

Marge taps the tip of her pen to the paper. "Got it." She flips over the page of her pad. "Give it to me." She looks at Leia. "He takes a whole page just for his order."

Leia's eyes widen. The fact they match mine stalls me for a second before Marge clears her throat.

"Vanilla, caramel and hot fudge sauce, whipped cream, nuts, Oreos, Heath bits, triple sprinkles both chocolate and colored."

"Whoa, going light on me tonight." She laughs. "Waters?"

"Please," I answer.

Her eyes linger a little longer, taking Leia in before venturing back to hand in the order.

Silence falls over the table for a moment.

I take a breath, then another, and lean forward on my elbows. "Leia?"

She glances at me. "Yeah?"

I run my hands together. "Can I ask you something, and it's okay if you don't want to answer?"

"Okay."

I nod, steadying myself, but I don't want to pretend we're not both struggling here. "How do you feel about me being your dad?"

Her eyes dip to the table, and I figure I'm not going to get an answer. Finally, she shrugs. "I don't know."

"That's fair," I say quietly. "You didn't get a say in any of it."

She blinks fast. "You're different than him."

I try to give her a reassuring nod. "I am. Does that bother you?"

She shakes her head, then she must be giving herself a little pep talk inside because she straightens her gaze to meet mine. "Is it bad that I still love him?"

That hits harder than I expect. I shake my head slowly. "No. Not at all. I'm sure he loves you too. Sometimes adults do bad things, but what he did has nothing to do with how much he loves you. Being a dad, I can guarantee that."

"But I'm mad at him too."

My chest squeezes. "Understandable."

"I like you." God, I feel like I'm in gym class and was the first picked for a team. "Wren loves you. You seem nice."

"Thank you."

After a long pause, she says, "I want to get to know you better."

"I'm happy to hear that," I say. "We can go as slow as you need. But, Leia, I want to be here. For real. Not just because I'm supposed to be. Because I want to know who you are. What you love. What you hate. Everything."

She smiles, and my heart warms like a ray of sunshine just rose over the horizon.

"I love butterflies," she says. "Did Wren tell you that?"

"She did," I say sheepishly, ashamed I had to ask anyone else what my daughter likes. "But I wish I had heard it from you."

"Did Wren tell you about Kayla beating the boys at basketball during recess today?"

"She didn't, but I'd love to hear it."

Leia starts in by wiggling in her seat to get more comfortable, then she gives me the whole story, much like Wren does but in a more methodical and less excitable way. I hang on every word, studying her cadence and little hitches or small words she adds.

God, she's a little Delaney.

Marge brings over our ice cream sundaes, and Leia gets onto her knees, picking up her spoon.

She eyes mine. "That's a lot of stuff."

"Do you want to try some?" I slide it closer, and she dips her spoon in and takes a taste.

"It's okay. I don't like those hard things," she says, scooping her own sundae on her spoon. Then she stops and glances at me. "Did you want to try mine?"

"If you don't mind. Sometimes it's the best way to find something new that you like, trying someone else's." I take a small spoonful, and she watches me the whole time. "I might have to try that cookie dough next time. That's a winner."

A proud smile crosses her face, and she digs into her sundae.

I take peeks after every bite or two. She's eating so fast I worry she'll get a brain freeze, but I don't say anything. I just enjoy sitting across from her, sharing ice cream with my daughter.

Chapter Thirty-Five

DELANEY

"You're going to wear out the carpeting," Levi says, sprawled out on the couch. "It's Bennett. She's fine."

I've almost bitten off all of my fingernails. This hour feels like a damn week. I wave him off, glancing out the window again.

"You act like he's going to kidnap her. Maybe you should've done a swap. Like you take Wren, he takes Leia, for extra security." He laughs to himself, his attention never leaving the television.

"I can't believe you talked me into this. I could've kept this secret."

He laughs. "You're delusional. I bet half of Willowbrook is already talking about how much she looks like him."

"You're not being helpful."

His feet drop to the floor. "Listen, don't you feel better knowing it's all out in the open? There are no more secrets to be discovered. I don't see how you thought you'd ever get back with him while keeping the existence of his daughter from him."

I stop and cross my arms. "Okay, we weren't getting back together, and I wasn't hiding."

He quirks his eyebrow.

"It wasn't like I was never going to tell him."

His eyebrow grows higher. How does he do that?

"What are you looking for? A thank you?"

"That would be nice." He relaxes back on the couch.

"Don't you have your own place?"

"You don't want to spend quality time with your brother?"

"Not when he's calling me out on all my shit. Believe me, I will be paying back the favor."

"Didn't Mom tell you? I'm perfect." He smiles wide, his two dimples shining proudly.

Headlights cast a glow on the front window, and I step forward.

"Don't," he says.

I whip back around. "Why not?"

"Let him get her out of the car and walk her up to the door."

An aggravated sigh escapes me. "Since when did you become Dr. Phil?"

"Didn't Mom tell you? I'm smarter than you."

I flip him off, and he laughs. I stay hidden behind the window, watching Bennett climb out of his truck and help Leia out of the back seat.

She slips her hand into his as they walk to the door. She didn't reach for his hand because Bennett offered, she did it on her own. Tears prick my eyes. She's talking to him, and he's staring down at her, laughing at whatever she's saying.

I shouldn't be surprised that after just one ice cream date, she's already comfortable with him. He makes it easy to be yourself. That's why I never stopped loving him.

The door creaks open, and I pretend to just be walking past.

"Mom! I'm home," Leia says.

Bennett steps inside with her, and we all stand awkwardly, unsure how this goes.

"What's up, B?" Levi calls from the family room.

"Hey, Levi. Heading out tomorrow, right?"

Levi joins our uncomfortable little circle looking completely unfazed by the tension surrounding us. "Yeah, just soaking up some sister time." He puts his arm around my neck and pulls me closer. "You two have fun?"

"Yeah, can we go again?" Leia asks. "Sprinkle Town is so good, and I want to try putting Oreos on my sundae next time."

She seeks out Bennett, and the two of them share a smile —an inside tidbit that happened tonight, I guess. My heart squeezes because I'm not a part of it. As if Levi can sense it, he tightens his hold on my neck.

It's good for her to have that. She never did with Sean. There are memories that should just be between a child and parent.

"And I need to try the cookie dough ice cream," Bennett says.

"Moving up from vanilla, huh?" I ask, as if I'm part of the joke.

"Leia's sundae convinced me that I might be missing out." He winks, and she smiles.

Again, my heart pinches. "Well, let's get you up to a bath, tell... say thank you," I stumble over my words, unsure how to refer to Bennett. He is her dad, but it sounds weird saying it out loud to Leia.

"Thank you," she says.

Bennett gets down on his haunches. "Could I have a hug? Only if you want to." He holds out his arms.

Levi's arm loosens across my shoulders. The weight of this feels too big, as if we shouldn't be an audience, but I'd never be able to strip my gaze away.

"Yeah." Leia steps into his arms.

They fold around her while she wraps her arms around his neck. Bennett's eyes close, and his back rises and falls with deep breaths.

God, what have I done?

"Good night," he says. "You'll probably dream about swimming in sprinkles."

Leia laughs. "Bye."

Bennett lingers for a moment, stepping back and stopping a few times before his eyes find mine, and he nods. "Good luck, Levi." Then he walks out the door, the screen door shutting behind him.

"So, sweetie"—I'm careful to keep my voice light—"you have fun?"

She nods, pulling her braid over her shoulder. "Yeah, the sundaes are huge."

I smile. "That's what makes it the best."

She walks into the family room, looking at Bennett through the window. I'm buzzing with nerves, but I don't want to crowd her.

"How was it?" I ask softly. "Being with him?"

She shrugs. Not in a dismissive way, but rather thoughtful. "He asked me how I felt about him being my dad."

I pause, sitting in the chair. Levi takes the couch next to her. "Yeah?"

Her eyes find mine. All I see is her as a baby, rocking her to sleep at night. As a toddler lining up her stuffed animals in a perfect row. The girl whose life has changed too much and too fast.

"I told him I didn't know," she admits.

"That's okay." I move to sit on the other side of her,

folding my hands in my lap. "You don't have to know yet. You can take all the time you need."

She picks at a piece of fluff on her pants. "That's what he said."

Levi looks at me over Leia's head with an expression that says told you so.

"He didn't get mad or anything."

"No," I say gently. "He wouldn't."

And that's the truth. Bennett is the kindest person I've ever known. He'd never rush Leia to accept him.

"I thought maybe he'd try to act like he was my dad. But he didn't." She says it as if it surprises her.

"What did he do?" I press, and Levi gives me a warning glare.

What does he know? He doesn't have kids.

She shrugs again, but the tiniest curve of a smile edges on her lips. "He just... listened. He said he wants to know everything about me. What I like and don't like."

I blink back the sting in my eyes. "That sounds like Bennett."

"He listened to my stories and asked questions about school as if Wren hadn't told him it all before." She looks at me. "I liked that."

I tuck a stray strand of hair behind her ear. "He sees you. That's good."

A beat of silence falls between us. Then, quieter than before, she whispers, "Do you think I'll like him?"

I swallow hard. "I think... if you give him a chance, he'll show you he's worth liking."

She nods slowly, then leans into my side long enough for my heart to crack open. "Can I go to my room?"

"Of course. I'll be up in a minute to get your bath started."

She heads up the stairs, braid swinging behind her, and I remain on the couch, watching her.

"You did good," Levi says once she's gone.

"We both knew he'd be gentle and patient."

"Yeah, now you two just need to get your heads out of your asses about each other, and you can be one big happy, annoying family." He heads into the kitchen.

Jeez, I wasn't ready.

I wasn't prepared to fall a little deeper in love with Bennett from seeing and hearing how he is with our daughter.

Chapter Thirty-Six

DELANEY

I should've known volunteering for the zoo field trip meant spending the day herding a group of first graders who act like caffeinated squirrels.

"Two feet on the ground. We can't climb the fence!" I call to Matty for the tenth time in five minutes. He's going to end up being one of those stories where the kid falls in the exhibit with the gorillas.

Bennett chuckles beside me, holding a wrinkled map of the zoo. "Gotta have a sharp eye on Matty at all times."

He looks far too good for someone surrounded by shrieking children and the smell of animal poop. His gray shirt strains along his biceps, and he's wearing shorts and gym shoes. Sunglasses block his gorgeous brown eyes, but I still feel them on me every once in a while.

Meanwhile, I'm a mess who can't stop sweating and heaving from making sure no kid gets out of my sight.

Wren's skipping ahead, her pigtails bouncing. Leia walks beside her quietly, holding her zoo scavenger hunt sheet as if it's the winning lottery ticket, wanting to make sure she turns it in and gets that prize she was promised, even though it's probably nothing big.

We pass through the reptile house, and I walk in the middle of the aisle, avoiding getting close to any glass case.

Bennett comes alongside me. "Trying to pretend they aren't there?"

He's been cordial with me today, and I wonder if we can turn things around again.

"Aren't you doing the same?"

"Hell yeah, I keep checking the ground to make sure one didn't escape."

I laugh, and his arm brushes along mine. I deny the pull to move closer to him.

"Delaney?" Wren says, voice shaky.

I look down.

She's holding her stomach. "My stomach hurts."

I crouch in front of her, Bennett right next to me. "What kind of hurt?"

She glances down, toeing the ground with her sneaker. "Like... sick."

"You didn't eat anything weird. Just snacks from home." Bennett's brow is furrowed.

I gently rub Wren's back. "Sometimes when you're excited or walking around a lot, your tummy acts up. Want to go outside with me and sit for a second?"

She nods, and I scoop her up in my arms, her legs wrapping around my waist.

"I can take her," Bennett offers.

"Nah, I got this." I smile playfully that I get to escape the reptile house, and he'll have to stay.

"She's my responsibility," he says, holding his hands out to take Wren, but she lays her head on my shoulder.

"Oh no, they're all our kids today. We're the chaperones,

so you get to watch Matty." I pat his chest, laughing and walking away.

"Matty, stop banging on the glass!" Bennett calls right before I push the doors open, smiling to myself.

We find a quiet bench outside, and I pull a water bottle from my bag and hand it to her, brushing a damp strand of hair off her temple. "Slow sips, okay?"

Wren nods, blinking at me with watery eyes. "I don't like being sick."

"No one does, sweetie. But we'll get you better soon." I shift on the bench, letting Wren lean into my side. Without thinking, I rub slow circles on her back. "Just relax."

Wren leans into me, the tension in her shoulders easing. Something that's been coiled up tight for weeks in me loosens too.

"My grandma usually gives me ginger ale," she says. "But I like this better."

"I can get you some—"

Her arms tighten across my stomach. "No, I like the circles."

"Okay then."

I've almost dozed off when I hear Bennett's voice telling the kids to stay together. When I look up, Bennett's stopped and watching me. His jaw tenses, but his eyes are soft. As though he's seeing something he's not sure he should enjoy.

He breaks the distance, and Leia trails beside him.

"Is she okay?" she asks about a sleeping Wren.

"Just a tummy ache."

"Oh." Leia frowns.

"It's time for us to go anyway. We need to make our way to the bus." Bennett checks his watch.

He picks up Wren with ease, and she lays limply in his arms. He whispers something to her, and she winds her legs and arms around him like a little koala bear.

"This leaves you in charge of the map." He hands it to me.

We all fall in line toward the front entrance, stopping at the gift shop for everyone to turn in their scavenger maps and get their prizes.

Bennett and I wait at the side, Wren still fast asleep in his arms.

"Thank you," he says, voice low.

"It's nothing. I feel bad for her." I run my hand down her back, and he watches the movement, then inhales a deep breath.

"She has a habit of over-exhausting herself. We couldn't be more opposite in that way. You'd think she was Emmett's sometimes."

I smile and look at Wren's angelic face. Without her big blue eyes open, you see more Bennett than Kristie. "Maybe it's that nature versus nurture thing. She gets it from being around Emmett, not from her genes. But regardless, she's amazing, Bennett. You've done a great job with her."

We hold each other's gaze, and the world of the shrieking kids and squawking birds fades away.

He steps closer, just enough that his knee brushes mine. His voice dips. "You're really good with her."

I feel that old, familiar pull. Gravity, like no matter how many years have passed or how many lies have been told, is dragging us together.

"I could say the same about you," I whisper.

His eyes drop to my mouth, and my breath catches.

Then he blinks, and his expression is neutral as he steps back.

He nods, and his gaze searches out Leia. She has a toy in her hand and is turning in another form, pointing at Wren. Wren didn't care about the scavenger hunt earlier, and I thought she had lost her sheet in exhibit two.

"You've done a good job too. Watching her take in the

world around her, the way she doesn't rush to react and... she's something... special."

"I'm sorry." I'm guessing the guilt of keeping her from him will never go away.

"I know." Our eyes meet, and I remove my hand from circling Wren's back. "I know you are, Delaney."

He might know I'm sorry, but he's not understanding or forgiving me. I can't blame him though.

Leia walks over holding small plastic figurines in her palm. "A butterfly for me and a flamingo for Wren."

"You got Wren one?" I ask. "She didn't have a sheet, did she?"

"I did both of them. She said she didn't care, but I knew she would have when everyone was getting their prizes." She shrugs and sandwiches herself between Bennett and me. "Is she okay?"

"She just has a tummy ache. She'll probably feel better when she wakes up." Bennett's hand falls down to touch Leia's back, but he hesitates for a second before he rubs his hand there. "Let's get to the bus."

I hang back with the other kids, watching Bennett holding Wren in his arms and Leia's hand in his, and the familiar anxiety of being abandoned resurfaces. They're a family. Blood will bind all three of them. Will we share holidays where he'll have both of them, and I'll be by myself?

Nausea washes over me as I imagine the future he once saw with me in it might now only be as a coparent and nothing more.

BENNETT

I'm just dropping off the damn pillow and getting out of here.

Wren insisted on the phone that she couldn't sleep without it and begged me to bring it over to Delaney's for her sleepover.

I pull into Delaney's driveway, pillow in the passenger seat, and give myself the same pep talk I do every time we do these drop-offs.

Don't linger. Don't look at Delaney as if you still want her to belong to you. Don't remember how many nights you dreamed about her coming back in your life. Don't forget what she kept from you.

No one comes out to get the pillow, so I climb out of my truck and make my way up to the door.

I rap my knuckles on the screen door, but there's no answer. Delaney mentioned that her parents were out of town this week, so maybe she and the girls are out back or something. I could easily toss the pillow inside then leave Delaney a text message and get the hell out of here. But then I hear laughter coming from the kitchen. Wren's giggle, Leia's quieter laugh, and Delaney's soft voice in the mix. It slides under my skin, makes me stupid, and fear of missing out pulls me toward them.

I knock again. This time louder.

"In here!" Delaney calls.

I open the door and step inside.

The scent of burned marshmallow, chocolate, and something vaguely smoky fills the air. There's a bag of marshmallows half-spilled on the counter, chocolate bars broken up on a plate, with graham crackers scattered in little broken pieces mixed in. The three of them are huddled around the gas stovetop.

You have got to be kidding me.

Wren's holding a skewer over the gas burner, her arm tucked in tightly, the flame licking the edges of a marshmallow already burned on one side.

"What are you guys doing?" I ask, or maybe more demand.

Delaney straightens up from behind Leia, her eyes going wide. "We're making s'mores."

"Over a gas flame?" I stare at the burner. "Jesus, that's not safe."

"We've always done it this way," Leia says, lifting her skewer. "Mine's on fire."

Delaney leans over and blows it out. "Perfect."

"This is fun, Daddy, want to do one?" Wren glances over her shoulder briefly before concentrating on her marshmallow.

"You're only inches from catching your hair on fire." I set the pillow on a chair and take the skewer from Wren's hand, turning off the burner with a click.

"Boo," Delaney says. The girls groan their agreement. "Why build a whole fire for a few s'mores? Leia and I have always done it this way." Delaney looks at Leia, and they both shrug.

I shake my head. "Where is your parents' fire pit and wood?"

Delaney tilts her head. "Outside. Wood is on the side of the garage. But—"

I walk out of the house, and Delaney tells the girls to sit tight.

She follows me out of the house. "I can make a fire, you know. I'm just choosing to do it over the stovetop."

"And burn off the girls' hair?"

She scoffs, and when I turn around, her hands are on her hips, and her mouth is set in a rigid line. "It's funny, you know. I've been a mom the same amount of time you've been a dad. Leia's hair is gorgeous and has never been singed once."

"It's only a matter of time," I say, going around to the garage and returning with wood.

She walks over and takes the wood from me. "You are not going to undermine me here. This is my night for a sleepover, and we were having fun. You should try it sometime." She circles and stomps back toward the house.

Right as her hand is on the handle of the screen door, I say, "Delaney."

She stops and glances over her shoulder.

"I'm sorry, I overreacted."

She circles back and keeps her arms crossed. "Want to tell me what this is really about?"

"Not really." I kick at the grass.

It used to come so easy with Delaney, telling her about my vulnerabilities, insecurities, but now we're lifetimes away from that, and I'm struggling.

"Okay then." She eyes the wood. "Build your little fire, and the girls and I will get the s'mores stuff together."

The door shuts behind her, and whatever she tells the girls

has them screaming with excitement. She returns with a lighter.

I want to be mad at her. I should be. She let me miss seven years of my daughter's life. Seven. That's every scraped knee, every bedtime story, every moment Leia needed someone and went to him.

I watch her situating the girls. Both my daughters, even though only one of them is hers. Wren represents everything that took me away from Delaney, and still, she treats Wren as if she's hers. Not that I'm surprised.

Damn it, I still want her.

That's the problem. Delaney still feels like home. Even when I'm furious with her, I want her.

I teach the girls how to stack the wood to get the best fire. They put the kindling on the bottom, the two of them working together better than Delaney and I do.

She sits in the chair, a silent observer, but it's too dark outside to read her expression.

"Gotta love a cowboy," Delaney says after a while, when the flames are crackling and the logs are just starting to catch.

The girls get comfortable under a blanket, sitting side by side, pointing as the flames increase.

I glance over at Delaney. Her hair's pulled into a messy bun, and she's wearing one of those threadbare sweatshirts that somehow is sexier than if she wore something tight. I want to know if she's wearing a bra or if my hands ventured under that hem, would I feel her bare breasts?

"I'm far from a cowboy."

She smiles, flames dancing in her eyes. "You might not corral cattle, but you're a cowboy at heart."

I scoff. "My cousins would disagree."

The fire casts a warm orange glow over her face. Makes her look softer. Younger. As though she could be seventeen again, when we were stupid and brave and thought love was gonna get us through. Such simple times.

"What do they know?"

The four of us are silent for a beat.

"Looks great. Sit down and relax. You wanna make a s'more?" She sits up to grab the stuff.

"I got it. Girls?" I grab two sticks and hand them each one with a marshmallow on it. I kneel by each of them, showing them how to keep it off the flames enough to not catch on fire. Wren is more familiar, though I've usually taken control of it for her, so she doesn't get hurt.

Delaney gets the graham crackers and chocolate ready, and between the two of us, we get them both assembled. They sit back in their chairs, eating over the small plates Delaney brought out.

"Want me to make you one?" I ask her.

"I can make my own s'more, thank you very much." She smiles. "Maybe in a bit. Sit."

I take the empty chair, and we all stare at the fire.

"I might be a tad overprotective," I admit in a quiet voice so only she can hear. The girls are busy laughing about something.

"You think so?"

I glance over, and she's got that joking smile. I shake my head.

"This is fun, girls, right? Do you have anything to say?" She changes topics, and I wonder if it's because she's scared by this dynamic between us.

"Thank you," they say in unison except Wren adds Daddy, and Leia doesn't.

As much as I want her to think of me as her dad, I know I can't push this. I tell myself it will come in time.

"You're welcome."

Leia takes off her blanket, picks up her skewer, and walks over to me. "Can you help me make another one?"

I swallow back tears, and I swear Delaney makes a noise.

"Of course. Let's go."

She puts the marshmallow on the stick, and she stands in front of me, both my arms around her, adjusting how she holds it over the fire.

Wren says something to Delaney about her grandpa and how he uses peanut butter cups and how Uncle Brooks does three-stack ones.

"I wanna see," Leia says.

I look at Delaney, and she's not smiling, but she does nod as if she's suggesting that's the next step. Leia needs to get to know my family.

After a half hour, Wren has to go to the bathroom, and Leia goes inside with her.

"Are you really okay with me bringing her around the family?" I ask.

"They're her family too. She should get to know them and vice versa."

I nod. "Okay."

Later, when the s'mores are done and the girls are sticky-faced and half asleep in their chairs, I get up to leave. "I can help you get them to bed."

"Nah, they'll wake up and pass out in Leia's room. But I'll warn you, there won't be any brushing of teeth or baths before bed. But I promise to return her clean tomorrow." She smiles wide with an expression as if to say, *I do what I want when it's my sleepover.*

"Not even a change of clothes?"

She shakes her head. "Lighten up, Owens."

I take one last look at the girls before turning toward the house.

"Thanks again," she says, walking me to the corner of the house.

"For barging into your night? You're welcome."

She leans along the side of the house. "You're lucky I know you mean well. I'll drop her off in the morning or text you if they try to swindle more time together."

"Daddy!" Wren shouts, clearly having woken up.

Both girls barrel across the dark lawn, and I force myself not to tell them to slow down so they don't twist an ankle in the dark. They run up to me and wrap themselves around my legs.

"Bye. Thanks for the fire," Wren says. "Love you."

I squat down and hug them both. My eyes sting with tears that are on the cusp of slipping. Delaney covers her mouth with her hand, unable to strip her attention away from us.

"Bye, girls, love you."

Leia doesn't say anything, but the hug is enough. It's her own way of saying she appreciates the fire and the s'mores lesson. That she's warming up to me a little more. I'll take it.

I force my feet to move toward my truck, the scent of smoke clinging to my clothes, my heart heavy. The last thing I want to do is leave them or Delaney, but I don't know how to forgive her. The problem is I don't know how to stop loving her either.

Chapter Thirty-Eight

DELANEY

The front bell jingles as the door to The Perfect Petal swings open, a rush of summer air trailing in. I'm trimming stems at the counter, and two sets of eyes now stare back at me.

"Hi, Mommy," Leia says, both she and Wren giggling.

Darla turns the corner and comes inside. I haven't actually seen her since the news got out. She could very well be mad at me for making her miss seven years of her granddaughter's life. Lord knows I would be.

"Day two of summer, and they're already bored." Darla groans and pats the girls on the back. "Go find something to do, I need to talk to Delaney."

The scissors slip from my grasp, falling onto the counter with a thud. "Lottie brought over some cookies from Laurel's. They're in the breakroom," I tell the girls.

They look at one another, squeal, and run off through the back doors.

"Is he here?" Darla asks, walking around the counter to join me.

Fear grips me. I've always loved Darla, but I'm not naïve

enough to think she's not angry at me. "No, he's at Blue Prairie. They don't really need me now—"

Her hands land on my upper arms, and she pulls me toward her, hugging me in a tight grip. "Welcome to the family," she whispers.

"But..."

She doesn't let me go, so I hug her back. "You are. If he can't get his head out of his ass, it doesn't matter. You're Leia's mom, and that makes you family."

Tears spring to my eyes. "Oh... well... you're not mad?"

She draws back, but her hands stay on my upper arms. "No. I'm just glad you're here now. Mother to mother, I want you to know, I love her. I would have loved her no matter what, but thank you for giving me another granddaughter to love." She wraps me in a hug again.

"Okay, Mom, give her some air." Lottie walks in with Poppy.

"You're going to suffocate her, Aunt Darla," Poppy says.

Both of them come over to the counter.

"Where are the little runts anyway?" Romy follows behind, a container of chicken salad in her palm and a box of crackers tucked under her arm.

How does she stay so thin?

"In the back. I bribed them with cookies," I say.

"Cookies?" Romy's eyes perk up.

"Jesus, do you have a tapeworm?" Lottie asks, sliding up on the counter.

Bennett's entire female side of the family is here, and none of them are giving me the cold shoulder or blatantly pointing the finger at me.

"When does Operation Bennett Gets a Swift Kick in the Ass start?" Romy asks, dropping the chicken salad and crackers on the counter.

"Leave it to me," Darla says.

I sigh. "You guys, it's complicated. Maybe we just let whatever is going to happen work itself out with time." I continue putting the flower arrangement together.

None of them say a word, and they're all staring at me with different faces of confusion.

"If we wait for Bennett to get a clue, you'll be on your death bed before he realizes what he's missing out on," Lottie says.

"Look who sounds so assured. Mom had to talk to you. Poor Brooks was like a dog behind a fence with a steak on the other side, panting to be let free." Romy picks up one of the caramel candies we sell.

Poppy smacks her hand. "Are you paying for that?"

"She thinks everything around the ranch is hers for the taking." Lottie raises her eyebrows. "Payback for throwing me under the bus. And you know how much I struggled with my feelings for Brooks."

Poppy puts her arm around Lottie's shoulder. "It's all in the past now. You're happily married."

"That I am." Lottie sticks her tongue out at Romy, but Romy only shrugs and searches the counter for something else to eat.

"Mom?" Leia runs out of the back room, Wren right behind her. She stops and stares at all the women, shrinking back into herself.

"Whoa, those eyes give her away," Lottie says.

"So does the nose." Romy points, then turns to Poppy. "How did you not see it?"

"Leave me alone, I didn't know about..." Poppy lets her words trail off. "What's up, girls?"

"Hi, Leia, I'm your Aunt Lottie, and the one with the mouth full of food is your Aunt Romy." Lottie points at herself. "I'm the cooler one in case you were wondering."

"Hi." Leia lifts her hand, and she meets my gaze behind them all.

Wren comes up to her side. "We want to make flower arrangements."

Lottie looks at Romy. "Us too. Get her hands busy so she can stop eating everything she sees."

Wren is already rushing toward The Stem Bar. "Do we get to cut stuff?"

Leia steps closer, her voice softer. "Can we really make our own bouquets?"

I crouch down between them. "Absolutely. You'll each pick out three flowers, then we'll go over the next step."

"You know, since Delaney started here, this little bar has been very popular," Poppy says.

I look at her over my shoulder. "I'm sure it always was. It's a great idea."

"I think they like that you guide them and help." Poppy smiles at me.

"I think you're saying that so I'll continue to work here."

We had a conversation about me moving on a few days ago. It's too hard to be around Bennett and not actually be with him. Neither of us can move into our new relationship roles when we're together all day. As it is, I'm not going up to Blue Prairie much. Once a week maybe, to direct the workers and help solve any problems. I miss doing it myself, but I think it might be hard for Bennett to look me.

"Are you thinking about leaving?" Darla asks, settling into one of the armchairs nearby.

I show the girls how to strip the leaves off the stems and let them pick whatever colors they love. Wren pulls out every bright hue under the sun, whereas Leia, more careful, compares them to each other and pulls out more pastel ones.

"You have your daddy's eye," Poppy says to Leia, and she freezes, staring up at Poppy. "He's just a very careful person, thinks things through. Not like our little Wren, who dives in and goes for what she wants and doesn't second guess her decision."

Poppy's trying to make her comment better, and the frown she gives me suggests she regrets it.

"Both are great qualities," I say.

"Does that mean I'm more like my mom?" Wren asks, her voice slightly shaky.

"It means you're like me." Darla raises her hand. "It's not good or bad, just unique to you."

Thank you, Darla.

"Did you know my mom was an artist?" Wren asks, positioning her flowers at different heights.

I hand her some greenery to fill it in. "I did. Have you ever seen her work?"

No one says anything, but whether I like it or not, Kristie is in my life. She's Wren's mother, and although I didn't care for the woman, I'm going to make sure her daughter knows she can talk to me about her.

"In the basement. Daddy has it down there."

No one says anything.

"It makes him sad to look at it, I think."

I catch Lottie glancing at her mom, but I can't see Darla's reaction.

"It's hard to lose someone. I'm sorry you never got to know her." I put my arm around Wren and kiss the top of her head. "Maybe you should ask your daddy to tell you some more stories about her."

The back door opens, but this time, there's no bell. Just the faint creak of wood and the weight of a presence that hits me before I even turn around.

Bennett.

The air shifts, as if everyone in the room took a breath and forgot to exhale.

He doesn't say anything right away. Just stands there, taking in the scene. He's wearing jeans and a soft, worn T-shirt that clings to his shoulders. His hair is messy, and he looks sexy as hell.

His eyes aren't on me though. They're on Wren and Leia. On the way they're sandwiching me. His jaw clenches as though he's trying to bite back a thought that's already halfway out.

"Hey," I say softly.

He clears his throat. "Hey."

Wren runs over to him. "Dad! Look what I made! Delaney helped me."

He looks at her bouquet, a bright mess of marigolds and snapdragons and one big sunflower. "It's beautiful."

Leia walks over, slower, holding her bouquet as if it will fall apart if she moves too fast. "Look at mine."

Bennett's voice gentles. "Beautiful as well." He looks between them. "You two are going to put me out of a job."

They giggle and come back to the table, filling in pieces and adjusting the heights.

All the women concentrate on their own bouquets, except for Darla.

"We've got two natural designers on our hands." I close my eyes when the words repeat in my head.

We.

Our.

As if we're a couple.

God, Delaney.

He nods, and I meet his gaze. Something behind his eyes softens, but the hesitation, the flicker of pain or memory or maybe just plain fear, also lingers there. The part of him that still hasn't forgiven me.

"Delaney, you good if I leave them here? I need Bennett's help with something." Darla abruptly stands.

"Now?" Bennett asks, his tone suggesting he does not want to go with her. "I just got back, and it was a long day in the sun."

"Sorry, yes, it has to be now. Come on. Lottie, we're taking the UTV."

"And how do I get home?"

"Call your husband," Darla says and walks out the front door.

Bennett steps alongside me. "Do you mind?"

"Of course not. Go ahead."

"Thanks." He goes to his office, drops his bags and comes back out with his cowboy hat, and heads out the front door.

"He's about to get a talkin' to," Lottie says, laughing. "Hopefully, she comes up with something better than being a weed."

The other two women laugh as if there's more to what Lottie said.

I try to concentrate on the bouquets, unsure how Darla thinks she can get Bennett to forgive me. Then again, I know better than to question a mother's tenacity when it comes to her child.

Chapter Thirty-Nine

BENNETT

My mom sits in the driver's seat of the UTV and pats the seat next to her. "Get in."

I stare at the seat and cross my arms. "Why? Where are you taking me?"

"You'll see."

"Is this the weed talk?" I heard all about how my mom took Lottie to Daisy Hill and gave her a "get out of your own way and see what's in front of you" talk.

"Does everyone have to make fun of me for that? It was a logical comparison." She fixes her eyes on me. "Now, get in."

She'll never let it go, so I slide into the passenger seat, and she throws it back in reverse before slamming on the gas to go forward.

"Jesus, Mom, you're gonna kill me before we get to the hill."

"Relax. Live a little." She rounds the corner, and I grab the top of the UTV, so I don't fall out.

She doesn't calm down until we're past all the houses and almost to the ranch's family cemetery on top of a hill of daises where my relatives are buried.

"I wasn't expecting to have to have this conversation today, so let's go. Your dad wants to do date night tonight."

"By all means, we don't have to do this. Go on your date."

"Nonsense, you've wasted enough valuable time."

"I have?"

She opens the gate, not holding it open for me, and trudges up the hill.

Emmett told me about when he was taken here by his dad, and his brothers as well. Clearly, it's a family tradition you only get the pleasure of experiencing when they think you're ruining your life.

I follow her and stand by my grandmother's grave. Aunt Daisy's has a fresh set of flowers on it, which means someone else has been up here recently.

"Sit," Mom says.

"I'm not a dog," I grumble.

She pats the ground next to her. "You're acting like a stubborn Jack Russell terrier, and if you don't change your ways, you're going to ruin everything you could be building."

I sit on the ground. "So, Lottie's a weed, and I'm a Jack Russell. You're stellar at these talks, Mom. You should practice now for whenever Romy's turn comes around."

"I wouldn't have to have any of these talks if you and your sisters didn't need so much guidance. I mean, I thought I raised you well."

"What have I done to show you I wasn't raised well? My bachelor's degree? Starting my own successful business? Raising a little girl on my own? Being a good cousin, friend, and community member? I fail to see where I've disappointed you, Mom."

She picks at the weeds surrounding my grandparents' graves. "You are a great man, Bennett, there's no doubt about that, but you're too proud."

"That's my flaw? If so, I'll take it."

"Even if it means losing the one woman you've ever truly loved?" She tosses a weed toward me and hits my hand.

"You don't know what you're talking about."

"I know more than you think."

I wait.

"Do you think I didn't see the way you and Kristie were when you came back to Willowbrook? I mean, Bennett, you barely touched each other. Sure, I was surprised by the news about you and Delaney while you were separated and the fact your marriage was in trouble, but I wasn't shocked. Truth is, I'm upset you didn't feel that you could come to me. I'm your mother. I would have understood."

"What, Mom? What would you have understood?" I stand, needing to walk off some of my anxious energy. "You and Dad are more in love with each other every day. You made it work. You raised three kids, built successful businesses, all side by side. You worked your way through the hard times. I failed." My voice cracks.

She gets up, putting her hand on my back because it hurts too much to look at her. "A lot of marriages don't work out. You can't blame yourself."

I turn around. "I was selfish, pissed that she took that grant when she promised that if I stuck around California for another year for her to graduate, she'd come back here. Then she started working all the time, late nights. So I did the same. I should've supported her, stood by her dreams instead of pushing the agenda I wanted."

She sits on the bench in front of the tombstones. "And now you know how to do it better next time. But none of that changes that she slept with someone else. Your friend."

I sit next to her, resting my forearms on my thighs and putting my head in my hands. "Because I drove her to it."

"Bennett, you have to let this go. She's been gone seven years, and you can sit here and say that and point a finger in your direction all you want, but it usually takes two people for a marriage not to work out. You need to stop the charade, even the one you're putting on for yourself."

"I'm not putting on a charade."

"The marriage and love you like to say you had for Kristie isn't true. At least not at the time when she lost her life. I should've pushed you to get out of your own way a long time ago, but I was being selfish."

"What do you mean?" I lean back on the bench and look at her.

She shrugs. "I liked having you and Wren all to myself. Kristie made that hard at times. Maybe it was easier to let you stay the way you were rather than pushing you, I don't know." She shrugs.

"What are you talking about?"

She blows out a breath. "Kristie seemed to like it to be just you and her. Sometimes she made the family feel as if we were imposing. Before Wren was born, I came to the conclusion that you wouldn't be here long. Her mom told me at the baby shower that this was a nice place to be pregnant but too small to raise a family. I told your dad that night that you were going to move again and that land we hoped you'd build a house on would sit vacant."

I open my mouth, but she continues. "Don't get me wrong. I was all for you going to college or traveling the world. I want you and your sisters to do whatever makes you happy, but my mother's gut told me you weren't. You never touched her or looked at her. You were different when Kristie was in the room and when she wasn't. I felt like she was going to take advantage of the good-hearted person you are. And now that I know about Delaney seven years ago, I'm telling you, Bennett, Kristie manipulated you. Because you felt you had to do what was expected, you left Delaney. So, you can go ahead and blame Delaney, not forgive her, but have you once put yourself in her shoes at any point?"

I stare at the tombstones, reading all the names, and blow out a breath.

"You have to start being honest with yourself. Take everyone and everything else out of the equation. What does Bennett Owens want?" Mom asks.

"I can't, Mom. Seven years. I think of how Wren grew during that time and everything I've experienced with her, and all I can think of when I look at Delaney is how I lost all that with Leia."

"You did, and there's no refuting that, but think about the future. Sure, I have no doubt you'll form a wonderful relationship with Leia, and she and Wren will be close sisters, but in a little more than a decade, they're going to be gone, off living their own lives. Where does that leave you?" She pokes me in the arm. "All alone with your pride, that's where."

I blow out a breath. "How do I just let the anger go?"

She leans forward and pats my knee. "That's something you have to figure out, but I see the way you look at Delaney. Whatever happened between you guys seven years ago solidified your connection. It would be a shame for you to miss out on your one and only because you couldn't see why she made the decision she did."

She stands up from the bench. "To really empathize with someone, you have to get in their shoes. Get in hers, and see if you can understand why she felt like she had made the best decision at the time. Right now, you're being a destructive Jack Russell terrier puppy about to chew up and spit out everything around him. Put your pride aside and decide what you want."

My mom walks toward the gate.

"She wouldn't even take me back anyway. There's been too much damage done," I say quietly.

"Bennett, that girl loves you. You're a fool if you think different."

I sit on the bench as the gate clicks closed. I hear another UTV pull up, but I continue to stare at my aunt's grave. She died too young, and Uncle Bruce never remarried because he loved her so much. I thought I was supposed to feel that for Kristie, but I was actually grieving Delaney. After we got back to Willowbrook, I was missing Delaney and wanting her while trying to pretend I was in love with another woman.

Fuck. I'm an asshole.

I stand and look around, seeing my mom and dad driving off in his UTV.

I run down the hill and slide into the seat of the UTV left behind, speeding off to The Perfect Petal and hoping like hell it's not too late.

Chapter Forty

DELANEY

Lottie and Romy demanded to take the girls, claiming they wanted to hang with their nieces. Leia beamed when she heard the word niece since she's never had an aunt before. Sean didn't have any siblings, and we barely saw his parents.

I'm turning off the lights and heading to the breakroom to make sure everything is shut off when the bell from the front of the store rings.

"Delaney!" Bennett shouts.

I stop, and the door to the back hallway shuts. He weaves around the table, and when he reaches me, he stops, staring into my eyes.

"What's wrong?" My heart rate picks up.

"Sorry... I... am... so sorry." He shakes his head back and forth.

"Did something happen?" I hear the panic in my own voice. "Is it the girls? Lottie and Romy took them."

He shakes his head, straightens, and takes my hand. "We need to talk."

I allow him to lead me to his office, where he stops in front of the couch. I sit and he slides into the spot next to me, keeping my hands tucked in his.

"Are you okay? You're sweating," I say.

"I'm fine. Obviously, my mom took me to Daisy Hill for the talk and—"

"What talk?"

"The same one as Lottie. Anyway, I've been so stubborn, not being willing to see your side of things. I couldn't stop harping on what I missed out on, when I should have at least tried to understand your reasons. Put myself in your shoes."

"It's fine." I go to stand, but he clenches my hands tighter.

"It's not. I've regretted leaving you in California since the minute I stepped out of your place. But I was too prideful to admit that my marriage had failed, or that I'd married the wrong woman because it's always been you, Delaney. The minute you showed up in that breakroom, I knew it. But I was ashamed that I was happy my marriage didn't work out and that it enabled me to pursue something with you."

"Please don't, Bennett." I blink back the tears welling in my eyes. "I can't. We can't."

"Why not? I'm telling you. I love you. It's always been you. This whole time when I couldn't move on, I thought it was from the guilt of not loving Kristie when she passed, but now I know."

"What... what do you know?"

"That I didn't want anyone else. I knew no one was going to compare to you. You are the love of my life."

I dislodge my hands from his and stand, rounding the coffee table. "I kept Leia from you. I allowed another man to raise her. You should hate me."

He meets me on the other side. "I never hated you."

I give him a look that says he's lying.

"I was mad, that's true, but I could never hate you. And it's upsetting that I missed out on all that time with Leia. I wish you'd made a different choice, but I can understand why you didn't. And I can see the role I played in your decision, even if I didn't know it at the time. I'm sad it took my mom to help me see that you were being protective of yourself and our child. God, I should've stayed with you then. I should've told Kristie that we'd coparent and that would have been that. I'm sorry. I told you I'd always be there, and I wasn't."

I suck in a shaky breath. "I wanted to tell you. I wished so many times I'd gotten to tell you I was pregnant before her and maybe things would have gone differently," I admit, never making eye contact with him.

He steps closer, putting his finger under my chin and raising it so our eyes meet. "Can you forgive me?"

"Can you forgive me?" I hold his gaze, and some of the guilt I've been carrying around slides away at what I see there.

"Yes. All I know is that I don't want to be apart from you. Do you think you're ready to start a new chapter?"

"My existing chapter hasn't closed just yet. I'm technically still married, in the legal sense."

He puts his hand over my heart. "Is this still attached to someone?"

I nod. His face falls, and he moves to step back, but I grip his wrist, keeping his hand covering my heart.

"It's attached to you. You've always held my heart."

He leans closer, invading my space. "What are you saying?"

"I'm saying I love you."

"And you want to give this a try?"

I nod. "I'm terrified, but I'm more terrified of living my life without you."

"God, me too. I'd rather have you and lose you than to continue to fight all these feelings. I love you so much, Delaney. You were my first love, and you'll be my last."

His eyes are on me as though I hung the damn moon, and

I lean in, already forgetting all the reasons this could be a bad decision. As if my body doesn't remember how badly it hurt when he left. I push it all away because I do love this man, so, so much.

He's standing so close, I feel the heat coming off his skin. One more step, and I can fold into him as if he's been mine for years.

"Say something," I whisper, because the silence between us is too weighted and charged.

"I missed you," he says, his voice rough. "I've missed you since the day I let you go."

My heart stutters. I never knew he felt even a fraction of the ache I've been carrying around.

And just like that, the space between us disappears.

His hands cradle my face, thumbs brushing under my jaw as if he's memorizing the shape of me all over again. Then his mouth is on mine, slow at first as if he's testing the waters, afraid to put himself out there in case I pull away.

I don't.

God, I don't even consider it.

I press into his body, starved for him. For us. For the way he makes me feel as if I'm the only woman in his world.

He groans against my lips, deepening the kiss, and I let his tongue through the seam of my lips. My fingers twist into the fabric of his shirt, pulling him closer. His hands slip down, one finding the small of my back, the other splaying across my hip, holding me to him.

Then the gentleness turns into a frenzy.

All the years of what-ifs pour out all at once.

He backs me toward the edge of his desk, and I go willingly, needing something to brace against. His mouth trails down my neck, leaving heat in its wake, and I gasp when he finds the spot just below my ear.

"Tell me you want this," he murmurs.

I do. God, I do.

Instead of answering, I tug his shirt, making it so there's no space between us. He exhales hard.

Bennett pulls back to look in my eyes as his hands slide under my shirt, warm and slow, one inch at a time. His mouth falls to my collarbone, his fingertips dangerously close to my breasts, causing my nipples to pebble.

"Laney," he whispers against my skin, and the sound of my nickname on his lips wrecks me.

Because this is it. We're promising ourselves to each other.

This moment is the culmination of everything we never said, everything we never stopped feeling.

And I'm done running.

From him.

From this.

It finally feels as if I've come home.

"I need you on a bed," he whispers.

"My parents are still gone, and Levi is gone. The girls are with your sisters."

"Perfect."

He takes my hand, but I tug him back, needing to kiss him one more time. He doesn't pull away, caging me to his desk, deepening the kiss further and spurring us to both moan.

I don't want to stop kissing him, touching him, but he has enough willpower for the both of us. He closes the kiss and rests his forehead against mine. "I'm only able to stop because my sisters will be watching the girls overnight, and we're going to make up for lost time."

He secures my hand in his, leading me out of the office and flicking off the lights on our way out.

I'd follow him wherever he leads me because I meant what I said. He owns my heart. He always has.

Chapter Forty-One

DELANEY

We don't make it past the front door.

Bennett kicks it shut behind us, his mouth already on mine, hands roaming every inch, as though he can't decide which part of me he wants to touch first. No one has ever made me feel as wanted as he does.

He presses me against the wall, one hand cupping the back of my neck, the other sliding up under my shirt. I'm already breathless, already burning for him.

"Upstairs?" I gasp between kisses.

He shakes his head, eyes dark and hungry. "No time."

I don't argue, instead grabbing the hem of his shirt and yanking it over his head. The fabric tears somewhere near the bottom, not that he seems to care.

"I love it when you strip me," he mutters against my throat while kissing lower.

"Maybe you should do the same." My fingers work his belt.

"Is that a challenge?" He flicks open the button of my jeans with one hand.

We stumble through the hallway, every step clumsy and

frantic, leaving a trail of clothes. Then he spins me toward the kitchen, walking me backward until the backs of my thighs hit the edge of the table. He lifts me in one fluid motion, and the thud of wood under my thighs sends a shiver straight through me.

"I've thought about you, doing this," he murmurs, dragging his mouth down my neck, over the collar of my shirt. "Every night for seven years."

"There were so many nights when you were the one I thought of when I touched myself." I gasp, dipping a hand into the waistband of my pants, tugging him closer. "Your mouth, your hands."

"I'm gonna need to see that." His mouth crashes into mine, hot and heavy, and I open for him without a fight.

His hands slip under my shirt, rough palms skating up my ribs, inching slowly as if he's relearning my body. When his thumbs brush the bottom edges of my bra, I gasp, arching into him, needing more.

"Let me help," I whisper, fumbling with the hem of my shirt.

"That's my job," he says.

"Then do it."

He draws back, and I miss his lips immediately. As if he's testing my willpower, a mischievous smile crosses his face and he grabs the bottom of my shirt, sliding it up my body and over my head.

His eyes darken, taking me in. "Jesus, Laney."

I would normally be self-conscious from the light stretch marks on my tummy from Leia, but with the way he's looking at me, there's no room for it. I don't need to cover myself because he loves me regardless of my post-baby body.

My hands run down his golden skin and taut muscles that I remember too well. He was all man seven years ago, but this feels different for some reason I can't explain.

His mouth returns to mine, more frantic, and his hand cups the back of my neck, holding me to him. I'm not complaining. I just want to feel him against me.

I slide my hand inside his jeans, and the low groan that escapes him sends heat pooling low in my belly. "Laney."

I bite his jaw. "Is there a problem?" I laugh.

"Do you want to play games?"

I shrug, giving him a flirtatious grin.

His hands hook into my pants, dragging them and my underwear down my legs before tossing them over his shoulder. Again, his gaze flows down my body, slow like honey, and the heat in his eyes undoes any control I have.

"Are you just going to look?"

He drops to his knees. "Hell no." His hands grip my thighs, spreading me open.

My whole body jerks with the first swipe of his tongue. He glances up at me—gauging my reaction or purposely teasing me, I can't be sure.

"I'll repay you when I'm on my knees."

He chuckles and buries his head between my legs. Bennett groans against my core, tongue teasing, tasting, ruining me for anyone else.

"B," I whisper, my fingers weaving through his hair, clinging tightly, pushing him in, on the cusp of coming.

He slides back and looks at me, chin glistening. "Say it again."

"B, more. Please, I'm so close."

As if he wants to take me to the edge, he teases my entrance with his fingers, not ever dipping in more than an inch as he sucks my clit.

"Oh shit," I say.

I come apart embarrassingly fast, but he doesn't stop. Not even when I gasp and tremble and try to close my thighs. He holds me there, drawing it out, savoring every last second.

"You taste so damn good." He rises, wiping his mouth with the back of his hand, his eyes feral.

"That was so—"

He doesn't let me finish. He grips my hips, dragging me to the edge of the table. "I'm gonna be honest, it's been a long time for me..." He looks shy, cheeks pink.

"I'm pretty sure you didn't forget how. You definitely didn't forget how to go down on me." I wrap my legs around his waist, yanking him to me. "Condom?"

"I've been tested, and it might sound crazy and not at all like me, but I could make another baby with you and not give one shit right now."

"Well." I put my hand on his chest. "We have a lot on our plates, so let's forgo that discussion for now. But I was tested after everything with Sean, and I have an IUD, so..."

"So I'm going to embarrass myself right now, I'm sure." He fists the base of his cock and lines it up with my opening.

The anticipation grows until he sinks into me in one deep, glorious thrust. I cry out, my hands clutching at his shoulder blades.

Perfect.

He's thick and hard, filling me so deeply my entire core clenches around him.

"Jesus," he breathes against my neck. "You're so damn wet. So tight."

My nails dig into his skin. "It's been a long time."

He groans, pulling almost all the way out before sliding back in, slower this time, as though he's savoring the moment.

But I'm desperate for him. "Don't be gentle. Not tonight."

He stills for a beat, leaning back, staring into my eyes.

Then he thrusts into me harder, slamming my hips against the edge of the table with each stroke. The obscene sound of skin-on-skin echoes through the kitchen, and I'm thankful there're no neighbors for miles, so I can be as loud as I want.

I spread my legs wider, angling my hips to take him even deeper, causing the next thrust to knock the air from my lungs. "Oh my god, B—"

His fingers dig into my hips, dragging me to meet him again and again, using my body exactly how he needs. Every time he thrusts into me, it's harder, hotter, and I grow wetter. I'm soaked, and feeling the slick slide of him in and out of me takes me right to the edge.

"You feel like fucking heaven," he growls, breathless. "We were always so good at this."

I can't find the words I want to convey how I'm feeling because I'm too busy falling apart with every one of his punishing and perfect thrusts.

The table creaks violently, the edge biting into the backs of my thighs, but let the bruises come, I don't care. His pace picks up, growing frantic and wild with need. I meet him thrust for thrust, chasing the orgasm barreling down on me. It builds like a tidal wave, cresting with every deep, wet stroke until I can't hold back.

I shatter with a cry, pulsing around him, body locking tight as everything in me releases in a rush. It's years of longing and heartbreak and need, all crashing through me until only peace is left behind.

He keeps riding it out, chasing his own release. His rhythm falters slightly, and I feel him throb deep inside me as he groans my name into my neck and spills into me with a final thrust so deep, I clench.

Then my mind stills. For the first time in so long, it's not filled with a million thoughts, a million worries, a million what-ifs.

We're both panting, slick with sweat, clinging to each other.

His forehead drops to mine. "Holy hell."

I nod, trying to catch my breath. "Yeah."

He cups my cheek, thumb gently brushing over my flushed skin. "You okay?"

I manage a breathless laugh. "I'm better than okay. That was..."

"Everything?" he whispers.

"More."

He kisses me slowly and tenderly, like a promise that this is it for us. And I'll take it.

I kiss him back, tasting his sweat and salt. It's a perfect moment.

The front door opens, and a bag drops on the floor.

"Jesus, the kitchen table? It's my favorite spot in the house, and now I'm gonna have to think about the two of you fucking every time I eat?" Levi grunts as the door shuts behind him.

We both laugh, and for the first time in years, I let myself believe that maybe it's not too late for our happily ever after.

Chapter Forty-Two

BENNETT

Her leg slides over mine, waking me. The warmth of her body tucks against my side, her cheek on my shoulder, her fingers running across my chest.

Delaney.

She's here.

It was all real. Not a dream.

Soft light pours in through her bedroom window. It's a new day that feels like the start of something exciting. A future with her.

There's so much we need to discuss. Telling the girls, people in town. Where do we go from here?

She shifts beside me with a sleepy hum, nuzzling closer. Her bare thigh brushes higher, and I bite back a groan. All those thoughts about how we'll handle things goes out the window.

She's still naked.

And so am I.

Memories from last night run through my mind. On the kitchen table, in the shower, in her bed multiple times. All through the night, the lightest touch from the other awoke a need that had to be taken care of.

I brush my lips against her hair. "Morning."

Her hand moves, slow and lazy, over my stomach. Tracing lines as she dips lower. Her fingers wrap around my hardened length, and I suck in a breath.

"Morning," she says with humor in her voice because she knows exactly what she's doing to me.

"Laney…" I warn, but there's no heat behind it. I'm ready to have her again.

She props herself up on one elbow. Her hair is wild around her face, her eyes heavy with sleep except for a wicked grin.

"I didn't get to return the favor last night," she whispers, voice rough and warm against my neck.

"You absolutely don't—"

She cuts me off with a kiss to my jaw, then my chest, moving lower.

My head sinks back into the pillow, and I close my eyes at the feel of her.

She slides down between the sheets, her lips trailing a path that leaves fire in its wake. My hands fist the blankets the second she grips my base, and her mouth wraps around me. I groan, lifting my hips. She teases me with long strokes of her tongue, her hand working in rhythm.

"Fuck."

She hums around me.

I look down at her lips stretched around my cock, her cheeks flushed, and the sight alone nearly makes me come.

I brush her hair back, my thumb skimming over her cheek. "You're gonna kill me."

She pulls off me just long enough to murmur, "You'll die happy then."

Then she takes me deeper, and I think I might just die.

The pleasure builds fast, my abs tightening, my breath shallow gasps. I'm so damn close. "Laney, I'm—"

She doesn't stop, nor does she slow. She holds me with her mouth and her hands until I groan her name, spilling down her throat.

When I open my eyes again, she's crawling over me, back up the bed, with a smug and satisfied smirk. I pull her to me, crashing my mouth into hers, tasting myself on her lips. I kiss her deep and slow and messy, rolling her onto her back, pressing my weight into her and wishing we could stay here all day.

"Your turn," I murmur against her mouth, kissing my way down her chest.

She laughs softly, breath hitching as I gently bite her hip. "You're insatiable."

"With you?" I look up at her, grinning. "Always."

❧

An hour later, we decide breakfast is a good idea.

I call Lottie and Romy to see how the sleepover went while she goes downstairs to cook breakfast.

When I get down to the kitchen, Delaney's wearing the shirt I took off last night—and I'm hoping nothing else.

"How are they? I was worried about Leia." She glances over her shoulder from where she stands at the stove.

I come up behind her, in my jeans, and wrap my arms around her waist, pressing my face into her neck. "There might have been a nightmare."

She whips around, the spatula flying across the room, hitting the wall, and falling to the floor. "We gotta go."

I tighten my hands on her hips. "Leia's good now. She's eating breakfast."

"But—"

"I know it's not ideal," I say.

"I'm a horrible mom. I should have waited until my parents were home or—"

I take her hand and lead her to the kitchen table. I'm half tempted to ask her parents to let me buy it since I'll remember last night every time I look at it.

She sits in the chair, and I hold her hands. "You didn't do anything wrong last night. You left her with her family." I tip my chin down and look into her eyes. "I was just as worried and was ready to grab my keys and drive you over. I don't want our daughter to be upset either, but I want her to feel comfortable with my family, with me. I want her to know that they and I can help her through the hard stuff too. Lottie said she set up a fort and slept with them. That she was able to soothe Leia back to sleep. Wren helped too, and Leia's good now."

She nods. "I know you're right. And I want her to be comfortable with your family and with you too." She kisses my lips. "But…"

I laugh. "You want to go have breakfast at my parents' place?"

She nods.

"Okay."

Delaney cringes. "I'm sorry."

I guide her to sit on my lap. "Don't apologize. I'd never be upset with you for wanting to make sure our kids are safe. But can we talk for just a second?"

She wraps her arms around my neck, and my hand falls to her outer thigh. "Of course."

I kiss her, trying to get that concerned look off her face. There's fear in her eyes, and I assume she's worried I'm going to take back what we did last night. I deserve it, but I'm going to prove to her every day that she can trust me again.

"Are we keeping this from the girls?" I ask.

"Well…"

"I'm good either way, but I want us on the same page." I really have no idea what's best for them. I hate to start us off by sneaking around again. We have nothing to be ashamed of, but I also don't want the girls to be hurt.

She opens her mouth, and I decide to be truthful with her.

"Listen, I'll go along with whatever you want, but I want them to know. I get that we could be cautious and see where this goes before involving them, but they're already in the mix. And I'm going to do everything in my power to make sure this doesn't end. I see you as my forever, Delaney, and I want our girls to be along for the ride."

Tears glisten in her eyes, and I run my thumb across her cheek. She's so beautiful. How did I ever get this lucky?

"How can I say no to that?"

"I don't think you can." I tighten my hand on her thigh.

"But maybe we hold off on sleeping at each other's houses for a bit."

"Then be prepared to be fucked in my office and in my truck on the regular."

"No complaints." Her hands cradle my face, and she presses her lips to mine.

I take the invitation and deepen our kiss.

Then she gets off my lap, flicks the button of my jeans and zipper before tugging them off me, with my help. She sinks down on me and fucks me so good I'm still hard after I come.

I'll never get enough of her.

Chapter Forty-Three

DELANEY

Bennett and I walk into his parents' house. It's newer and decorated nicely in the same style Darla had in their previous house. There're lots of pictures of the entire crew who live on the ranch, but mostly her own children through the ages. The only new ones seem to be of Wren, then Lottie and Brooks at their reception.

"Hello!" Bennett says, his hand tight in mine as he leads me into the house.

"In here," his dad calls. We turn the corner as Brad says, "Go fish, Leia." He taps her nose with the tip of his finger. "Maybe next time."

She puts her single card down on the table and giggles.

As if Bennett feels the same as me, we stand a little out of sight, watching his dad interact with her.

Brad turns to Wren. "All right, card shark, do you have any threes?"

Wren's head goes back, and she gives him one of her cards.

Brad triumphantly pairs the cards and holds one card in the air. "I got your numbers."

They both laugh.

Darla comes out of the kitchen and sits down next to them, until she sees us spying.

"We've been saved, Brad," she says.

The girls turn around, look at one another, then run to us —Leia to me and Wren to Bennett. I go to slip my hand out of Bennett's, but he grips it tighter, leaving us both to hug them with one arm.

They pull back and look at one another again before they zero in on our linked hands.

"We have something to tell you," Bennett says.

The girls jump up and down in excitement, the two of them hugging one another so tightly.

"Aunt Lottie was right!" Wren screams. "We're sisters."

"You were already sisters," I say, chuckling.

"Yeah, but now we get to share a room," Wren says.

I glance at Bennett. Maybe we didn't think this through as far as we should have. Of course the girls are going to want to live together right away.

"Actually..."

"Shoo, you two, let them eat." Darla comes over and pats them on their backs. She steadies her gaze on us. "What can I make you?"

"Eggs or pancakes?" Bennett asks me.

"I don't want you going to any trouble. I can just pick something up when Leia and I leave."

Bennett slides his arm around my waist, his hand molding to my hip, then leans in and whispers, "My bed is going to be lonely tonight."

Darla rolls her eyes, probably seeing my beet-red face, before she heads to the kitchen. "I'll make both."

"I'll help." I leave Bennett, but he slyly pats my ass.

"Thank you. I appreciate that," Darla says over her shoulder.

I go into the kitchen with Darla, and from what I hear, Bennett joins the Go Fish game.

"Lottie had to leave this morning to open the store, but she said the nightmare wasn't too bad." Darla cracks eggs into a bowl.

"Thank you so much for all this." I help her crack some eggs into the bowl.

"You don't have to thank us. We're just happy to get to know her. It's amazing how opposite the two of them are." She glances over her shoulder.

"Leia's quiet and more reserved."

Darla smiles at me. "There's nothing wrong with that. I have one of those too." She nods toward Bennett. "She's very smart and polite, and not that my opinion matters, but you did a great job with her."

Pride swells in my chest. "I'm still so—"

"No more of that." She holds out a fork for me. "No more sorrys. We're going to move forward now and leave all that in the past." She puts her arm around my shoulders. "You make my son really happy, and you're a good mother to one of my granddaughters. That's enough for me."

The words *one granddaughter* repeat in my head.

I'd love to be a mother figure to Wren, but maybe she doesn't want that. I'll have to see where our relationship goes.

"Now beat the eggs." She points at the bowl.

Darla makes the pancakes, and I wonder how many times she's measured that flour out because she doesn't even use a measuring cup anymore.

"Don't worry, I'm not one of those mothers-in-law who won't share recipes or omits one ingredient. You want it, it's yours."

"But—"

She side-eyes me. "If you're about to say that you're not

his wife, that's ridiculous. You're his future. A mother knows."

After we eat breakfast and say goodbye to Darla and Brad, Bennett drives all of us over to The Perfect Petal where I left my car.

"I don't understand," Wren says to her dad. "If you guys are together, why can't they move in with us?"

Bennett glances at me. "We're dating, we're not married."

"Aunt Lottie said that doesn't matter. Briar lived with Emmett before they were married."

"Aunt Lottie got married in Vegas, so..." Bennett says.

I place my hand on his, turning to face the girls in the back seat. "The time will come when we're all under one roof. I see it for us, but right now isn't the right time. Let your dad and I go on a few dates first. We need to take our time."

They look at one another. "Then go on a date now. We'll stay at Grandma and Grandpa's." Wren smiles wide.

"I'll tell you what. Why don't you both come over for dinner tonight? I'll cook."

"YAY!" the girls cheer in unison.

I turn to Bennett. "And how about you?"

"You don't even have to ask." He winks.

I wonder when it will be okay to give him a quick kiss in front of the girls. Jeez, I need to get myself under control.

I leave the truck, letting Leia out. As we stand at my car, it feels weird and not right that we're about to leave them. But we have kids to think about. We can't go rogue and move in together right away, right?

Still, saying goodbye feels so wrong.

Bennett crouches, and Leia hugs him. He tells her how proud he is that she stuck it out and spent the night with Lottie and that he understands how scary it is to wake up from a nightmare somewhere you've never been before. She nods and goes in for another hug.

Tears cling to my eyelashes. I distract myself by saying goodbye to Wren, giving her a hug of my own and telling her I can't wait to see her tonight.

Bennett kisses my cheek and pats my ass behind the girls' backs, and I climb into the car, leaving my heart with him.

How long we can do this, I have no idea, but as I look in the rearview mirror at Leia, I know I have to be patient for her. She needs time to adjust too. But I meant what I told them. I'm certain the day will come when we're all under the same roof.

Chapter Forty-Four

DELANEY

The lasagna is still steaming when Brad sets the dish on the table.

It's the weekly family dinner at the Owens', and Leia and I were invited. Since it's our first time, I took the seat next to Leia with Bennett across from me, which is slightly disappointing since I was kind of hoping for some leg squeezes under the table.

We've been doing a lot as a family since we told the girls, not wanting them to feel left out. We've taken walks around the lake at night, built fires, and made s'mores. We've done dinners and gone out for ice cream. But the only time I'm really alone with Bennett is when we're both working.

Sure, the quickies in his office and the long make-out sessions in his truck have been nice, but they haven't nearly satisfied me, or him I'm sure. I keep reminding myself that we have a lifetime together as long as we get a solid foundation with the girls. We're not early-twenty-somethings anymore, with little responsibility except for ourselves. We have two little ones to think about now.

"It's so good, Leia," Wren says. "My grandma is a better cook than Uncle Jensen." She whispers the last part.

"I'm gonna tell him you said that," Lottie teases, her smile showing that she's joking.

"It looks delicious, Darla," I say, catching Bennett staring at me.

A smug smile plays at the edge of his mouth. I tilt my head, wondering why. Lottie helps dish out kid-size portions of lasagna to Wren and Leia as I feel my phone buzz in my pocket. I glance at Bennett. He already has his fork in hand.

Not that many people text me, and I don't want be rude, so I pull it out and casually check under the table to make sure it isn't an emergency. With Levi competing in the rodeo, I always fear I'll get a call from the hospital one day.

> Tell me you're not wearing panties under that dress.

I nearly choke on my own breath from surprise.

I catch him watching me, his eyes full of mischief, pretending he didn't just light a fire in me.

When I shift in my seat, every inch of fabric clinging to my skin feels too tight. I threw on this sundress because I was done with the shorts and T-shirts and jeans I have to wear at work all week. It felt nice to dress up a little, but now I want to go buy a whole lot of them if they get Bennett to look at me as though he wants me to meet him in the bathroom.

I take a slow sip of lemonade, then type back with one hand, using the other to steady my phone beneath the tablecloth.

> Maybe you'll find out later. ;)

Across the table, his mouth twitches. He's chewing,

nodding along to whatever Brooks is saying about the house they're building, but he glances in my direction every few seconds. Then he nonchalantly rests his fork on the table and looks down at his lap.

Another buzz hits my thigh where my phone is tucked under my leg.

> Make an excuse and meet me upstairs.
> There are four bedrooms to choose from.

I press my thighs together, heat curling low in my belly.

> And say what exactly?

> That their son feels like he's seventeen
> again and can't get enough of his girlfriend.
> How about the second on the right? I could
> be between your thighs making you come
> in less than five minutes.

My fork slips from my grip, hits the table, and falls to the floor.

Leia glances at me. "Are you okay, Mommy?"

"Yeah," I say too quickly, ducking my head and pretending the fork just slipped, and it's not because of the man directly across the table.

Bennett's smirk widens, already pushing back from his chair. "Want me to get you another one?" His voice is full of charm and sweetness.

I narrow my eyes. "No, I've got it." I rise from the table.

"Please, it's my family's home."

Everyone's eyes are volleying between us as we both walk into the kitchen.

He's definitely using this as an excuse to get me alone.

He's going to be the death of me.

"Nice game," Romy says.

I think she's calling us out, but the closer I get to the kitchen, knowing Bennett is going to take full advantage of having me alone for a few minutes, I can't find it in myself to care.

Sure enough, he beats me into the kitchen, and when I walk in and am out of sight of the dining room, he wraps his arm around my waist and cages me against the wall.

God, will there ever come a time my body doesn't want him?

One hand lands beside my head, palm flat against the wall. The other cradles my hip. The heat radiating off him, the desire coursing in his eyes... I won't fight him on this. I'll take every millisecond I can get with him.

I swallow. "They probably know what we're doing."

"I know," he murmurs, not backing off. His mouth is inches from mine. "Did you wear this dress to torment me? If so, it's working."

My fingers run down his chest, feeling his muscles through the thin fabric. "I think there's a different question you want the answer to, no?"

The hand on my hip inches lower, slipping beneath the fabric, deliberately slowly, as if there isn't a table full of people in the other room. His fingertips curve up my thigh, and I press back into the wall. My skin pebbles as his palm glides higher, skimming along my inner thigh.

He teases, brushing his finger along the outer edge of my panties, and I'm desperate for him to pull the fabric to the side, to touch me.

Bennett's mouth falls to my neck as that finger doing all the work runs down the center of me, and he stills for a moment. Quickly recovering, he brings his mouth to my ear and groans.

"You're soaked," he murmurs, voice rough with awe.

"Disappointed?" I whisper, since I'm not bare under my dress.

He pulls back, locking his eyes with me once more. "Never."

His thumb brushes over the damp fabric, and I squeeze my eyes shut, biting my lip to keep from moaning. Our mouths crash together in a frantic kiss that's all teeth and hunger. His hand on the wall drops to my waist, pinning me to the wall as if he can't trust himself not to drag me upstairs and rip off this dress.

He kisses me like that first kiss in his office only weeks ago.

My head tilts, lips parting, and his tongue instantly slides against mine. I whimper when he removes his hand and replaces it with his thigh. I shamelessly grind against it.

"I need a sleepover," he growls against my lips. "An entire night."

My fingers tangle in his hair, tugging at the short strands. He dips his head, trailing kisses along my jaw, then down to the sensitive skin beneath my ear.

"Fuck, take whatever you need."

"We can't," I breathe, dizzy from his hips pressing into mine.

Understanding that we're probably on our last second before curious little feet search us out, he slows the kiss, but it does nothing to stop my desire from building.

"Did you get lost finding a fork?" Lottie hollers from the other room.

He pulls back, chest heaving, then drops his forehead to mine. "Later. You're not going home without an orgasm."

I smile, breathless. "I'm already halfway there."

His eyes flash. "Oh, just you wait."

"Oh, Leia, sweetie," Darla says loudly.

We straighten just in time for Leia to pop her head around the corner. "Mommy?"

I clear my throat and pray she doesn't notice my swollen lips and flushed skin. "Coming."

Bennett opens a drawer, grabs a fork, and hands it to me. Right before we enter the dining room, his one hand lands on my stomach, pulling my back to his front. His lips land at my ear.

"I love you," he says sweetly, as if he wasn't seconds from devouring me against the kitchen wall moments ago.

He weaves by me, leaving me barely holding on and already craving the next time we can be alone.

Everyone at the table eyes us as though they're saying they know what we were doing. Wren ignores us as we sit at the table, telling a very animated story about something that happened the other day with Mack. Leia adds in quiet additions, and I try to focus, I really do, but then Bennett sends another message.

> You have no idea the restraint it is taking for me to remain seated at this table.

I squeeze my knees together, hoping to quelch the ache.

Wren reaches for more garlic bread and tips her cup. Bennett lunges to steady it, and while everyone is distracted with the chaos, I hammer out a reply.

> You started it.

I hit Send, then add:

> Now, keep your hands off your phone and stop eye fucking me across the table with our daughters here.

The word *our* slips out so easily.

Again, his eyes dip to his lap, and he checks it with a little tilt of his head as though he already knows he's been caught. When his eyes lift to mine again, they're darker.

"Wren," he says, turning to her as if he hasn't just wrecked me, "did you tell everyone about you and Leia helping at the golf course?"

Wren's forehead crinkles. "We had to go help Daddy and Delaney at the golf course." She couldn't sound less enthused.

Leia cringes. "It was boring."

Bennett gestures with his fork. "It wasn't that bad. You got to hit the balls into the holes."

"Until that man yelled at us," Wren says, and Leia nods.

They continue their story, a little more animated now, about the mean old golfer with hairy ears.

Bennett looks down at his phone again. If he keeps playing this game, my willpower is going to be shot.

> I want to be between your legs so damn bad.

My breath catches, and a flicker of heat travels from my head to my toes and back up.

> You're killing me.

> That's the point.

I try to act as if I'm not seconds from squirming in my seat.

> I could have gotten my own fork.

He casually leans back in his chair, one arm draped over the back. The muscle in his jaw flexes once before he types again.

> Where would the fun be in that?

> Take your phone to the bathroom and send me a picture.

> You like to torture yourself.

> Yes, especially since seeing you makes me all proud caveman cause you're mine.

My whole body goes still.

I should say no. I should shut this down. But who am I kidding? I like this game too.

I excuse myself with a quiet, "Be right back," and slide my phone into my hand.

Darla glances up. "Everything okay? You two have been on your phones this whole dinner."

"Business," we say in unison.

"Blue Prairie stuff," Bennett adds.

"I just need to use the washroom." I give Darla a smile and push my chair back in before I step away from the table.

Bennett doesn't look at me as I pass.

I close the door to the downstairs bathroom and lean against it, heart racing. I've never sent a dirty text before, but I trust Bennett. I stare at my reflection in the mirror. I'm not fooling anyone in that room. I'm completely flushed, my skin pink.

It feels odd to just take a picture of my pussy. What fun is that? So, I lift the skirt of the sundress, focus more on my inner thigh and the edge of my panties, so he can see the wet spot, and snap a photo.

My finger hovers over Send, second-guessing it, but then I press the button. The moment the message says *Delivered*, the air leaves my lungs.

My phone buzzes instantly.

> Fucking hell, stay right where you are, I'm coming.

I hurry out of the bathroom, not needing him in this small, confined space. If so, his entire family will hear him fucking me because I have no more restraint left.

Right before I enter the dining room, I send one more text.

> I expect the same in return just so you know.

> Well now's the time because he's standing tall and proud at the moment.

Everyone finishes eating, and thankfully, our text exchange stops—probably because we took ourselves to a level we needed to come down from.

When I set a serving bowl in the sink, Bennett steps up behind me.

"Laney," he says, voice low and dangerous in my ear, "I'm going to rip those panties off of you tonight."

I glance over my shoulder. "And how do you plan on accomplishing that?"

His hand skims the back of my thigh. "I'm finding us a babysitter."

"Oh my god, get a damn room," Romy says, coming in the kitchen, holding dishes.

Lottie comes in and stands next to Romy. "For the entire night."

Darla breezes in. "It's cute. The girls will stay with us tonight."

Bennett winks at me.

"I'm going to send a text to Nash and Jensen to clear the house," Romy says, pulling out her phone.

"Or at least drop off earplugs." Lottie smiles at us.

"It's the polite thing to do," Darla says with a chuckle.

Bennett isn't embarrassed in the slightest, putting his arm around my waist and bringing me into him, kissing the nape of my neck.

We'll need to figure this out eventually, but right now, I just want him to make good on his promises.

Chapter Forty-Five

BENNETT

We pull into the softball field's parking lot, and I realize I'm a little nervous about playing in front of Delaney. I want to impress her, but I'm not a home-run hitter like Ben or a scrappy double hitter like Brooks. I'm a solid player, but if I play shitty, I don't take it home with me.

"Yay, we're here!" Wren screeches from the back seat.

I park and cut the engine. Wren's going on and on to Leia about the games and how fun they are to watch, and she hopes their cousins Colter and Daisy are here.

I shift in my seat to face Delaney. "You sure you don't mind watching Wren?"

She gives me an annoyed look and rolls her eyes. "No, for the millionth time."

"It's just—"

She cuts me off with her hand on mine, then climbs out of the truck. She opens the back door and tells the girls to unbuckle. Since we're in the first parking spot next to the field, she asks them to go say hi to Aunt Lottie and Uncle Brooks and to stay there until she gets there.

Once they're gone, she climbs back in the cab of the truck

and shuts the door. "Listen, because I'm only going to say this once. Yes, Leia is my daughter, I share blood with her, but I'm hoping Wren will be my daughter one day too. I'm hoping she'll welcome me as another mother to her. With us comes them. There is no yours or mine, it's us, so I'd much rather you didn't ask me to watch her or ask if I'm good with watching her. She is part of us, and I don't want it any other way."

Fuck, how did I get so lucky with this woman? I push back the nugget of guilt that hits me every time I think about letting her go all those years ago.

Instead, I grip the back of her head, pulling her toward me and smashing my lips to hers. She moans, and I take it as an invitation to slide my tongue through the seam of her lips.

She inches forward. I really wish we weren't in a parking lot with trucks pulling in and people walking by. Otherwise, I'd pull her onto my lap and get her off with my fingers.

A loud bang on the window interrupts us. "You're parents, for Christ's sake."

I close the kiss and rest my forehead on hers, both of us catching our breaths. "Emmett," I whisper.

"He'd be the one."

I give her one more quick kiss, and we leave the truck, me rounding the back to grab my bag.

"So, are those, like, speciality items?" Delaney asks.

I glance over my shoulder to see Briar wearing an "Emmett's girl" T-shirt.

"You want a 'Bennett's girl' shirt?" I swear my chest puffs out on its own.

She shrugs and flutters her eyelashes a little. "I mean, I'd wear it, I suppose."

"Then I'll talk to Jude and get you one."

She leans up on her toes and kisses my cheek.

I hold out my hand, and she slides hers in it. God, this feels so good.

Leia runs up to us, tucking her hand in Delaney's free one. She's still hesitant with my family since they're so big and overwhelming. She can take all the time she needs. I'll never rush her into accepting them as her own.

"Check out this new Willowbrook couple," Sadie says, holding Daisy to her chest. "It looks good on both of you."

Gillain sidles up to her sister-in-law, with a smile so big you'd think she was as happy as us. Not a chance in hell she is.

"Finally, Owens gets some." Walker Matthews comes from around the fence line by the other team's dugout. "Delaney, heard you were back."

My back goes up. If he thinks he's going to say anything shitty to Delaney, we're going to have a problem.

"You should come visit Wild Bull Ranch sometime," Walker says.

"Why are you even here?" Briar asks him. "We're not playing your team."

"We have the next game, and since it's winding down to championship time, I figured I'd see if you guys have improved." Walker looks out at the parking lot. "Looks like you might be down a player."

We all turn to see Romy walking up on crutches and her ankle wrapped. My mom is wearing her Plain Daisy Ranch team shirt.

"What happened?" Delaney asks.

Wren runs up to Romy, asking her a million questions.

Mom raises her hands. "I've been waiting for my chance to show you kids how the game is played."

"What's going on?" Jude comes out of the dugout. "Why is Aunt Darla wearing Romy's shirt?"

"I could've gotten Nash to be our tenth," Poppy says.

"I'm sure you'd like that." Scarlett eyes her, and Poppy ignores the look.

"Oh, Jude, get that look off your face. I'm a good player, just ask Brad," my mom says. She thumbs behind her, and my dad emerges, having parked the truck.

"Sorry, guys, we flipped a coin." My dad shrugs.

Mom narrows her eyes at him.

Everyone laughs, and I turn to Leia next to Delaney. It's a lot of noise and chaos, and Delaney told me the other night that Leia's just not used to it after growing up as an only child with very few extended family members. She says that Leia enjoys them all, but back in California, there were a lot of times it was just the two of them. I hate thinking they didn't have the support of any family out there, and from what I've gathered, most of Delaney's friends ditched her after Sean's arrest.

Delaney bends and scoops Leia up in her arms. "Good luck."

I kiss her briefly on the lips. Something we started last week and neither of the girls have said anything. "Don't expect a home run or anything," I murmur.

I hold out my hand to Leia, and she smacks it with a smile.

"Good luck," Leia says, mimicking Delaney. Then she holds out her arm that's not wrapped around Delaney's neck.

Delaney's eyes shine as I lean in, giving her a half hug. I'll take whatever she offers.

Wren runs over and attaches herself to my legs. "Good luck, Daddy."

We're all entwined, and this feels really fucking good. I never want this to go away.

I head to the dugout where Emmett is relaxing on the bench, his feet out and his hands laced behind his head. "I'm disappointed, Danson. I talk you down from the ledge, and I gotta hear from your mom about you and Delaney?"

Since school's been out, we haven't been going to The Getaway Lodge for breakfast. Mom watches Wren and Leia most days, splitting the time with Delaney's parents.

"We're together," I say, sitting down to change my shoes.

"I got that when your tongue was shoved down her throat in the truck. I guess you're not being discreet?"

"Nah, damn the consequences." I tie my shoes.

"This town isn't going to give you shit. They've wanted you happy forever."

"But with Leia being mine—"

"Again, they're not going to care, and if they do, who gives a shit? You're happy, she's happy, I know the girls are happy. Fuck the rest of 'em."

Having my family on my side means a lot to me. I'm not sure why I ever felt as though I had to make my marriage appear perfect.

Jude rounds us all up, and of course there's an argument about the batting lineup and position play.

"Hey, I want one of those shirts for Delaney. Where do I get one?" I ask Jude.

"He's not going to tell you," Emmett says.

"You should get one that says, 'Lottie's guy,'" Lottie says to Brooks, who looks none too thrilled with the idea.

"How about you get 'Brooks's girl'?"

"It's a family thing, and we're the family." She circles her hand around the group.

"So I'm not part of the family?" Brooks crosses his arms and widens his stance.

"Of course you are, I just meant... oh shit, that's on me." She throws herself on him, practically climbing him.

Brooks shoots a victorious grin at all of us over her shoulder.

"Man, that's come full circle," Poppy says.

"Can we please focus?" Jude says.

"It's not like we're playing Wild Bull." Ben shrugs, and we all go down the line with the same reaction.

"And that's how we don't make it to the finals." Jude narrows his gaze. "We have to win this one to get there."

We all give him our attention because if we don't, he'll get pissy.

Eventually, Jude goes out to talk to the umpire and the coach for Safe Haven.

Finally, we start playing. The game is more competitive than I thought it would be, and I'm worried we might lose. If we do, Jude will lose his shit. Did we all come in too confident?

It's the final inning, and Jude is on third. If I don't bring him in, it will be left to my mom. Even though she talks a good game, her skills are rusty, and she's struck out at every bat. All my cousins give me pats on the back as I make my way to the plate, as if it's over, and we've already lost, and they're silently saying sorry I'll get the wrath of Jude.

"Go, Daddy!" Wren shouts.

"Go, go, go!" Leia chimes in.

Their faces are plastered to the fence, and Delaney gives me a big smile and claps as if she thinks I've got this.

I so do not. Baseball was never my sport. I played football like the rest of my family. I can catch a ball and run, but hitting a softball is harder than it looks.

I get set up as the girls continue screaming for me.

I take a strike, two balls, and foul off the other one.

Jude's clapping and trying to be encouraging, but I can see his face from over here, like he's saying, *hit the damn ball and get me in for the winning run.*

Another ball, and I'm even more anxious than when I first walked up to bat.

I foul another one, and everyone is chanting, mostly my girls.

The next pitch comes in, and there's a huge lump in my throat. I swing, and the ball sails high and long. I'm running to first, legs and arms pumping. Jude runs home as everyone rushes out of the dugout.

I fear it's going to be caught, but the ball sails over the fence, and someone shouts home run.

Holy shit, I did it.

I run the bases, and my family comes out to congratulate me, but it's the two little faces in the crowd that make my heart pinch.

I touch home plate and grab each of them, swinging them around.

The home run was great, but holding both of my girls is the real win.

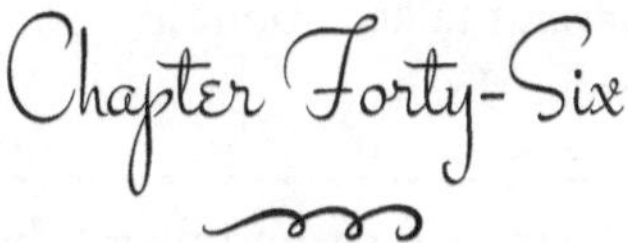

Chapter Forty-Six

DELANEY

Bennett drives us over to the stables and parks. The girls cheer in the back seat, both taking off their seat belts and going for the car handles.

"Whoa, hold up," Bennett says, giving his stern dad expression.

I've been taking note of all his parent looks. The stern one like now, the worried one when one of them says they fell, the happy one when they show him attention. He is a great dad, which I knew he would be.

Leia is becoming more relaxed around him, and I'm pretty sure the day is coming when she'll seek him out over me.

"You're not riding Biscuits or Sparkles. You're riding with us," Bennett says.

The girls look at each other, then get out of the truck.

"Why can't I ride Biscuits?" Wren asks.

"You're not ready to go on the trail yet, but you can ride with Delaney or me," Bennett tells her.

She looks at Leia, and the two of them walk to the barn. I glance at Bennett, unsure if he would like to experience this with Leia and have Wren ride with me, but he only takes my hand, allowing the girls to walk ahead of us.

"So, you want to tell me about why you learned to ride?" He knocks his shoulder into mine.

We actually haven't talked about it.

"Nash is a snitch," I say.

"Hey, why didn't you tell me? I'm proud of you."

"I just wanted her to learn, and then I thought what fun is it if she knows and I don't? So, I learned too."

He squeezes my hand. "I wish I could've been the one to teach you."

I roll my eyes. "Don't be jealous of Ray. He didn't much care for teaching. Not sure why he signed up to run lessons."

"I guarantee you he admired your ass when he taught you how to trot."

"He was, like, seventy and married."

He shrugs. "It's a great ass."

I shake my head and chuckle. Once we're inside the stables, he goes into Cedar's stall, where Wren is already waiting, Leia standing next to her.

Bennett comes with me to Junebug's stall, holding the saddle. "So, I'm thinking we should pick out a horse for you," he says, eyes not meeting mine while he concentrates on getting the horse saddled.

"I don't need a horse, and I cannot afford one." I give Junebug a pat and am rewarded with a nuzzle into my hand.

"It would be a gift from me."

"No, Bennett." I glance out the stall at the girls and back at him. "You will not be buying me a horse."

"How will we go on family rides?"

"Poppy doesn't mind me using Junebug, so we'll go with that."

He follows my line of sight to the girls, who are now at the stall door. "Conversation for another time."

I help Bennett saddle both horses, but let's face it, I don't do nearly enough.

The girls decide who they want to ride with, and Leia waits by Cedar while Wren stands next to me.

I try to mask my surprise and act as though it's perfectly fine that they switched it up. This is what we want. One day I'd like to have the conversation with Wren about where our relationship stands, but Leia hasn't even referred to Bennett as Dad yet, so it's probably a little early for that.

Slow and easy. We'll get there.

We take the trail I'm familiar with and come to the same spot I brought Leia to when I told her Bennett was her father. On the other side of the field is where I lost my virginity to Bennett when I was seventeen.

We all climb down off our horses. The girls have been doing an excellent job since they've been riding a couple times a week this summer. In that regard, dating an Owens has had its perks. Leia isn't being charged for lessons, and she goes out with Wren all the time, even when they don't have lessons.

I was too busy making sure the girls were safe that I never noticed the blanket and picnic basket, along with some games spread around for the girls. There are even little glass mason jars filled with battery-operated tealights.

"Bennett," I say with a huge smile.

"Look!" Wren and Leia run over to one of the games.

Bennett takes my hand. "This place is where we've made a lot of good memories, and I want to continue them. I haven't been this happy in a long time."

"It's been a dream."

He stops us at the blanket, and I sit down before taking off my boots. He does the same. The girls are completely occupied going through the games, so he opens the picnic basket and takes out a bottle of champagne.

"What are we celebrating?" I watch him open the bottle.

"Us. All of us." He pours two glasses. "I love you, Laney, and I can't wait to make so many more memories with you."

I clink my glass with his. "I love you too."

I turn to watch the girls play cornhole, not really knowing the rules and running back and forth to toss the bags. Leia stands where she should, but Wren runs closer then tosses it.

I laugh at them. "They're so opposite. Which is a good thing."

"That's what Principal North said."

My head tilts. "When did you talk to him?"

"It was before we got together. He compared Leia to me and Wren to Emmett, saying Wren was bringing Leia out of her shell. But now that I watch them, I don't think Leia's shyness and hesitancy to try something new is bad. I think it's a great quality to have growing up."

"She's coming around, I see it. When she started—" I stop, embarrassed that he wasn't there.

"Go ahead, Laney, I want to hear the stories."

"It's just…" I inch closer, my throat getting tight. "I hate that you missed that part. Like how I'm telling you a story about your own child. It's not fair."

His hand cradles my cheek. "Please tell me."

My hand covers his, and I squeeze. "You're too good of a guy."

"I'll take it." He winks. "But you're wrong. Now go ahead and tell me."

I stare into his beautiful brown eyes a second longer before starting my story. His soft smile says he really has made peace with the past and does want to move forward.

"It took her two months to talk to anyone in kindergarten. She wasn't even one of those kids crying and clinging to me. She'd give me a hug and go in. The first day, I peeked in, and she just sat at her desk and watched all the other kids running around and playing with things. Like a little observer. The teacher would give me weekly updates, but it was like the click of a switch two months later. Leia was never the one to talk nonstop, but she would smile and wave and laugh with the other kids at drop-off and pick-up. It just took her some time. But once she's comfortable, she's all in."

Bennett urges me to lean back into him, and I do, both of us watching the girls.

"She'll get there, B, just be patient. I promise one day she's going to jump in, and I know you'll be there to catch her."

His hands run down my arms. "I will be. Let her take all the time she needs. But, Laney..."

I look over my shoulder.

"With all the past, are you okay, I mean with Wren... I know what you said at softball, but I just want to make sure. I mean, she's Kristie's..."

The torment in his eyes tugs at my heart, so I straighten and turn around to face him. This time I cradle his face with my palm. "I already love her like she's my own. And I will love her for Kristie because that was the most important thing to her. She wanted Wren raised—"

His face twists, and I quickly realize I never told him about Kristie's visit. He doesn't know.

"Did you talk to Kristie?"

I look at the girls. We really need to clear this up, but right now, I don't want to spoil our day by delving into the past. "Would you be mad if we delayed this conversation for later tonight?"

His expression says he wants me to answer now, but his voice says, "Okay. Tonight."

"Thanks, and I promise to tell you everything when we get home."

He hums.

"What?"

"Home. I want us to have a home that's *ours*. I'm thinking it's time I build on my plot of land."

The girls run over, both of them grabbing our hands and tugging us off the blanket.

For the rest of our time in the meadow, we don't talk about Kristie or our future. We just enjoy the moment, the memories we're making—together. We play games with the girls, eat the cupcakes and get frosting on our noses. When the girls are distracted with the sparklers Bennett brought, he holds me, kissing me as if it's a promise that there will be many nights like this one.

Chapter Forty-Seven

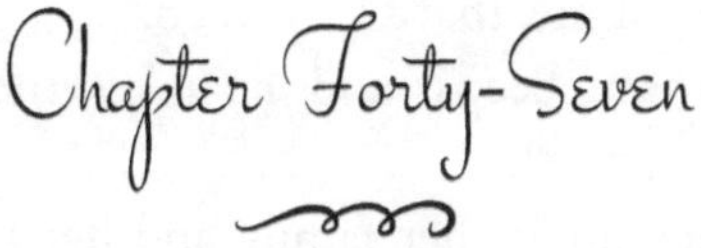

DELANEY

The house is quiet. The girls were exhausted and went down easily. Leia is spending the night here, and I'll come back tomorrow. I'm not sure how much longer we can play this game of separate houses.

Bennett asked me to stay and have a beer on the front porch, and I made the mistake of laughing at one of his stories, leaning into his arm. One story led to another, and I can tell we're both dodging the one story that will shift the vibe of our night.

It's after midnight now, and Bennett suggested popcorn, so I'm perched on the edge of the kitchen counter, bare feet swinging. He stands between my legs, his palms flat on my thighs, while the popcorn pops in the microwave.

"You always were a night owl," he murmurs, his voice a low rasp that makes my stomach flip.

"You're mistaking that for you keeping me up at night," I shoot back, smirking.

His eyes drop to my mouth. "My favorite thing to do."

Our eyes lock, and that familiar tension snaps into place

between us, meaning we're about to forget all about the conversation we need to have.

"Kristie came to see me right before you did that day." My eyes search his, and all I find there is surprise. "She asked that if you didn't fight for me, that I let you go."

The microwave beeps, and he takes the popcorn out, dumping it into a bowl.

"She told me about her family and her parent's divorce. How she wanted to give her daughter a normalcy she didn't get growing up. I was confused and upset, and then you came over."

"And I didn't fight for us." His voice is quiet and laced with regret.

"I don't want to go over all this again. It's over and done with."

"Why would she do that? How did she even know where you lived?"

I tilt my head, and he sighs. It's not hard to find people nowadays.

He looks away from me, almost as though he's ashamed of his next words. "I told her I loved you and that I was happy, but she begged and pleaded. I understood it. My responsibility to my unborn child."

I hop off the counter and put my hands on his cheeks, turning him to look at me. "Exactly. And I understand too."

He nods.

"We move forward. Nothing good is going to come from us constantly looking back. We leave the memory of Kristie alive for Wren, but everything else stays back there."

He nods again, and I raise up on my toes, pressing a kiss to his lips.

"It's us now. Where we are now is all that matters."

His hands grip my hips, and I press my lips to his once more. The tension hums between us, growing heavy.

Bennett picks me up and places me back on the counter. "You're amazing," he whispers. His fingers brush my knee, sliding up as if he's testing the line.

"Keep talking." I laugh, but his eyes are heavy with lust.

"I want you." His voice is thick.

I'm not sure if it's because of Kristie being the center of our conversation, or if it's the fact she came to see me reminding us of what we gave up, but if he needs me, he can have me to remind him that I'm here, and I'm not going anywhere.

I tilt my head, lips parted. "Take me."

That's all it takes.

He steps between my knees. His hands grip my hips as his mouth crashes into mine. It's messy and hungry and claiming. I wrap my arms around his neck, and he steps closer, grabbing my ass and bringing me to the edge of the counter.

His tongue finds mine, transitioning our kiss to slow and deep, and when I roll my hips against him, his groan vibrates through my chest.

"Upstairs," he breathes against my mouth.

I nod breathlessly, heart pounding. He lifts me as if I weigh nothing, and I cling to him, willing to go wherever he wants me to.

He walks into his bedroom, where I've only been one other time—to grab his phone when he forgot it up here. He shuts the door with the softest of clicks, walks me over to the bed, and gently sets me down.

"The girls," I whisper, reaching for the hem of his shirt.

"I'll cover your mouth." He tugs it the rest of the way off.

I'll never grow tired of seeing him without a shirt.

My fingers run down the valley of his abs. "What about you?"

"You're the loud one."

"Excuse me?" I raise both eyebrows.

He strips his mouth off my neck to give me a wicked grin. "I say it as a compliment."

When he does that thing with his tongue along my collarbone, I forget all about our playful arguing, though I'm half tempted to act as if what he's doing isn't driving me wild with want.

The desire snaps, and our hands are everywhere. His mouth on my throat, my hands buried in his hair. He nudges me up the bed, crawling up over me until his body presses me into the mattress.

Nothing could be more perfect than it is with him. The way he's able to slow our pace, wanting to take his time.

Bennett undresses me one painfully slow touch and kiss at a time, and when he pushes into me while gazing down at me, it almost brings tears to my eyes. He whispers sweet promises, and my fingers dig into his shoulder blades as I meet him thrust for thrust.

By the time we both come on a strangled whimper, making sure not to wake the girls, exhaustion takes over my body.

THE ROOM IS A COCOON OF CRUMPLED SHEETS AND early morning light. I blink, disoriented, trying to remember where I am. I feel the warm body at my back, see the picture of Wren and Leia on the nightstand, and it all comes together.

I search for my phone, but I have no idea where it is.

"Shit," I whisper, hitting Bennett's arm.

He mumbles something but doesn't get up. I hit him again.

Knock. Knock.

"Daddy?"

Bennett jerks beside me, sitting up as though the word *daddy* is a blaring alarm clock. I'll have to remember that for next time. His hand flies out as though he's searching for his phone too, but I'm thinking it must be downstairs with mine.

"Shit," he hisses, sitting up and running his hand over his face.

Knock. Knock. Knock.

I freeze. "Is that—"

"Wren." He presses his palms over his face. "It's Wren."

"Daddy, are you awake?"

I scramble, grabbing my shirt from the floor and shimmying it on backward before fixing it. "Where are my, oh my god, my underwear—"

"Laney." He reaches for me. "Just stay still a second."

I'm half out of bed, shirt on, crouching to find the rest of my clothes. I shoot him a frantic look. "Where do I go?"

"Maybe we let her know you're here," he whispers, rubbing his face again, clearly trying to shake off sleep. If he was in a panic like me, maybe his heart rate would get him to wake up and get dressed.

"I can't be in here."

"I mean, you *are*," he says dryly.

"Not helping," I mutter, pulling up my pants.

"Dad?" Wren tries the doorknob. Thank God it's locked. "I'm hungry."

Bennett throws on sweatpants, still shirtless, and moves to the door without telling me the plan. He turns and gives me an apologetic look and an expression as if saying, *this is our life now.*

He cracks open the door. "Hey."

"Can I come in your bed?"

"No, um... let's head downstairs. Give me a minute, okay?"

"Okay, Leia is still sleeping."

He shuts the door and comes over, sitting on the edge of the bed with me.

"Where am I supposed to go if you sent her downstairs?" I ask.

He takes my hand. "I think we just tell them that we're having sleepovers. I know it hasn't been long, but we're committed to each other, and honestly, I don't want to spend our evenings apart anymore. We can do it this way, or we can find a place for just us. I guess what I'm saying is I want us out in the open. I want the girls to see our love for each other."

"I do too, but—"

"It's been too long, too much wasted time." His gaze searches my face.

I nod because he has a point. "So, what, I just go down there in yesterday's clothes?"

"I could lend you some. I love seeing you in my clothes." He waggles his eyebrows. He stands and holds out his hand. "Come have breakfast with us."

I take his hand, inhaling to give myself some reassurance.

He throws a shirt on, then we walk downstairs, him first.

Leia comes out of Wren's bedroom while we're on the stairs. "Mommy, did you sleep over too?"

Bennett purses his lips.

"I did," I say and hold out my arms. She walks into my open arms, and I pick her up.

"You should have packed an overnight bag," she says.

Bennett laughs, which makes Wren come to the bottom of the stairs and see us all coming toward her.

Her eyes widen. "Can we go to The Getaway Lodge for breakfast?"

Bennett laughs. "I'm thinking breakfast at home. You girls can help us."

"Yay!" Wren yells, and Leia squirms to get out of my hold.

The two of them go into the family room, and Bennett wraps his arms around me, kissing the hollow of my neck. "Easy peasy."

He chuckles, but he's right. That went a lot smoother than I thought it would.

BENNETT

We're over at Delaney's parents' house.

"I say we buy your parents an RV and we move in here." I sit on the couch.

"I know they're retired, but I thought they would be here more. Not that I'm complaining." She sits next to me, and I inch a little closer, never as close as I want to get with her.

"I went to the property today." I'm hesitant to bring it up, not sure what Delaney's reaction might be. "I'd like you to come visit it with me." She opens her mouth, but I keep going. "Before you say anything, our sleepovers have become consistent, and I'm really tired of the term sleepovers. I've waited years to have this. I want the crazy mornings where the girls jump in our bed, and we get them ready for school together. I want dinners where they complain about what we made. I want to settle down next to you on the couch after we put them to bed. I want to make more babies with you. And I want to be able to do it in a house by ourselves."

Her gaze floats upstairs to where the girls are. "I'm not even divorced yet."

"You will be in two months. I don't care about that

though. I want you to marry me, and I intend to ask you, and I don't give a shit about rings or government declarations. I just want you in my bed, my home, my life." I inch even closer, leaving no space between us. "The land is mine, and I want to build a house for our family on it."

"I can't contribute, B. The little amount of money I've made has been from working for *you*. I know you're going to say you'll take care of it, but I don't want to be in the situation I was with Sean. I can't do that again."

I stare at her, understanding what she's saying, but we're at a crossroads. "Do you want me to charge you rent?"

From the look on her face, she doesn't find my joke funny.

"I understand your reasons, but I would never do what he did to you. If you don't want to work for The Perfect Petal or work with me, fine, but regardless, we..." I wave my finger between us. "We're a team. This doesn't work unless we're together, side by side. If I have to float the expenses right now, then that's the way it will be, but you know it will change."

"I just don't want to feel so out of control of my own life, so in the dark again. I've really enjoyed working again, and I don't want to give that up."

"I would never ask that of you. Ever. And I won't ever do that to you." I cradle her head in my palm, my thumb running across her neck.

She nods. "Okay. But as soon as I'm making more money, I'm paying half our mortgage, and we're separating all our finances."

"Deal," I agree. I'll give her whatever she needs to trust that we can make this life one we're both proud of.

"Uh oh," Wren says.

A box falls down the steps, opening midflight, and about a hundred little stuffed Hello Kittys scatter at the bottom of the stairs.

"Girls?" Delaney stands from the couch and walks over.

"What are these?" I follow her, seeing every Hello Kitty is dressed differently. Some appear to be from different countries.

Delaney's too busy looking up the stairs to answer me. "Come on, you two."

"Your mom voice is getting me all hot," I whisper, picking up the box and putting the small stuffed animals inside.

"Not the time."

"Just saying maybe I need some discipline tonight."

Her nose scrunches up. "Ew, stop."

I chuckle.

Both girls come downstairs, heads hanging low.

"We were bringing it down to show you," Wren says first because she always speaks up for the both of them.

I hope with time, Leia finds her voice a little more, but I might have to have a conversation with Wren about giving Leia a chance to speak for herself.

"Leia?" Delaney asks.

"I was packing them up."

"Why?" she asks, her voice a little softer now.

I finish putting them all back in the box and push it aside, waiting for one of the girls to answer.

"Because he's not my daddy," she says quietly, peeking up at me.

I start to understand that the Hello Kittys represent something more than just her outgrowing the stuffed animal.

"Oh." Delaney glances at me. "So..."

"I still love him. Miss him, but I..." Leia seeks me out again, and my heart squeezes. "Love you too."

My nose stings, and my eyes well as I try to push back tears.

"I love you, Daddy," she says in a whisper.

I bend down and hold out my arms, needing her to say it again while I'm holding her.

She walks over, and I hug her so tightly that I fear she'll struggle to breathe. "I love you, Leia. So, so much." I pull back and run my hand over the side of her face like I do with Wren. "Can I ask you to say it one more time?"

She laughs. "I love you, Daddy."

"The best ever." I hug her tightly again.

Delaney sniffles, and I close my eyes, so damn happy to have gotten to this point. I believed it would come, but at the same time, I feared it never would.

Delaney comes over to me, and I bring her into the hug, holding my other arm out for Wren, but when I look over Leia's shoulder, Wren isn't there.

"Wren?" I call, searching the room.

Leia and Delaney step back and all of our eyes scan the area.

"Maybe upstairs?" Delaney jogs up the stairs but returns shaking her head.

"Where did she go?" Leia asks.

Delaney and I rush around the house, but I can't find Wren anywhere, so I burst through the screen door to search the grounds.

Why would she run off? That's not like her. Where would she even go? This isn't Plain Daisy Ranch where she has specific hiding places she knows.

Delaney follows me, both of us searching. Our eyes catch one another's as my stomach sinks. While trying to get one daughter to find her love for me, did I not tell the other one that she's just as loved?

Chapter Forty-Nine

DELANEY

Where would she go?

I see the frantic expression on Bennett's face, and my own heart practically beats out of my chest from fear. He goes one way with Leia, and I go the other. Wren couldn't have gotten that far.

Rounding the back of my parents' house, I continue down to Levi's small coach house, and the sound of sobs calms the beating of my heart. I peek around the corner of his house to find Wren huddled on the back stoop, knees drawn to her chest, arms wrapped around them with her head buried, crying.

Bennett comes along the other side, obviously hearing what I did, and I put my hand on my heart, silently asking if I can be the one to talk to her. He nods and disappears around the side of the building.

"Wren," I say gently so she doesn't run again. I sit down next to her without touching her. "Do you want to talk about it?"

"No." She shakes her head.

This is so unlike her. She usually owns her feelings so well.

She always speaks what she feels, so this must be worse than we thought.

"Okay, you don't have to."

She cries harder, her back racking. My hands itch to comfort her, but at this point, I think she'd push me away.

"Why does she have to have my daddy? He's all..." More tears fall from her eyes. "He's mine."

"I'm sure it's hard sharing his attention." My hand reaches out, but I retract it when she picks up her head.

"She gets a daddy *and* a mommy, and now I have to share him and everyone else. They're *my* family."

"I get it. I do, Wren. This situation is hard. I think it was all exciting in the beginning to find out your best friend turned out to be your sister."

"Half sister," she corrects.

I inhale deeply because she heard that from someone, and I wonder who it was. My bet is one of the kids at school before it let out, or she overheard someone in town gossiping.

"Regardless, she is your sister, and your daddy is her daddy."

"Yeah, and she gets both of you, and I only have half of a daddy now."

I slide a little closer. "You have a full daddy. He loves you both, and as far as you only having a daddy, I would like that to change."

"How?" she asks, tears still in her eyes.

I wrap my arm around her back and rest my head on top of hers. "I would love to be your mommy. I know you have one already, and I would never try to replace her, but I'd like to be an extra one."

She lifts her head, so I lift mine, our eyes meeting. The surprise she's reflecting back to me says I did a shit job of making my intentions clear to her.

"I love you, Wren, like you're my own."

"That's just because you love Daddy. Johnny said that's what happens. Women fall in love with daddies, and they pretend to love the kids until they don't love the daddy anymore."

Fuck you, Johnny.

"That's not true for me. Sure, I would've never gotten to know you or grown to love you had I not fallen in love with your daddy first, but I want all of us, all four of us, to be a family. I want us to support and love one another like a family. Blood doesn't bond people together. It's your heart that does that. I think the four of us are pretty great together."

She rests her head on the back of the house, her tears having subsided a little. "But I'm the odd one out. You three are a family, and I'm only Daddy's."

My heart squeezes painfully. "There is no divide. It is four of us, and that's it. You live with Jensen and Nash, right?"

She nods.

"And you love them both?" I arch an eyebrow.

Wren nods again.

"But Jensen is the only one related to you. Nash is the family you chose." I let her think that over for a moment before I speak again. "The way I see it, there is no half or full. It's just family, *our* family."

She catches her breath, still taking deep breaths. "You really want that?"

I run my hand down her hair. "Want what, honey?"

"To be my mom?"

I smile and cup her cheek. "More than anything."

"I've never had one before," she says quietly.

Now there are tears in my eyes. I wrap my arms around her and bring her into me. "Oh, Wren, I want to braid your hair in the morning, I want to read you bedtime stories, I want to hug you good night and give you a pep talk before school when you're nervous for a test. I want to be your cheering squad and your psychologist. I even want you to be sassy to me in your teen years. I might leave driving lessons to your dad though."

She tilts her head up to look at me. "That sounds nice."

I push back a strand of her hair sticking to her forehead, "I think so too. So, yes, you have to share your daddy, but Leia has to share me with you because you are mine."

"Yours?"

I nod. "Forever. I love you, my sweet, spirited daughter."

She smiles, and I hug her tightly.

Bennett comes along the side of the coach house with Leia in tow. "Can we interrupt? We feel like this is the time for a family hug."

I draw back and wait for Wren to answer. She nods, and Leia comes in fast, wrapping her arms around Wren's neck. Bennett squats, his eyes on me with a smile of pure joy as he completes our family hug.

"I'm sorry, Leia. I'm happy you're my sister," Wren says.

Leia squeezes her neck harder. "I know. I love you, Wren."

"I love you too." Wren looks at each of us. "All of you."

We all cling a little tighter to each other.

I feel so blessed to have come here during the worst time of my life and found exactly where I belong and who I belong to.

Chapter Fifty

Sean,

I hope you understand why I felt the need to give you the story of how Bennett and I came to be. He is the love of my life, and it's always come back to him.

Thank you for supporting Leia and me for seven years. You gave us a life I never would have dreamed. Although I'm not sure I will ever really know your true intentions, I like to think I knew you on some level.

You loved Leia. I know you did. I saw it in your eyes. So, I'm hoping you'll find it within yourself to sign the Adjudication of Facts of Parentage papers that your lawyer will be bringing to you so that Bennett can be her father now. Yes, we found each other once again, and this time, nothing is going to tear us apart.

There is another letter accompanying this one, it's from Bennett, and I'm asking you another favor... please read it. Hear it directly from him. He's going to give us a good life.

I do wish you the best, Sean. I wouldn't be where I am now without you.

Delaney

DELANEY

We break ground on our house tomorrow, so Bennett said it's only fitting that we go on a horse ride at sunset. The sky is brushed in soft, sleepy watercolors of pinks and golds. Bennett's ahead of me, his shoulders relaxed, one hand on the reins and the other resting loosely on his thigh. He thinks he's not a cowboy, but he's wrong.

Somehow, after all this time, all the ups and downs, he's mine.

We follow the familiar trail that winds along the edge of the old cornfield, the one that leads to the hilltop we used to sneak away to in high school. It was a lifetime ago. Sometimes though, it still feels like yesterday that I was riding in front of him, his arms around me, making me feel safe.

But now I like to think we both give each other that feeling, and our girls too.

I glance to Wren and Leia, with their little helmets on, their ponies clopping along. Wren is chattering nonstop to Leia, who listens with that quiet patience she got from her father. Wren inherited none of his calm demeanor, but she wouldn't be her without all the fire and constant questions.

"Are we almost there?" Wren asks for the third time.

Bennett smiles over his shoulder. "Almost. Just one more bend."

I would never ruin the surprise, but I know why we're here tonight. He's been acting a little off today. Somewhat nervous. He's checked his saddlebag at least three times, and if I had to guess, there's a ring in there. But he must've kept it from the girls, otherwise it probably would have spilled from one of their lips by now. A calm anticipation makes my stomach flutter.

We reach the top of the hill, and my breath catches as it always does. From up here, the whole world stretches out as if it's only for us. The trees below are thick and green, and I eye the curve of the creek. This spot will always be ours.

Someone's already set up a picnic like always when he plans our family trips up here.

The blanket is spread wide beneath the oak tree, a little wicker basket beside it. In the middle of the blanket is a jar of peonies, my favorite flower. The ones he brings me whenever I've had a hard day.

We finished the golf course, and because of that job, Bennett has been asked to bid on some bigger projects, which left him needing a partner. So I do a little of both—working in the shop and on the landscaping portion of the business—but the days where we get to work alongside one another, arguing about what to plant where and why, are my favorite days.

Leia and Wren dismount, slipping off their ponies with ease.

I join them, and we walk my horse and their ponies over so Bennett can get them tied to the tree with enough slack to roam.

"Can we eat the cookies now?" Wren asks, bouncing on her toes.

"Who said there were cookies?" I ask.

"Daddy," Leia says with a smile.

"Let's wait for him," I say, my hands running down my daughters' hair.

Bennett ties up the horses and joins us, holding his hand out for me to take. "You girls go. I need to steal Mommy for a minute."

Wren's eyes light up, and she shares a look with Leia. "Oooooh, are you gonna kiss?"

Leia rolls her eyes but grins. "Come on, Wren."

The girls plop down on the blanket, heads bent together, giggling over the cookies like the best of friends. Which they are, but I'm not naïve enough to think we won't have our fair share of problems as they grow older. My heart swells watching them though. *Our* girls.

Bennett takes my hand and leads me toward the edge of the hill. We stop where the sun kisses the horizon, casting a glow that any painter would want to recreate.

"I used to stand up here and remember you and us together and wonder if I'd ever find it again," he says. "If you'd ever look at me and not see all the ways I failed you."

I squeeze his hand. "You didn't fail me. And what's past is past."

He nods slowly. "But even in all that mess, I never stopped loving you. Not once. Even when I didn't deserve to."

Tears blur my vision.

He pulls in a breath, then slowly lowers to one knee.

The girls gasp as though they had no idea what was happening tonight.

"I've loved you in every version of my life," he says, eyes locked on mine. "When we were kids sneaking out to this hill. When I didn't know how to breathe without you. And now, standing here with our girls laughing behind us, I know this is it. This is home. This is the life and love I want forever."

He reaches into his pocket and pulls out a small box, then

opens it to reveal the most beautiful, simple ring. A gold band with a diamond tucked in the center.

"Laney... will you marry me?"

The boy who held my hand the first time I was brave enough to dream is proposing.

When I was lost, he was there to help me stand back up.

"Yes," I whisper, my voice cracking. "Of course I will."

He stands, and I throw my arms around him. The second he kisses me, the girls scream and shout behind us.

"They're kissing!"

"We're flower girls!"

I laugh into his mouth, tears of joy streaming down my face. He lifts me slightly and spins us in a slow circle. After another kiss, we walk back to the blanket hand in hand.

Leia looks up at me with those big, steady eyes. "Congratulations, Mommy and Daddy."

Wren beams. "I wanna wear a dress with sparkles."

"I want butterflies on mine," Leia says.

The two of them run around us in circles.

Bennett squeezes my hand. We're surrounded by the life we built from the pieces left behind after everything fell apart —proof that sometimes the best things come after the fall.

WE DROP THE HORSES OFF AT THE STABLE, AND THE girls see a butterfly and run off after it, giggling as they chase it.

I hear hushed voices in one of the stalls. I peek my head in to find Nash.

"Hey, you," I say.

Poppy comes out from the other corner of the stall he was working in.

"Oh, and you too?" Bennett and I share a look.

"I was just here because well..." She looks at Nash. "Scarlett told me that Zander Shaw is going to be filming his country music video here." She puts her hand to her lips. "But it's hush hush, so don't tell anyone, especially Romy. Scarlett can't wait to surprise her."

"And yet, you've told Nash *and* us. Remind me never to trust you with a secret." Bennett puts the saddles back. "Maybe she won't care. Seems she's obsessed with someone else these days. Does anyone know the guy she's seeing?"

I lift my hand and swat Bennett's shoulder. My ring catches the light from the overhead lights in the stable, and Poppy screeches.

"Clearly I'm not a vault like you." She tackles me, seesawing us back and forth. "Congratulations, you guys."

Nash comes over and shakes Bennett's hand, then gives me a hug.

We chat for a little longer before saying our goodbyes. We find the girls outside the stables grinning with excitement because the butterfly has landed on Leia's finger. It flutters away as we approach, and Leia frowns. They want to chase after it again, but we each scoop up one of the girls.

On the way back to the truck with Bennett holding Leia and me Wren, I ask, "Is Romy a big fan of Zander Shaw?"

"That's an understatement. They went to the concert a few months back, and she got herself backstage and didn't get home until six. She's very hush hush about what happened. I think she's dating a roadie or something."

We strap the girls in and climb into the front seat, driving back to the guys' house. Thankfully, Nash and Jensen are cool with us all staying there until the house we're building is ready.

We get the girls to bed, then head to our bedroom. I climb under the covers, curling into Bennett's side.

"It was a perfect night," I whisper, kissing his chest.

"And there's a lifetime more to come."

He kisses the top of my head, and we drift off to sleep. I only have sweet dreams these days, but even they aren't sweeter than the life we're building together.

The End

Also by Piper Rayne

Plain Daisy Ranch

One Last Summer

The One I Left Behind

The One I Stood Beside

The One I Didn't See Coming

Chasing Forever

Chasing Love

Chasing Home

The Baileys

Lessons from a One-Night Stand

Advice from a Jilted Bride

Birth of a Baby Daddy

Operation Bailey Wedding (Novella)

Falling for My Brother's Best Friend

Demise of a Self-Centered Playboy

Confessions of a Naughty Nanny

Operation Bailey Babies (Novella)

Secrets of the World's Worst Matchmaker

Winning my Best Friend's Girl

Rules for Dating Your Ex

Operation Bailey Birthday (Novella)

The Greene Family

My Twist of Fortune

My Beautiful Neighbor

My Almost Ex

My Vegas Groom

A Greene Family Summer Bash (Novella)

My Sister's Flirty Friend

My Unexpected Surprise

My Famous Frenemy

A Greene Family Vacation (Novella)

My Scorned Best Friend

My Fake Fiancé

My Brother's Forbidden Friend

A Greene Family Christmas (Novella)

Lake Starlight

The Problem with Second Chances

The Issue with Bad Boy Roommates

The Trouble with Runaway Brides

The Drawback of Single Dads

The Complication with the Best Man

The Nest

Mr. Heartbreaker

Mr. Broody

Mr. Swoony

Mr. Charming

Hockey Hotties

Countdown to a Kiss

My Lucky #13

The Trouble with #9

Faking it with #41

Tropical Hat Trick (Novella)

Sneaking around with #34

Second Shot with #76

Offside with #55

Chicago Grizzlies

On the Defense

Something like Hate

Something like Lust

Something like Love

Kingsmen Football Stars

False Start

You Had Your Chance, Lee Burrows

You Can't Kiss the Nanny, Brady Banks

Over My Brother's Dead Body, Chase Andrews

Modern Love

Charmed by the Bartender

Hooked by the Boxer

Mad about the Banker

Single Dads Club

Real Deal

Dirty Talker

Sexy Beast

Hollywood Hearts

Mister Mom

Animal Attraction

Domestic Bliss

Bedroom Games

Cold as Ice

On Thin Ice

Break the Ice

Chicago Law

Smitten with the Best Man

Tempted by my Ex-Husband

Seduced by my Ex's Divorce Attorney

Blue Collar Brothers

Flirting with Fire

Crushing on the Cop

Engaged to the EMT

White Collar Brothers

Sexy Filthy Boss

Dirty Flirty Enemy

Wild Steamy Hook-up

The Rooftop Crew

My Bestie's Ex

A Royal Mistake

The Rival Roomies

Our Star-Crossed Kiss

The Do-Over

A Co-Workers Crush

Holiday Romances

Single and Ready to Jingle

Claus and Effect

Merry Kissmas

Yule Be Mine

Cockamamie Unicorn Ramblings

Surprise, surprise, this book didn't go as planned. If you've been reading us and our end-of-book notes for a while, then you know this is a common occurrence with us.

One day, you're going to be reading one of our CURs, and we're going to tell you that we planned the whole thing out. We knew from the very first page of the series that this is how it would be. But not today, Unicorns, not today!

So... back when we were plotting this series, Bennett was a widower and a single dad. We didn't really flesh anything else out except that Kristie was to be the love of his life, and he was struggling to move on.

After finishing Chasing Forever (Brooks and Lottie's book), we realized we needed more to make his story engaging and compelling enough for readers to want to continue.

So... our original idea was that the heroine was going to be Kristie's enemy in high school who had just returned to town, and he'd hate her on behalf of Kristie. Then we tossed around the idea of heroine being a nanny, being Kristie's best friend. At this point in our plotting, Kristie grew up in Willowbrook. There was no Leia, there was no Sean, and there was no seven-years-later affair.

As we dug deeper and tried to dig into Bennett and his

grief, and thought about why he couldn't move on that's when we really started to feel the pulse of the story. Who doesn't love second chances, and we didn't have one in this set of three books (The Owens). It was decided Delaney would have a daughter, too, and she'd have to return to town.

Newsflash, Leia wasn't going to be Bennett's until both of us, at the exact same time, as we were plotting, said, "Wait." Actually, Piper started saying it, and Rayne said I thought the same thing before she could even finish. So, it had to have been our most intelligent decision ever to make Leia be Bennett's. LOL

As you can imagine, though, it snowballed after that with a million backstory questions we had to answer.

All in all, we love this story so much. The four of them as a family. Wren is gaining a motherly presence in her life with Delaney and a sister in Leia. Bennett gains a daughter with the woman he always thought he was meant to be with. Heart-warming, right? (It's in our tagline, after all.)

We hope you enjoyed their story and were rooting for them all along like we were.

As always, we have a lot of people to thank for getting this book into your hands...

Nina and the entire Valentine PR team. The organization, the promotion, and the way you keep us on point with dead-lines. We appreciate you SO much!

Cassie from Joy Editing for line edits, who is still taking our book days late. Which is becoming a habit we hope to break. Please know you have our heartfelt gratitude for always working with us to shift things around.

Ellie from My Brother's Editor for line edits and proofreading. We give you barely any time, but you always come through.

Olivia Weston, for being our second proofreader. You're an awesome addition to our team.

Whiskey Ginger for our illustrated cover, which speaks perfectly to Bennett and Delaney, bringing them to life.

All the bloggers who choose to read us with so many options out there. We are appreciative and honored to be on your list of must-reads and love reading all your reviews, edits, and more.

All the Piper Rayne Unicorns who support us every day, all day. We'd be lost without you answering our polls and telling us what you love and hate. We strive to give you the best Piper Rayne experience each and every time. We can't say much else except that you're awesome!

You, dear reader, have an abundance of books to choose from. Thank you for picking up one of ours. We do hope you enjoyed the story.

Next up is Romy, as we're sure you've guessed. Do you have any suspicions about who the baby daddy is? We're sure you do, you're too smart not to have figured it out! ;)

See you soon back on the ranch!

xo,
Piper & Rayne

About Piper & Rayne

Piper Rayne is a *USA Today* Bestselling Author duo who write "heartwarming humor with a side of sizzle" about families, whether that be blood or found. They both have e-readers full of one-clickable books, they're married to husbands who drive them to drink, and they're both chauffeurs to their kids. Most of all, they love hot heroes and quirky heroines who make them laugh, and they hope you do, too!